Out of the

Since escaping ————————————————
riage, Fleurette ————————————————,
has reveled in her freedom—turning the
heads of the *ton* with her unrestrained enjoy-
ment of life. But her extravagant purchase of
the statue of a fourteenth-century Celtic mer-
cenary seems beyond the pale, even for the
vivacious young beauty—especially when a
powerful, breathtaking, and oddly familiar
stranger mysteriously enters her world . . .

Comes a passion undimmed by time

The warm caress of an exquisite lady has
awakened Killian, Sir Hiltsglen, the legendary
"Black Celt," from his centuries-long slumber.
To end the curse that encased his spirit in
cold stone, his destiny is now bound to the
infuriating lass who set him free—and who
tempts the great warrior with a smoldering
sensuality that inflames his barbarian desires.
For Fleurette is hiding a dark secret and is in
dire need of a champion—and Killian's mission could be compromised by an unbidden
love that transcends time.

"Greiman's writing is warm, witty,
and gently wise."
Betina Krahn

By Lois Greiman

TAMING THE BARBARIAN • SEDUCING A PRINCESS
THE PRINCESS MASQUERADE
THE PRINCESS AND HER PIRATE
THE WARRIOR BRIDE • THE MACGOWAN BETROTHAL
THE FRASER BRIDE • HIGHLAND HAWK
HIGHLAND ENCHANTMENT • HIGHLAND SCOUNDREL

Lois Greiman

Taming the Barbarian

An Avon Romantic Treasure

AVON BOOKS
An Imprint of HarperCollinsPublishers

AVON BOOKS
An Imprint of HarperCollins*Publishers*
10 East 53rd Street
New York, New York 10022-5299

Copyright © 2005 by Lois Greiman
ISBN-13: 978-0-06-078394-5
ISBN-10: 0-06-078394-X
www.avonromance.com

First Avon Books paperback printing: September 2005

Avon Trademark Reg. U.S. Pat. Off. and in Other Countries, Marca Registrada, Hecho en U.S.A.
HarperCollins® is a registered trademark of HarperCollins Publishers Inc.

Printed in the U.S.A.

10 9 8 7 6 5 4 3 2 1

To Erika Tsang,
who manages to tread that fine line
between honesty and kindness.
Thanks for all your hard work.
My books shine brighter because of you.

Chapter 1

❦

"**M**e? Marry again?" Lady Glendowne tilted her head as she stroked the petals of a perfect yellow rose. It was as bright as a canary and peeked with precocious optimism out from amidst dark, scalloped leaves and thorny companions.

The fragrances of Jardin de Jacques were heady and ripe, teasing the nostrils, awakening slumbering senses. The sun felt warm and sensual against Fleurette's neck and bosom, for her frock, the exact shade of the impetuous rose, was cut fashionably low beneath her small, peaked chin.

She was on holiday, it was early summer in Paris, and she was accompanied by four of her closest friends, but she hardly needed those heady excuses to show such daring cleavage. Fashion and her own advancing years were reason enough. After all, she was nearly four-and-twenty.

"No. I do not think I shall choose to marry again," she said.

"You jest." Frederick Deacon's tone was stunned as he curtailed his admiration of a cluster of blushing columbine. He was short and narrow and known to flirt with anything that donned skirts. Indeed, it was sometimes whispered that he flirted with some who wore breeches.

"No," Fleurette countered. "I do not. My husband meant the moon and the stars to me, as you well know, but I have little reason to marry again."

Quirking a brow and reaching for her hand, Deacon gave her an elegant bow. "My dearest lady, if you do not yet comprehend the advantages of wedded bliss, I feel it is my responsibility, however tedious to . . . help you understand nuptial pleasures."

Fleurette laughed, allowed one dawdling kiss,

and drew her hand carefully away. She was no prude, but she was hardly a *demirep* either, parading about in dampened gowns that showed every peak and dimple. "You are too kind, good sir, but that would hardly be proper."

"Propriety," said Lady Anglehill, distractedly eyeing a nearby statue, "is highly overrated." Jardin de Jacques was valued for its magnificent blossoms, its ancient statuary, and its lack of prejudice against artistic nudity. Not necessarily in that order.

"Be that as it may," said Fleurette, skimming her fingers along the undulating wall of stones beside which Lucy led them, "Thomas has been gone such a short while and . . ."

"Seven years," interjected Lord Lessenton.

"I beg your pardon?"

"Seven years." Stanford Henry, the third baron of Lessenton, was fair-haired, handsome, perfectly groomed, and impeccably dressed. "This coming August."

Fleurette's steps faltered, and her eyes became misty. "Has it been so very long?"

"Yes," Stanford said, catching her gaze. "It has."

She turned toward him, taking his hand between her gloved fingers. "But of course it has.

My apologies. At times I forget he was as dear to you as he was to me."

"Such a senseless loss," Stanford said. "First my Clarice, then her beloved brother."

She squeezed his hand. "Indeed, I shall never . . ."

"Here now," Deacon cut in, with smooth aplomb. He scooped his arm through hers, but allowed her time to do the same to Stanford, so that they stood three in a line, linked side by side. "Let us speak of happier things."

She gave him a half smile and forced her mind from sadness. After all, they were on holiday. "And what would you suggest?" she asked.

"Well . . ." Deacon paused as if thinking, then, "oh yes, your lucky bridegroom to be. Whomever shall you choose?"

"My dearest Frederick, you're dreadfully obvious," she said.

"I beg your pardon." He drew back as if aghast, splaying elegant fingers across the crisp white of his freshly laundered cravat.

She gave him a look, then skimmed her gaze back to the meandering path. "I fear your need for funds is well-known."

Deacon pulled his companions to an abrupt halt. "Might you be suggesting that I love you for your bank account alone?"

"Yes," she said, and tugged them gently along in her wake. "That is exactly what I am suggesting."

"Well," he puffed and stared into the unseen horizon as if highly insulted. " 'Tis entirely untrue. I also happen to very much admire your tilbury phaeton."

"You mustn't forget her horses," Amelia added from behind. The fifth daughter of a struggling baronet, she had been hastily engaged to a promising young banker from Hendershire before, as her father put it, she went entirely to buttermilk. Her mother, it was said, had gained a good five stone since her marriage, but Amelia Engleton was hardly concerned. For she had eyes like an angel and hair like a goddess, or so vowed her besotted betrothed.

"The horses," Deacon repeated dreamily. Sighing, he stared foggily into the distance again, as if imagining them even now. "I admit that seeing you seated behind the grays makes me want to strangle you in your sleep, my dear." He shook his head and caught her gaze. "No offense meant, of course."

"None taken," Fleurette said, and smiled as she thought of her horses. She had purchased the team as matched weanlings and seen to their training herself. "They are a lovely pair.

You know their strides are matched to within a quarter of an inch."

Deacon's mouth pulled down sharply at the corners. "Now you're simply being cruel."

"True," she admitted, "but you did threaten my life."

"Threaten your . . . I would do no such thing," he vowed, then leaned conspiratorially close, "Not until after we have become lovers at the least."

"Frederick," she scolded. "I must implore you to keep a civil tongue."

"I have always believed it quite civil to speak of love," quipped Deacon. "What I find completely unacceptable is for a handsome woman such as yourself to be alone in the world."

"I am hardly alone," she argued. "I have Lucy and Amelia, you, and Stanford." She gave her brother-in-law's arm a gentle squeeze. "Who is my rock."

"I am speaking of an entirely different kind of loneliness," said Deacon.

"Truly?" She glanced at a bower of honeysuckle that graced a stone archway. The blossoms sprouted in spikes of white and pink, heavenly scented and as numerous as the stars. "And all these years I was under the impression there is only one kind."

"I am speaking about being alone in one's bedchamber as you very well know. Which you are, unless you and Stanford have an arrangement I know nothing about."

Stanford gazed past Fleur to give Deacon a scathing glance.

"Just as I thought," Deacon deduced. "Poor Stan is as alone as you."

"Perhaps some of us still maintain a modicum of moral fiber," Stanford said. The two men were generally congenial enough, but tempers flared now and again.

"Moral fiber," Deacon repeated, as if he'd not heard of such a preposterous thing. "Amongst the peerage? I very much doubt it."

"Nevertheless, I must insist that you cease insulting Lady Glendowne's reputation."

"I am hardly insulting it. I am merely inquiring when she plans to take a lover. Indeed, if the truth be known, I am complimenting it by offering my services," he said, leaning close and speaking to her again, "should you lack suitable options."

"And I'm certain if she desires the companionship of a boring wastrel with not a penny to his name, she will be quick to call upon you," Stanford suggested.

"I may be penniless, and I am most certainly

a wastrel, but I take exception to being called boring. I am never boring."

"I am bored as we speak," Stanford said.

"Perhaps it is your own disposition and not my presence at all that predisposes you—"

"Gentlemen," Fleurette interrupted. "I must insist—" she began, but her sentence was interrupted by a gasp from the far side of a carefully pruned hedgerow.

Dropping their arms, the threesome rushed around the bend to find Lady Anglehill staring upward in silent awe. Fleurette took one moment to ascertain that all was well, then flitted her gaze toward the towering statue that had speared her friend's attention with such resounding finality.

Her breath caught immediately in her throat, for the statuary was all-consuming.

Chiseled from solid granite, the sculpture looked as old as life itself. Moss grew upon the rearing steed's shod hooves, and weathered stains marred its rider's boots, but the warrior's legs were perfect. As large and unyielding as oaken tree trunks, they hugged the stallion's barrel with ferocious strength. Muscles hewn of ancient granite bulged beneath the horseman's kilt. In his fist he held a battle-notched sword and his gigantic arm, straining beneath the timeless weight of his weapon, was knotted with venerable strength.

A helmet shadowed his eyes and hid his cheeks. His teeth were gritted in a struggle as old as sin. But it was neither the statue's towering size, nor its maker's obvious talent that took one's breath. It was the sheer force of its presence, for it seemed almost as if the thing was the barest breath away from life.

"My Lord!" Amelia gasped, stepping up like one in a trance.

"Or a demigod at least," Lucille corrected, rounding the statuary with revered awe.

"Surely, you must have heard of the Black Celt," Deacon said.

"The what?" Amelia breathed.

"The Black Celt. History claims him to be the fiercest of all ancient warriors."

"Since when have you ever shown an interest in history?" Stanford asked.

"Since it was filled with murder and betrayal and lust, of course."

"From the beginning of time then," Lucy murmured, still circling the statue.

"Or very nearly so," Deacon agreed, watching Fleurette join Lucille. "And that is just about the time when the Black Celt lived, according to the tales." Amelia's eyes were wide and chocolate dark against her milky complexion. " 'Tis said he was the deadliest of all mercenaries, hiring out his sword to the highest bidder . . . until he met the fair mademoiselle who stole his heart."

"The tale does sound familiar," Stanford admitted.

"But of course. It is as old as black pepper. He met the lovely lady and became infatuated with her beauty even before he knew she was his liege's adversary."

"Ahh, and thus trouble brewed," Lucy said.

"Indeed yes, when your liege happens to be dabbling in the black arts."

Amelia hissed. Deacon smiled, glad for the appreciative audience. "Thus, our stony fellow here vowed to protect the lady from all comers and broke his alliance with his dark overlord."

"I have the feeling this tale may not end happily ever after," Amelia lamented.

"Happily ever after. What boring tripe. Of course there are ferocious battles and constant tribulation. The Celt's master was enraged by his bold knight's duplicity and spat forth a dreadful curse. The warrior would be turned to stone, never to breathe again until he could right the wrong he had perpetrated against his lord."

"A difficult task for a boulder," Stanford mused.

"So this statue was once the Black Celt himself?" Amelia asked.

"Certainly," Deacon said, lowering his voice dramatically. "And he may, at any moment, spring forth into full raging life once again."

Amelia rolled her lamb-soft eyes toward Deacon, who smiled and took her hand.

"But you need not fear, my dear, for I am here to protect you from one and all."

"Or at least from rocks and the like," Stanford quipped.

Amelia grinned at the baron, then turned narrowed eyes toward Deacon. "Might you be forgetting that I am betrothed to be married in a matter of weeks?"

He smiled. "Then there is no time like the present."

"But weren't you just now flirting with Fleurette?" Amelia asked.

"Don't be ridiculous. You know you're all that I see."

"So long as Lady Glendowne turns aside your advances," Stanford said.

"Or at least until she gives me some kind of encouragement," Deacon admitted, and leaned close to Amelia as if he shared a great secret.

"You know she's amassed a fortune since her husband's death."

"You're shameless," Amelia tsked, but laughed just the same.

"I do hope so," he admitted, then raised his voice. "Lady Glendowne, might you at least give me a small hint who intrigues you?" When she failed to answer, he turned and found that she stood perfectly still, one palm laid flat upon the warrior's bulging thigh. Her gaze was lifted to his granite features, and her lips were slightly parted, as though she had been just about to take a breath before forgetting her intentions.

"Well, it looks as if you have your answer," quipped Lucille.

"Ahh, of course," Deacon agreed, scowling in puzzlement. "But what might the question be."

"Who intrigues *la petite fleur*."

"No!" Deacon placed his hand over his heart as if mortally wounded. "Tell me 'tis not so. Our little flower could not be interested in such a hulking barbarian."

"Whyever not? He is most . . ." Lucille skimmed her gaze down the Celt's gargantuan chest, bare but for the bunched strip of cloth that crossed his bulging shoulder and disappeared beneath his belted plaid. Her nostrils flared. "... intriguing. Don't you agree, Fleurette?" she asked.

Lady Glendowne did not answer.

"Fleurette?" Lucy repeated, louder this time.

Fleur snapped to attention as if struck.

"I'm sorry. What?"

Lucy laughed. "I said, the Black Celt is quite intriguing, is he not?"

"Oh, yes, beautiful..." She skimmed the statue again as if not quite able to resist. "Artistry."

Lucille's eyes danced with mischief. "And he's so large."

"Yes," Fleur breathed.

"It makes one wonder if he is just as impressive in other areas. Does it not?"

"Yes," she said again, then jerked her gaze from the Celt and felt herself blush despite her advancing years and widowed state. Surely she was well past the age of such foolishness.

"No!" Deacon said, sounding aghast. "Ladies of quality could not possibly be interested in an overgrown barbarian with a fractious horse and a ..." He glanced toward the hocks of the rearing steed and winced. "Is that a hound?"

"It almost appears to be a wolf," Lucille said. "And a good-sized wolf indeed."

"But of course." Deacon spread his hands

wide as if surrendering to the inevitable. "He would be accompanied by a wolf, would he not?" he asked, then reached out and grasped Fleurette's hand. "But surely you're more interested in an elegant bloke with a slim figure and ready wit."

"Certainly," said Fleur, and smiled at Deacon. He had a pretty face, but it was generally accepted that he was built rather like a cricket mallet. "Might you know of any such fellow?"

"How amusing. And what of you, Miss Engleton?" he asked, but she, too, was staring wordlessly at the statue.

"I am struck to the very quick," Deacon said, and placed his hand over his broken heart once again.

"Don't be idiotic," Lucille said. "Elegance is all well and good for a ball at Almack's or a nice turtle dinner. But for one mind-shattering night alone in the dark . . ." She paused and sighed heavily as she tilted her head toward the Celt. "There's not a woman on earth mad enough to refuse that."

Fleurette felt her attention tugged inexorably toward the Celt again. It seemed almost, that he watched her, that he could see her no matter where she stood. His eyes were hidden in shadow beneath his stony helmet, and his lean cheeks were mostly concealed under the tight rows of metal rings that served to protect his face. But it mattered little, for his demeanor was everything—boldness and bravery, chivalry and honor. A life that would be given without question or regret.

"That's it then," Deacon said. "I shall return to my room straightaway and slice my wrists. Messy, yet effective, I'm told. But wait, perhaps I should drown myself in the Seine. Ghastly inelegant, but oh the drama. Then again—"

"Oh, Deacon, do shut up," Fleur insisted, drawing herself from her reverie.

He grinned at her. "So you do care for me?"

"Of course I care," she said, her tone offhand.

"And you wouldn't want some barbaric Celt in your bed?"

Her scowl was thoughtful. "I really don't think he'd fit. His charger alone would take up the entire mattress, and the wolf—"

"Very amusing," he countered, his tone dry and his expression nonplussed. "I meant if he were alive . . . and conveniently detachable from his steed."

"Oh, well . . ." She glanced at the Celt again and found that he still drew her. But she pulled her gaze resolutely away. "That would make all the difference, wouldn't it?"

He gave her a look that reminded her a bit of Henri, her overly sensitive spaniel, who was most probably still moping about being left behind in England.

"I jest of course," she said. "It's the nineteenth century, Deacon, and I've no wish to abandon my freedom. Not that I wouldn't do anything to have Thomas back, of course." She paused as a pang of memory smote her. "But I could hardly give up holidays such as this for a man with bulging biceps and a snarl."

"Even if he has a wolf?"

She laughed. "Even if," she said, but as they traversed the mossy trails toward the garden's trellised entrance, she could not help but turn to take one last look. The Black Celt stood alone, rearing above the heads of mortal man, alone, dark, and shrouded in purpose.

Chapter 2

〜∽∾∿〜

"**B**ut you must come see the Pantheon with us," Amelia argued. "Tell her, Antoinette."

Antoinette Desbonnet was a countess, a widow, and the woman with whom they were staying while in Paris. Her rambling estate offered a distant view of the Jardin Des Tuileries and the ancient palace that accompanied it. She was also, very possibly, the most beautiful woman Fleurette had ever seen.

"*Oui, certainement,*" she said. "How could one live without seeing a cluster of moldering

17

graves?" She said the words with absolute sincerity, yet managed, somehow, to convey the exact opposite attitude. The Comtesse de Colline was the epitome of pedigreed class. Always dressed in immaculate white, her wardrobe was flawless, if monochromatic. Her coiffure was *au couture*, and her complexion glowing. She should be an easy woman to hate, and yet Fleur had not been able to manage it.

"Yes," Lucille agreed. "You should definitely come. We'll not see a single thing without you there to distract Deacon. He may even become so desperate as to believe *I* might wish to marry, if he doesn't have you on whom to concentrate his attentions."

Fleurette forced a smile. "I am so very sorry. But I fear my headache is worsening."

"Mon dieu," said Antoinette, lifting a slim hand. Her gloves were made of white kid. Not a single speck of dirt dared show against the pristine leather. "I shall order up a tonic straight away."

"Yes," Amelia agreed. "In a matter of minutes you'll be right as rain."

"Thank you," Fleur said, fighting her conscience. Had she not known better, she would have thought she had pummeled the damn thing into submission many long years ago.

"But I fear I didn't sleep well, and I am mad to spend the day abed."

"Oh dear." Amelia's expression turned from enthusiast to worried in a matter of seconds. "Was it talk of Thomas that disturbed you?"

"Perhaps," Fleurette admitted, then touched her young friend's arm and gave her a brief smile. "But you needn't worry. I shall be fine if left to my own devices."

"I am so very sorry," Amelia said, covering Fleur's hand with her own and gazing into the other's eyes. "Lord Lessenton means well, you know."

"I do know," Fleurette agreed, doing her best to lighten the mood. It seemed to work, for Amelia sighed and gave her an optimistic smile.

Since her engagement some weeks before, Amelia tended to see the world from the rosy precipice of impending matrimony. "You must miss Lord Glendowne so. I know if anything happened to my Edward . . ." She paused, unable to go on.

"There now," said Lucille, coming up from behind and patting the girl's arm. "Edward is as healthy as a hound." And looked similar by all accounts, despite his impressive bank account. "You needn't worry. But we must rush on now. I promised your *mère* that you would return to London as cultured as a marchioness."

Amelia shifted her wide-eyed gaze from one to the other. In reality, she was no more than a few years younger than Fleurette, and yet, at times, the difference seemed vast indeed. "But surely we cannot leave Lady Glendowne unattended."

"I think she can brave a headache," Lucille said, and, fetching their shawls, draped an Indian silk across the girl's shoulders. "Come now."

Amelia scowled but allowed herself to be herded relentlessly toward the door. "Are you certain there is nothing I can fetch you? A cup of tea? A cool cloth for your brow?"

"You are kind," Fleur said. "But truly I am quite well. Just fatigued. I am sorry," she said again, and after she'd repeated that sentiment several times, Amelia relented and stepped outside, followed by the comtesse, holding her immaculate skirt just so.

But Lucille stopped in the doorway, her shrewd eyes somber as she rested her hand on the latch. Their gazes met. "I am told repeatedly and emphatically that they are not all alike."

"Who?" Fleur asked.

"Men," Lucille said. Her husband, the aging earl of Anglehill, had been bent, bald, and as cantankerous as a toothache. But despite it all, Fleurette suspected at times that Lucy still missed him, regardless of the cavalier front she so carefully maintained.

"Go now, Lucy," Fleur scolded. "The others are waiting. Hurry along, or you'll be late."

Lucille shook her head, sighed, and drew herself to her full height. She stood five-eleven in her silk stockings, a daunting height for any man. The earl, riddled by rickets and a number of other ailments, had never reached the five-six mark. He'd resented it deeply. "There is no such thing as being late when one is on holiday. One is either spot on time or early for the next engagement."

"I shall keep that in mind," Fleur said, and smiled at her departing companions. But as they traipsed down the steps to the cobbled street, she realized her hands were shaking. Pressing the door shut, she retreated to the parlor and assured herself that all was well. The nightmares were nothing new. They were only dreams conjured up by a foolishly overactive imagination. All was as it should be. She needn't worry.

But she dare not return to bed. Neither could she eat, though the breakfast she had ordered waited on the sideboard.

She tried to read, but the words swam before her eyes, and dark images crowded in. Finally, vexed and restless, she donned her favorite riding habit and wandered alone to the comtesse's stable. The buildings were immaculate, as were the steeds. Although Antoinette had never been known to ride, she kept several fine hacks. Requesting a leggy bay be saddled, Fleurette finally rode the wending streets of Paris alone.

It was nearly dusk when, to some surprise, she found herself at Jardin de Jacques. Fond memories of the day before drew at her until she left her mount with a squire and wandered the mossy paths. It was not long before she came once again upon the statue of the towering Black Celt.

The sun was low in the sky and cast a gentle glow on the upturned blossoms of the nearby roses, but it did little to lighten the Celt's granite face. Instead, he stood imposing and dark, as if the light never quite reached him. As if he stood perpetually alone despite the many visitors who stopped for a moment, then bustled past.

He was not entirely unlike herself, Fleurette thought, then laughed at her melancholy mood. In that instant a shadow loomed over her. A scythe swooped down. She gasped and jerked about, but the shadow materialized into nothing more deadly than a wizened old man bearing a gnarled staff.

Fleur pressed a hand to her pounding heart and sought to calm her breathing.

"Me apologies, lass." The old gaffer was dressed in rough garb, his knobby hands bent with age and placed one atop the other on the curve of his cane. "I did na mean to frighten ye."

Fleurette pinched back harsh words. Fear tended to make her sharp-tongued. "No. No." She forced a weak smile. "The fault is entirely mine. I must have been daydreaming."

"Aye. 'Twill happen." He returned her smile, showing stained teeth and a kindly tempera-ment. "'Tis easy to do in the shadow of the braw Celt." He nodded toward the statue. "One tends to remember things long past and some-times things best left forgot."

She watched him, wondering what he meant, wondering if he could read her thoughts, could guess the images that haunted her nights. Or did he have dark memories of his own that came tumbling back in the Celt's stony presence?

"Are you the keeper of these gardens?" she asked.

"Me? Nay," he said, and gave a gravelly chuckle. "I am na but an old man what comes to visit the Celt now and again."

"An admirer of ancient art?" she guessed.

"I would na say so," he said, eyeing the statue. "But more an admirer of ancient times."

She turned her gaze toward the venerable sculpture. It seemed to watch her even now, its thoughts unspoken, its purpose suspended, but only for an abbreviated moment. "When was he sculpted? Do you know?"

"Sculpted?" said the old man and gave her a glance from the corner of his rheumy eye. "Have you na heard the tale, lass?"

She smiled. "Surely you don't believe that foolishness about his being cursed," she said, though she admitted to herself that in the lengthening shadows of the Celt all things seemed possible.

"A sensible young maid are ye then?" he asked, and canted his head at her.

She laughed. "Sensible yes. Young . . ." She shrugged, and he chuckled.

"The Celt lived back when the world was new. When druids roamed the Highlands and chanted beneath an ancient moon. Even ye are probably young compared to him, aye?"

"Fourteenth century?" she guessed, studying the chiseled links of the warrior's lower helmet.

The old man cocked his head as if impressed by her knowledge. "Ye ken yer history."

"I am fond of ancient artifacts. Indeed, I collect some pieces from that era and before."

"Do ye now? And what of the dark Celt here? Does he strike yer fancy?"

She tried to pull her gaze from the statue but found she could not quite manage it. There was something about it, something that spoke of honor and duty and virtues lost long before her time. "Yes," she said, "I suppose you could say that he does."

"Then ye should take him home with ye."

"What?" She jerked her gaze toward the old man. She was certain he was joking, but his expression suggested otherwise. It was as somber as a stone.

"I have been visiting the Celt for nigh on sixty years now. And afore that me da did the same." He nodded ruminatively, then sighed. "Me own time grows short. But ye . . ." He eyed her askance, then nodded as if deep in thought. "Aye, he would do well in yer care."

She laughed, startled and breathless. "I am certain his curator has no wish to see him gone from this place."

The old man squinted as he gazed up at her from his wizened height. The light from the sinking sun gleamed in his marble-bright eyes. "Certain of that are ye, lass?"

"Ancient art as fine as this is not easily parted with," she said, and motioned toward the statue. It called to her, and she stepped nearer. The hound seemed to be laughing, its pitted eyes rolled up to watch her approach. The stallion all but quivered on the brink of release. And the warrior . . . Dear Lord, the warrior . . . Reaching up, she touched his solid arm. It still held the heat of the sinking sun. She smoothed her fingertips along the corded muscle. "I doubt any would part with such a piece," she breathed, but even as she said the words, she imaged him in her own gardens, imagined him watching over her at night, shielding her from the world beyond her windows. "He would not be easily replaced. Indeed," she added, skimming along his massive forearm to his hand, fisted tight about his etched sword, "I doubt if there is another like him in all the world."

A dove crooned at the oncoming night, but the old man remained silent. She pried her gaze from the Celt. "Don't you agree?" she asked, but when she turned, the old man was nowhere to be seen. "Sir. Sir?" she said. Nothing answered but the sound of the wind in the nearby willow. Its trailing branches waved gently as if moved by unseen hands.

She tightened her grip on the Celt's fingers.

They were as solid as forever, as unyielding as the earth beneath her feet, and for a moment, for one brief lapse of time, she felt truly safe.

But someone giggled from a path nearby, snapping her from her reverie. Feeling girlishly foolish, she pulled her hand from the Celt's hewn grip and slipped unnoticed from the garden.

Chapter 3

⁓⁓◦◦◦◦⁓⁓

"Lady Glendowne." Mr. Finnegan bowed over her hand, squeezing her fingers and placing a sloppy kiss somewhere in the vicinity of her knuckles. "You look absolutely bedazzled this evening."

She could only assume he meant dazzling, for despite the mind-boggling amount of work and the nightmares that had plagued her since her return from Paris, she herself had thought she'd looked quite fetching when first she'd seen her reflection in her bedchamber mirror. Her gown was made of salmon brocade, beribboned at the hem and laced tight below her bosom. Tessa had used her magical skills to sweep her hair into an intricate coiffure embedded with faux pearls. Small ringlets cascaded to her breasts, which, though humble in stature, had been persuaded by somewhat deceitful means to reside just below her chin.

She looked quite charming, Fleurette admitted silently. And she wanted nothing more than to return home and toss the entire ensemble into the cook fire.

"Thank you," she said instead, and, smiling prettily, pulled her fingers firmly from his grip. Mr. Finnegan was short, as round as a turnip, and married to a woman who could wither an adversary with one glance. He was also sloppy drunk. "You look enchantingly besotted yourself."

He beamed at her. "You've noticed."

" 'Twould be impossible not to."

"You're too kind," he said, and staggered a little. He was sweating like a draught horse, but he owned a small fleet of ships that regularly carried Fleur's coveted carriages across the Channel and beyond.

Shortly after Thomas's death, Fleurette had sold off everything but Briarburn's floor tiles and bought a floundering company. Eddings Carriages, as it was now called, was, to date, her greatest success. "Have you lost weight as well?" she asked.

"A bit perhaps." Finnegan patted his expansive belly. "One has got to watch his figure, or the maids will surely not, aye? Why just last week I—"

His voice droned on like a pesky insect. Fleurette smiled, glanced up, and caught Stanford's attention from across the room. The slightest widening of her eyes had him easing away from Deacon to come to her aid.

"Lady Glendowne," he said, and bowed elegantly at the waist. His hair glowed like autumn wheat in the bevy of candles that graced the width of the ballroom. "I have been searching for you all this long evening."

"Truly?" She feigned surprise, "My apologies. Had I known, I would have sought you out straightaway. Please excuse me, Mr. Finnegan."

"Oh." The Irish merchant scowled at the intrusion, his mouth still open from his ongoing soliloquy. "Very well. But you must promise me a dance before you leave."

"Most certainly," she said, and, taking Stanford's arm, eased into the milling crowd of revelers. Well out of earshot, she clasped her companion's hand as he led her into a waltz. Stanford settled his fingers comfortably against her waist and held her gaze with his own. He was a fine dancer, well tutored, considerate, and graceful. "I am, once again, entirely in your debt. Whatever would I do without you?"

"I am certain you would do very well on your own," he said, and swept her about an elderly couple near the towering double doors that led to the formal gardens beyond. "In fact, that is something I had hoped to speak to you about."

"Oh?" She tried not to stiffen with apprehension and prayed quite fervently that he had no hopes of furthering their relationship. She adored Stanford like a brother, and he had been a tremendous support to her in the months following Thomas's death, but she had no desire to marry again. As it turned out, independence suited her far better than she had dared hope.

He studied her face for a moment, and she felt her breath hitch.

"I wish you would not drive so much alone, Fleurette," he said. "Especially to Hampstead."

She laughed with relief and he scowled.

"'Tis no laughing matter," he assured her. "It can be quite dangerous, even during the day. I know your business endeavors are important to you, and I applaud your success. Truly I do, but you must implement caution."

She gave his hand a grateful squeeze. "'Tis sweet of you to be concerned for my welfare," she said, and leaned back slightly so as to study his face more closely. "But you needn't be. Truly. If I feel there is the slightest risk, I make certain to have Mr. Benson accompany me."

"Mr. Benson," he said, spinning them around a drunken gentleman who seemed to be dancing alone, "while a formidable overseer, is the approximate age of the equinox."

She laughed despite the fact that her slippers were pinching and her head was beginning to pound. "I would disagree, but I've no idea what the equinox is."

He gave her a charming smile. "Neither do I, but I'm quite certain Mr. Benson was present at its birth."

The music led them easily across the marble floor. She sobered somewhat. "You always make me feel better, Stanford. I want to thank you for that."

"You should not spend so much time alone, Fleurette. Indeed, despite Deacon's deplorable . . ." He paused as if searching for a kindly euphemism, then said, "self. I must agree with his sentiment. You should consider marriage again."

She stared at him. Thomas and Stanford had been as close as brothers. So close, in fact, that it was difficult for her to believe he was prepared to see her put his death behind her. "I'm not yet ready," she said. "Surely you can understand that."

"Fleurette—"

She interrupted him quickly. "Thomas was . . ." She paused, fighting to give him a misty smile. "It would be impossible to replace him." The young baron of Glendowne was well-bred, elegant, and intelligent. He had been a fine catch for a young lady with no one to see to her future. She'd been no more than fifteen when her parents had died in a carriage accident. Alone and utterly lonely, she had been thrilled when Thomas began his courtship. The days had been filled with picnics and laughter. The evenings had been afloat with dancing and earnest conversation.

He was charming and witty and irresistible.

Unfortunately, he had also been a devout gambler. But his hobbies were no hardship, for she'd inherited a modest fortune, one she was more than happy to turn over to the charming baron who asked her to be his bride. They'd had money and to spare. Or so she had thought.

The devastating truth had come quickly upon the startling news of his untimely death.

But she had been unable to bear making the news of their financial failure public. Thus she had emptied every room in Briarburn, the only property she'd been able to retain, and quietly sold the goods overseas. Except for the parlor. Into that one chamber, she had poured every bit of remaining treasure. It was, after all, the place where she most often entertained guests— friends and business acquaintances alike. And she was not foolish enough to allow others to glimpse too much truth. No matter how much she trusted them.

Stanford was watching her with the slightest scowl marring his elegant brow. She caught his gaze, and he sighed. "You know I loved him as a brother," he said "But he was not perfect."

Memories knocked at her consciousness, but she honed them carefully. Thomas had been exceedingly handsome, she remembered. Everyone had said so. "But I fear he was as close as I am likely to get," she said.

Stanford's scowl deepened.

She squeezed his hand and gave him a tremulous smile. "Seven years is not so long a time. Is it? Say, shorter than the . . . equinox."

He stared at her for a moment, then shook his head and gazed past her shoulder with disapproving solemnity. "I'm quite certain you're using the term entirely incorrectly."

She laughed, and he returned her smile.

"I simply want you to be happy, Fleurette. Nothing more."

"I know you do, Stanford. And I am. Truly."

"But for a woman such as yourself to live alone . . . It seems . . ." He shook his head, at a loss for words.

"I enjoy being alone. And when I do not, I seek the company of friends."

"Your business endeavors . . . they are a strain on you. Why must you—"

"If not for Eddings Carriages, whatever would I do with my time?" she asked, interrupting smoothly. "There are only so many items one can embroider. Without my business holdings, I would have embellished everything I own by this time."

"Honestly," he said, watching her with wry interest, "have you ever embroidered a single article in the entirety of your life?"

She blinked, all innocence. "Of course I have."

"When?"

"Back when I was seven I—"

"Oh for heaven's sake!"

"Back when I was seven," she began again, patiently stifling a laugh. "I embroidered a shawl for my mother. Gave it to her for her thirty-second birthday." She made an expression as if she were thinking back. Her parents had been the center of her universe, always happy, always kind, and deeply, madly in love. She had somehow assumed she would be the same. "It was hideous. I use it as a rag in the stables. The horses hardly ever complain."

"You're looking at this with entirely too much levity."

She watched him for a moment, feeling a sweep of fondness. "But that is how I prefer to look at things, Stanford. Better with levity than with fatalistic woe. Don't you agree?"

He sighed. "I worry."

"Well, you needn't. All is well. I'm healthy. I'm happy . . ."

"Are you?" He searched her face.

She drew forth a careful smile. And it was not so very hard. "You are most dear to care."

"I'm your only kin, and that by marriage. I have to worry for all those who've prematurely abandoned their posts."

"And you do it well," she said, and noticed, from the corner of her eye, that Lord Lampor was making his way through the crowd toward them. "Oh. Damn. Stanford, dance me toward the door."

He did so without inquiry, and, once hidden from the looming lord's view, she eased to a halt.

"Is something amiss?" he asked, and glanced surreptitiously about.

"No. I just . . ." She shook her head. "I've heard Lampor is on the prowl for a new wife."

Stanford glanced through the crowd but seemed to see nothing alarming. "Lord Lampor would not be a hideous choice. He's got a lovely home near Hyde Park and—"

"I have a lovely home near Earlsglen."

He quirked his lips at her. "Which boasts what now? Two goats and a prizewinning turnip?"

"You heard about the turnip?"

He didn't bother to respond. "Lampor is his father's firstborn and certain to inherit the old man's estate."

"I don't want the old man's estate."

"Very well then," Stanford said, growing peevish. "He harvests excellent tomatoes."

"Tomatoes." She gave him a look. "You're suggesting I marry a man who looms like a bent gargoyle and smells perpetually of fish oil because of his garden vegetables?"

"You seemed impressed with the turnip."

"Well . . ." She shrugged. "That was entirely different. Did I tell you it has won actual awards?"

"He also makes a damnably good mulberry wine."

"I'm lucky he doesn't have an orchard, or you'd sell me to him as a slave."

"Be happy," he said, and she rose on her toes and kissed his cheek.

"If I were any happier, they'd have me committed, but just now I have a pounding headache and a bunion the size of Lampor's lovely tomatoes. I'm going home."

"You sound ecstatic. I'll escort you to your carriage."

"Lord Lessenton!" From across the room, Lord Sebastian motioned rather wildly with his lace-scalloped handkerchief. He always kept it close to hand, as his nose and eyes tended to leak on a surprisingly regular basis. "Might I have a word?"

Fleurette turned to await the marquess's arrival, but seeing Lampor wading along in his wake, she whispered her good-nights and turned away.

"One moment," Stanford entreated, but she shook her head with a smile.

"I believe I can find my own conveyance. Take care. I shall see you soon." And with that she fled the house.

The air outside felt damp and lovely against her bare skin. Rain was brewing on the coast. Off to her right, a pair of rented coachmen smoked cigars and chatted quietly together as they waited for their masters. A horse nickered far off, and even through the darkness she could see her matched grays. They were a beautiful pair. She'd found them in a decaying hamlet in Suffolk, where they'd been bred by an aging gentleman with more debt than good sense. He'd been happy enough to part with them in exchange for a two-wheeled gig and a tractable cob. He'd even—

"Lady Glendowne."

She started at the sound of her name and pivoted about. A man stood a few feet away, his face hidden in the shadows.

"Lady Glendowne?" he repeated.

She forced herself to breathe and straightened her back. "Yes," she said, her voice carefully steady. "I am she."

He stepped forward another stride. It took some power of will to resist backing away, even though she knew she was being foolish. She was, after all, in Madame Gravier's front yard, surrounded by hostlers and her own dedicated driver.

"Allow me to introduce myself," he said, and inclined his head the slightest degree. "I am William Kendrick."

She waited a moment for him to continue, but he did not. Her heart thrummed nervously in her chest, but she dare not show it. "Is there something I can do to assist you, Mr. Kendrick?"

"You can tell me of your husband's death," he said, and stepped forward again.

This time she did retreat, for there was something in his tone that frightened her. Something in his looming presence. "I beg your pardon?" she breathed.

"Your husband," he said, and gave her the ghost of a knowing smile. "Surely you remember him."

Her knees felt suddenly weak and her chest restricted. "If you'll excuse me, I have a terrible headache," she said, and turned away, but he hurried around her, blocking her retreat.

"I know the truth," he murmured.

"I've no idea what you speak of."

"Then either you are not so smart as I have heard, or your memory is short indeed. Was he so insignificant to you?"

"Who are you?" It was difficult to breathe, all but impossible to keep her hands steady. "What do you want?"

"Oh, did I not introduce myself appropriately?" he asked, and bowed with sardonic elegance. "I am your husband's cousin." He straightened slowly. "As for what I want . . . Revenge would be sweet but . . . revenge is mine, or so saith the Lord."

Her heart was hammering against her ribs in earnest, and her limbs felt wooden, but she lifted her skirts in a careful hand and raised her chin. "I thank you for that biblical reference. I'm certain it shall come in quite handy, but as I've said, I must be getting home."

She turned away. He snatched her arm, his grip hard and unyielding.

"The wicked will surely die," he hissed.

Anger spewed through her with unexpected vehemence. Damn him and his thinly veiled threats! She'd endured too much to allow an unknown intruder cow her with a few foolish words. She jerked her arm away with a snap and turned on him. "And the demmed meek shall inherit the earth."

"Maybe so," Kendrick snarled, stepping close. "But you are not the meek are you, Madame? Indeed, you are nothing more than a harlot who has—"

"What's this then?" a burred voice rumbled.

Fleurette jerked her attention to the newcomer, ready to flee toward whatever safety he might offer, but when he stepped out of the shadows, she actually leaned away, for he was the approximate size of a seasoned draught horse. Silent and impossibly large, he dwarfed Madame Gravier's carefully sculpted arborvitae.

But Kendrick was not cowed. "Who the devil are you?" he asked, and yanking a pistol from his vest, pointed it at the stranger.

Fleurette gasped, but the giant stood unmoved. "I asked a question of ye," he reminded, his voice low and quiet. "I would have an answer."

"It so happens that I have business with the lady," Kendrick said. The gun gleamed dully in the silvery moonlight. "And that business is no concern of yours."

The stranger stepped closer. Fleur caught her breath.

"Ladies do na conduct business with vermin." His Highland burr was deep and quiet. "And I dunna care for liars."

"You dare call me a liar?" snarled Kendrick.

"I dare call ye vermin."

"Damn you!" Kendrick cursed, and raised the gun. But suddenly it was gone—snatched from his hand and spun into the darkness near Fleur's feet. She scooped it up in shaky hands.

The stranger stood inches from Kendrick, his hand wrapped about his wrist and his head lowered toward the others.

"*And* a liar," he said evenly.

Kendrick yanked at his arm, but only his own body moved. The giant's remained exactly as it was. Even in the darkness, Fleur could see the terror in the smaller man's eyes. He jerked again and stumbled suddenly backward as he was abruptly released.

Catching his balance, he rubbed his wrist frantically and retreated. "I would suggest that you mind your own affairs, Scotsman," he warned, but his voice quivered. "Or you shall surely regret the outcome."

The Scot stepped forward, his stride long and steady. "And I would suggest that ye understand this, ye sniveling cur. Trouble *is* me affair, and I dunna fear the outcome."

Kendrick jerked back, his gaze darting toward Fleurette. "You've not seen the last of me, my lady. The wicked shall surely pay," he said, and fled into the darkness.

Fleurette steadied her hands against her skirt and turned breathlessly toward her savior. "Well, he was rather rude wasn't he? Though quite well versed in theology." She locked her knees and tried to see the Scotsman's features in the darkness. "I believe I owe you—"

"Where is your master?" he asked, and stepped toward her.

She stumbled back without thinking. "I . . . I beg your pardon."

"Your lord," he said. "Why has he allowed ye to venture out unchaperoned?"

"Allowed me?" She straightened her back with a snap. "Listen! I appreciate your intervention, but as it turns out, I do not have a *master*, and I did not need your overbearing assistance. In truth—"

"What did he want?"

"I . . . What?"

"The well-versed vermin what spewed biblical verses like venom. Was he after coin or was it your virtue he hoped to steal?" he asked, and stepped closer still.

She crowded backward. In the diffused light of the moon, she could see that his clothes were rough and his hair unfashionably long. "Who are you?"

"Or do ladies in this place have no virtue?"

She drew a sharp breath and held her ground with hard-won determination. "What do you want?"

"Mayhap I want the very thing your quivering friend wished for," he said, and, advancing further still, glared down through the darkness at her.

She lifted her chin and tightened her fingers on the pistol. Damn him and all his ilk. Gentleman or pauper, it made no difference. They were often one and the same. "And *mayhap*," she gritted, "you should crawl back into whatever hole you've just emerged from, because I'll be damned before I'll give you so much as a farthing."

He stared at her. His expression was chiseled, but his eyes gleamed like a rogue wolf's in the moonlight. "Mayhap 'tis not coin I'm after, lassie."

"Then you'd best be on your way," she said, and pressed the pistol's muzzle against his groin. "Or you'll never have that again either."

He glanced down as if curious. His lips lifted the slightest degree, and then he stepped closer still, forcing her backward. She retreated, breathing hard.

"'Tis a strange place you've got here," he mused quietly. "Where the men quiver and the women growl."

"I'll do more than growl," she vowed, and though her voice shook, she pressed the gun more firmly against his crotch. "If you hope to continue your questionable line, you'll back away."

"As it turns out," he said, and pushed her farther still. "I dunna."

She jerked the gun up, planting it below his jaw. Apparently oversized Highlanders with antiquated speech patterns didn't much care if their nether parts were blown to kingdom come. Strange. In the past, she'd found men to be quite protective of everything between their navels and their knees. "If you've no wish to join your ancestors you'll leave me be."

"Lassie," he said, and suddenly he was gripping her hand and easing the muzzle toward the sky. "Threats of death dunna move me, but if ye canna say the same I would suggest ye find yourself a well-smitten champion to come at your beck and call. For if I hoped to harm ye . . ." He tightened his grip. There was only a hint of discomfort, and yet she knew beyond a shadow of a doubt that if he wished, he could snap her bones like writing quills. " 'Twould be no hardship," he said.

She opened her mouth. But whether she planned to scream or plead or pray, she couldn't be sure, for suddenly her hand was miraculously set free. The gun bobbled in her fingers. She struggled to steady it, but the barbaric intruder was already gone, disappearing like a nightmare into the shadows.

Chapter 4

Fleurette's journey home was long, dark, and riddled with misgivings. Horace, her well-trusted driver, deposited her at the end of her cobbled walkway, and she hurried through the darkness, for even her own estate seemed suddenly fraught with danger.

Henri met her at the door, bounding ecstatically about her feet. She stroked his ears as Mr. Smith hurried up, apologizing profusely for his tardy greeting. But she wanted nothing more than the safety of her private chambers and hurried up the stairs, Henri in her wake.

Tessa, sleepy-eyed and quiet, was there in a moment to undo her mistress's upswept hair.

"Did you enjoy the party, my lady?" she asked, then hung away her gown.

"I've a bit of a headache," Fleur lied. "I fear it ruined the evening for me."

" 'Tis a shame," proclaimed the maid, but immediately launched back into her usual merry mood. "Oh, I almost forgot—the strangest thing 'appened today. Did—"

"Forgive me," Fleur interrupted, and rubbed unsteady fingers over her eyes. "But might it wait until the morning?"

"Certainly, my lady," Tessa agreed. "My apologies. Shall I get you a tonic?"

"No thank you. I just need to sleep," Fleur assured her, but after the maid's departure, the room seemed unnaturally quiet. Which was silly, because Fleur enjoyed the silence. Indeed, she reveled in solitude. After Thomas's death, she had moved from the master's chamber into smaller quarters. She was unsure what others made of her decision, but neither did she care. She loved her own private space. Oil paintings of bucolic tranquillity graced the walls. An ancient tapestry hung in a place of honor near the lone window, and an intricate figurine of Pegasus resided on a small commode near the door. But despite the time and funds she had expended on her precious art, it was the bed's shabby coverlet that she cherished the most. Tattered from her childhood, it draped her each night in kindly memories, and even now, with her nerves raw and tattered, it worked its usual magic when she pulled it close to her chin and bid Henri good night.

Morning found her rested, her mood restored and her nerves soothed. Outside, the sky was washed blue and the sun peeped merrily over the eastern woods. Rising from her bed, Fleurette wandered toward the window that overlooked her gardens. But she had not yet pulled on her robe when she stopped dead in her tracks. For there, looming above the fawning flora, was the Black Celt.

"Tessa!" Fleur yelled.

Henri scurried under the bed.

The maid appeared in a heartbeat, her eyes wide as she rushed into the room.

"What's wrong? What—" she began, but Fleurette was already motioning toward the window.

"When—How—"

"Oh! I tried to tell ye last night. Isn't it

grand?" Tessa breathed, joining her mistress by the window.

"Why?" Fleurette turned woodenly back toward the statue. It loomed above the nodding roses as if accepting their blushing obsequiousness with silent dignity. "Why is it there?"

"I thought . . ." Tessa turned to her with wide eyes. "I thought you purchased it while in Paris. The gentleman said—"

"The gentleman. What gentleman?"

The maid scrunched her face in thought. "He was smallish. Old. Irish maybe. Or—"

"The old gaffer came here?"

"So you do know him. I thought . . ." Tessa began, but Fleurette was consumed by the statue.

Snatching up a robe, she hurried down the stairs and outside. The stones on the path felt cool and rough against her bare feet, but she barely noticed, for the Celt was there, silently gazing down at her.

She reached up to tentatively place a hand on his thigh. It felt warm and solid. "What are you doing here?" she breathed.

And though it did not answer, its very presence seemed to speak of guardianship. Of honor and bravery and courage long dead.

It was some time before Fleurette was able to

tear herself away. Even longer before she forced herself into her study to rifle through the paperwork her overseer had delivered during her time in Paris. But she could not concentrate. She wandered out into the garden again, and in the shadow of the dark Celt, the world seemed quiet and serene. She gave herself a mental shake. It was only a statue, after all, a slab of stone and nothing more, no matter how well crafted.

Why it had been delivered to her, she could not guess, but that hardly gave her an excuse to dawdle the day away. She had work to do. And yet, she could not seem to force herself back into her dim study. Thus she determined to pursue another effort.

Ordering her mare saddled, she changed into her riding habit, settled the matching chapeau upon her head, and mounted the restive bay. Beneath her, *Fille de Vent* pranced as they turned from Briarburn's sweeping drive onto the humble thoroughfare. London was some miles to the north, but Fleurette had no interest in that bustling metropolis. Instead, she turned the mare's elegant head toward the west and pressed her into a rocking canter.

The surrounding woods were still after the previous night's rain and *Fille*'s high-stepping footfalls were muffled against the damp earth. Sweet clover scented the warm air and troubles dropped away, and though Fleur wished she could ride forever, her mission lay close at hand. Yes, she would allow herself this break from paperwork, but she would not waste the day entirely, for despite the frivolous airs she displayed for her posh friends, she would not forget the years when she was hungry and alone. Security, she well knew, meant the ability to take care of one's own finances, for without funds, she was at the mercy of others.

Off to her right, a warbler piped its afternoon song. Fleur glanced into the woods there. Deep in the verdant forest, the Nettle River wound its haphazard course. It was a lovely sight and hosted an aquatic bounty, but it was neither its pastoral beauty nor its trout that fascinated her. It was the land itself—the earth, dark with silt and heavy with nutrients—the land that undulated gently in shades of green until it fell quietly into a small quarry set amongst the ancient oaks.

Some years before Thomas's birth, it had all belonged to the Eddings estate. Financial problems had forced its sale, but according to the records Fleur had rooted out of the old lord's office, the stonery had once brought in a decent income. With any luck and a bit of skillful bargaining, it would do so again, for Lord Gardner, its present owner, was floundering in debt. Indeed, he had gone so far as to beg a loan in an effort to cover his mounting troubles. And Fleurette had complied. After all, it was impossible to dislike the jovial baron; but if she were to be honest, that was hardly the entire reason for her capitulation.

She had long hoped to buy the land that lay between her property and his. Hence, she had done all she could to lay friendly groundwork toward that end.

Fille's footfalls clattered restively onto Gardner's drive. Horse chestnuts lined his road, obscuring the view of his estate, but in a moment the trees parted, affording a glimpse of the ancient house. Built of native rocks, it stood against a lovely backdrop of sweeping hills. A stone fence stood guard beneath the towering trees and in the front yard, a swaybacked sorrel stood with cocked hip and drooping head.

Fille gave the aging gelding a disdainful glance, arched her neck to even more impressive heights, and pranced to a halt. Jumping from the saddle, Fleurette drew the reins over the mare's neck and walked the short distance to a tying post. But even before she had the mare secured, an elderly servant bustled from the house.

"My lady," he said, and bowed, stiff with old age and formality. "Shall I have a squire stable your mount or will you not be gracing us with your presence for so long a time?"

"Mr. Sitter," she said, and smiled. Gardner's butler had an old-world panache that Fleurette had always found appealing. "'Tis good to see you again. You are feeling well, I hope."

He nodded, and his rigidity softened slightly. "Her ladyship is most kind to ask. I am doing well."

"And your wife, how is she?"

"Well also, and doting on the little ones whenever possible. Our Evie gave us a grandson this month past. A strapping lad he is."

"I'm certain of it, if he's anything like his grandfather."

The old man blushed with guileless appreciation. "Do you wish to secure your mount and accompany me to the parlor?"

She glanced at the sorrel gelding. It lifted its bottle-shaped head and gave her a disinterested stare. Its bottom lip drooped loosely, and its toes pointed in. Had Gardner's affairs sunk so low that he rode this poor beast? Fleur wondered. Slipping her reins through a nearby ring, she tied the mare and followed the servant. "I've no wish to disturb your lord if he has company."

"A . . ." Mr. Sitter paused for a second, then hurried on, doing his best to cover his obvious uncertainty. "A . . . gentleman arrived some time ago. But I am certain my lord will wish to know of your presence. Please, if you will follow me."

With one last glance at the horses, Fleur strode up the walkway and into the house. The parlor was small but sunny and welcoming. She seated herself in a brightly patterned armchair as the butler hustled off for refreshments.

"Lady Glendowne." Lord Gardner hurried in not a full minute later. He was a short, squat gentleman with a bulbous nose, watery eyes, and a smile like a mischievous cherub. He employed it now with honest good mirth. "Aren't you a picture?"

She rose to her feet and extended her hands. He took them in his own and kissed her cheek.

"Lord Gardner. You look well."

"Ach," he said, and eyed her askance.

She could smell the whisky on his breath. 'Twas a funny thing, some men were mean whether they were drunk or sober, and some only got merrier when deep in their cups.

"You're full of flattery as usual," he said. "When Sitter came to announce a visitor I knew it was you straightaway. Blushing like a debutante, he was."

She laughed. "You'd best be good to him," she said, "for I have every intention of stealing him away from you."

"Aye, well, he couldn't go to a kinder lady. But what can I do for you this day? I doubt you've come to snatch my butler from under my nose."

"Actually, that is a secondary mission," she said, and cleared her throat. Now that it came to it, she felt somewhat edgy. But business did that to her. Like a she wolf over a fresh kill, Lucy had once said. Fleurette had never particularly cared for the analogy. "I've come—"

"Ahh, there you are, Mrs. Edward," Gardner said, as an elderly woman hobbled into the room with a tray. "Please, my lady, sit. Have a sip of tea and a sandwich. Cook's cucumbers are the envy of all England."

"Oh, no. Thank you. I've come on a bit of business as it were."

"A biscuit then?" he asked.

"No. Thank you." Fleur waited for the elder servant to depart, then launched back into business. "I know you've had . . . Well, finances have been difficult for everyone of late, have they not? What with the king's current ailments." And the Prince Regent, of course, who was an extravagant ninny, though she did not say so aloud.

Gardner took a tiny triangular sandwich between his thumb and forefinger and downed it in one bite. "Times are hard, and that's the truth of it," he said, seeming unperturbed by her bluntness.

"Yes, well," she said, smoothing her skirt. "I was hoping I might make them a bit easier. For you at least."

He lifted a cup from the tray and swallowed noisily. "That is ever so kind of you, my lady," he said. "But things have been going along well enough, considering. Why just today—"

"I'm speaking of the woods that adjoins our property," she interrupted smoothly.

He had reached for a second sandwich, but stopped his hand halfway to the tray. "The woods?"

"Yes." She said, breath held as she watched him. "I thought you might wish to sell it."

"The woods with the quarry?" he asked, bobbling his cup back onto its saucer.

She nodded. "As you know, it belonged to my husband's family some years back."

"Yes indeed. Father was more than happy to buy it when old Maynard made those bad investments years ago and . . . Well," he said, blushing slightly at his lack of diplomacy, "you've turned things about nicely for yourself since then."

She gave him a modest smile for the compliment. "It was Thomas's efforts that made it possible, really, and yet he didn't live to harvest the fruit of his well-laid plans. He had always hoped to restore Briarburn to its former holdings. And now that Eddings Carriages is doing well, I was hoping to do just that."

"Yes, certainly." He took his second sandwich, but held it in his hand as if forgotten. "But well . . ." He chuckled and rubbed his neck with his free hand. " 'Tis a funny thing, to be sure."

"What?" she demanded, then smoothed her voice and smiled. "What is funny, Lord Gardner?"

"Well, I just now . . ." He chuckled as if embarrassed. "I just today had a visitor. We had a bit of a chat about . . ." He cleared his throat, looking sheepish and flitting his gaze to her and away. "Well about a good many things, truth to tell. It seems he appreciates a fine horse, though his own mount was far and away the sorriest—"

"Lord Gardner," she interrupted, patience fraying as she preened a smile. "What has this to do with my—"

"I got another offer on that land."

"Another offer?" she snapped. "From whom?"

"As I said, 'tis a funny thing." He looked anxious now, anxious and fidgety. "I was out for a gallop with the hounds. Fritzy whelped just last week. As handsome a litter as ever I've seen. Six bitches and the same number of dogs. Can you believe it? Twelve all told and—"

"Lord Gardner," she prodded, careful to smile through her gritted teeth, "about the land."

"Ahh, yes, well, the land." He cleared his throat. "As I said, just this morning a gentleman comes to visit. Rides up through the chestnuts on the saddest-looking gelding I've seen in some time. Long in the tooth and low in the back if you take my meaning. The horse that is, not the rider. As for that gentleman, I'd not met him before, or his ilk, I'll wager. Big man, he was. Twice my size. And he was dressed peculiar. Truth to tell he looked as if he hadn't two pence to rub together, but—"

"Who was he?" Fleur rasped, but before the baron spoke, a figure loomed in the doorway.

" 'Tis meself," rumbled a voice.

Fleurette turned with a start and stumbled backward, for not five feet away stood the towering Scot from Madame Gravier's front yard. "What are you doing here?" she breathed.

Sometime during the night she had convinced herself that the irritating Scotsman had not been as large as she remembered. She had been entirely wrong.

"I've a need for the wee quarry," he said. "And the land what surrounds it."

She breathed a shocked hiss and turned toward Lord Gardner with a start. But the baron giggled and shrugged as if too embarrassed to speak. She jerked back toward the Highlander.

"That's ridiculous," she snapped, then drew a slow breath and gave him a well-groomed smile. "I'm afraid that's impossible, Mr. . . ." She waited in silence . . . as did he, showing a detestable lack of good manners and no embarrassment whatsoever. From what murky depths had he slithered?

"Hiltsglen," Gardner supplied nervously. "Mr. Killian Hiltsglen, wasn't it? Truth to tell, Mr. . . . Hiltsglen . . ." He giggled again, then cleared his throat and seemed to go rather pale. "I thought you had ridden off."

"As I see it . . ." The Scot didn't turn toward the baron, but kept his gaze steady on Fleurette. His hair was long and dark. Tied in a queue behind his muscular neck, it boasted a single narrow braid behind his left ear. A scar slanted through his right eyebrow and across the bridge of his nose at an obtuse angle. "Ye've na need for more land, lass," he rumbled.

She huffed in outrage, then lowered her

brows and glared at him. "If you'll excuse me, Mr. . . . Hiltsglen, I don't believe it is for you to decide what my needs might be."

He remained silent for a moment. His brows were low and dark, shadowing his narrowed eyes. " 'Tis just yerself ye look after. Ye've no bairns to care for, have ye?"

"Bairns?" she blustered, wondering madly just what Lord Gardner had said about her.

"Wee ones," he explained, and let his gaze drop to her breasts. They were well covered that morning by her deep blue riding jacket and singularly humble in their unembellished state. "Ye are nursing na bairns."

For a moment she was actually speechless, then, "That is hardly any of your—"

"Why are ye na wed?" he asked. "Ye are na uncomely."

"I—You—" She closed her mouth with a snap and turned toward their host, pointedly ignoring the barbarian who studied her like a prize Thoroughbred. "Lord Gardner . . ." She would have liked to smile, but she was afraid she was incapable of such an extraordinary feat at that precise moment. "I should like to purchase your land for ten thousand pounds."

"Ten thousand!" he breathed. "That is most generous of you, my lady, but I—"

"Payable into your private account this very day."

"I . . ." Gardner snapped his gaze from one to the other, his face as red as an autumn apple. "I'm afraid, Mr. Hiltsglen here offered . . ." He swallowed. "More."

"More!" she rasped.

"My apologies, my lady. I—"

"Then I shall give you the same plus a hundred guineas."

The baron opened his mouth like a gasping trout.

"I shall match her offer," said the Scot, not turning toward Gardner, "And vow to keep yer borders safe from brigands."

"My borders . . ." The inebriated baron was breathing hard. "That's most kind of you, I'm sure, but I hardly think—"

"I'll give you eleven thousand pounds plus an Eddings viceroy, straight from the factory. Two horse with a curved dash and velvet seats."

"Well I . . . I do love those velvet seats. They're as soft as butter when you—"

"Ye may tek the sorrel for yer own," the Scot rumbled.

"Your mount?" Gardner asked, blinking. "That's really—"

"Your gelding?" Fleur huffed a laugh. "He is not worth a pile of pebbles."

The Scotsman's eyes glowed as he looked her up and down "Mayhap ye judge a thing too much upon its appearance, me lady," he suggested. "And na enough upon its ability."

"Thank you for that invaluable lesson, Mr. Hiltsglen, but I fear I do not need—"

"Sir," he rumbled.

"What!"

"Ye may address me as Sir Killian of Hiltsglen. I am a knight, fully dubbed and spurred."

"I don't care if you're the bloody king of the trolls," she snarled, stepping up to him and raising her chin so as to meet his glare. "That woods belongs with my estate, and I'll not see it fall into the hands of an antiquated cretin who has neither the manners nor the breeding to behave in a civilized manner when—"

"My lady! My lady," Gardner rambled and, grabbing her arm in a gentle grasp, turned her abruptly toward the door. Pressing his other hand against the Scotsman's endless back, he prodded the giant along ahead of them. "I do so very much appreciate your gracious offer. And yours, too, Mr. Killian Sir. 'Twas ever so generous, but I fear I simply need a bit of time to give due consideration to the situation. Thank you ever so much," he said, and, depositing them unceremoniously on his front stoop, closed the door behind them with a snick.

Chapter 5

Killian watched the baroness turn, watched her eyes narrow, watched her watch him. Gone was the gracious maid who'd first arrived on Gardner's property, and in her place was this snarling she-wolf.

"Who are you?" she snapped.

Who indeed? Truth to tell, he remembered his name and little else since awakening beside the road some days ago. Since that moment nothing had been as it should be. Everything was changed, different, confusing. When had he journeyed to England? He had been in France. He was certain of that, for he could remember the lilting sounds of cultured voices, the sweet scent of cranesbill and alyssum in the Parisian gardens.

How and why had he arrived in England? And what did his sojourn there have to do with Lady Glendowne? That he did not know, and yet their lives were somehow entwined. That much he knew, felt in the very marrow of his bones.

Thus he had learned what he could, asked questions where he dared. Subtle inquires about the lady. The answers had set his mind racing, and none more than from the besotted Lord Gardner.

It seems she had married well. Lord Glendowne had been "'andsome as a god and well-bred to boot, if a bit free with her funds," or so said Shanks, the scrawny wainwright Killian had drunk with in a London pub.

Further inquiries had suggested the young baron had been "a fine chap, ready to buy a bloke a pint when he was out and about," which was a fair amount by all accounts.

Everyone agreed with shaking heads and morose expressions that his death was a bloody shame.

And yet Killian wondered whether the lady felt the same. If rumors were correct, it had been her coin that had bought the pints and financed the gambling. Might not a woman of her caliber resent such a thing?

"Why do you bedevil me?" The lady's back was as straight as an archer's arrow, and her lips were pursed with disapproval.

"Bedevil," he repeated and though she was well covered this day, he could not help but remember how she had looked on the previous night, with her glorious hair unhidden and her breasts all but bare to his parched gaze. What kind of men would allow their women to traipse about half-unclothed? "Is that what ye lowlanders call it when another comes to your aid?"

"Aid!" Her face was flushed pink from the tiny coil of her ears to the slim column of her neck. A few strawberry curls trickled out from beneath her silly hat and lay like pinkened gold against her ivory flesh. How soft would that flesh be beneath his fingertips, he wondered, and found that he was tempted almost beyond control to find out.

The idea made him grit his teeth against his own foolish desires. He was here on borrowed time. That much he had ascertained, though little else.

Her lips moved breathlessly for a moment, but when she finally spoke, she seemed to be in control once again. "Aid." She nodded once, the movement sharp and crisp. "In the quagmire where you were conceived, is that what they call it when one tries to steal another's land out from under her very—"

He stepped up to her, close enough to feel the warmth of her body, to smell the intoxicating sweet pea scent that wafted like summer magic from her elegant form. "Nay, lass," he said, " 'tis what I call it when I save ye from some sniveling coward intent on doin' ye bodily harm." He let his gaze rest on her heaving bosom, then slide slowly downward. She was built as fine and sleek as a prized mare. But a beautiful form did not necessarily speak of a good heart. That much he knew. Still, the temptation was as sharp as a spear. "Or mayhap men are free to do what they will with yer body."

Perhaps she had been angry before, but fire filled her eyes now, and her nostrils flared with rage. "You, Mr. Hiltsglen, are a bastard and a rogue," she said, and turned away.

He caught her arm, though he knew he should not. It had been a long age since he had felt a woman's skin against his own, and his defenses were weak, his instincts thrumming like pounding hooves. "Are they?" he asked. And though he tried to imbue his tone with scalding criticism, he found that he half hoped he was right. That she was the sort to offer herself to a man in aching need if the price was right.

But her teeth were gritted, her eyes narrowed to sparking green slits, and if he remembered correctly, women for hire tried to present a more congenial mien. "Release me," she hissed, her voice low and angry.

"Are ye offering yerself?" he asked instead, because, dammit, he was desperate.

He would not have thought she could stand straighter, but she drew her shoulders back and turned toward him, as slow and regal as a conquering queen. Pulling her arm from his grasp, she pursed her lips and held his gaze with a lethal glare. "I do not, nor shall I ever, *offer* myself to the likes of you."

Angry frustration brewed slowly in his own gut, but he would not let it dictate his actions. He must be patient. He must be wise. Indeed, he must turn away, let her go, say no more. "But ye dunna say the same of a prince such as Kendrick?"

"Kendrick," she said, then seemed to remember of whom he spoke and gave a thoughtful nod. "Tell me, Scotsman," she said, "do you think him so different from other men because he dared to threaten me outright?"

He scowled, his mind churning to override

the agony of his long suffering desires. "Aye," he assured her. "I do."

"Then you are a fool," she said, and, lifting her skirt in one gloved hand, marched down the stairs toward her mount.

He paced after her. "I dunna care to be cast into the same basket as a coward who would accost a woman," he said.

"Don't you?" She turned when she'd reached her mare. "That is unfortunate then, for I see you just the same."

"I've not threatened a maid," he said, and although he tried to keep his restless thoughts at bay, broken memories stormed ruthlessly in. "Though in truth, I believe I may have had some reason."

She smiled, but her eyes remained glittery hard. "Believe this," she said, and untied the bay without glancing down, "men will ever believe they have good reason." Easing the reins over her mount's elegant neck, she turned the iron toward her.

He grasped the mare's bridle in one hand. "Reason for what?" he asked.

"For whatever atrocities they choose to perform." She was no longer blushing. Indeed, her face was pale, her eyes huge in her neatly sculpted face. He watched her closely, for if he had learned aught, he knew enough to study his adversaries. And that was most certainly what she was. For though he remembered little, he had immediately recognized her title . . . Lady Glendowne. But there would be no more of her husband's line, for he had died and left her childless.

"What drives ye to labor like a man?" he asked.

For a moment she showed her surprise, and maybe a flicker of fear, but it was gone in an instant, hidden behind her cat-bright eyes. "I do not believe that is any affair of yours, Mr. Hiltsglen."

"Yer husband," he said, his mind finally taking precedence over his body's insistent demands. "Did he na see to yer needs?"

Her eyes were narrowed, her fine body tense.

"How did he die?" he asked.

"That is none of your—" she gritted, but he interrupted her.

" 'Twas na a love match," he guessed.

She stood breathless for a moment, her lips parted, and in that instant he saw the fear, long denied and hard fought, but there nonetheless.

"How dare you assume to know anything about me?" Anger brewed in her stormy eyes again, and he found that he was glad to see it, was thrilled to watch the fear be replaced by the blaze of her vibrant eyes. "Release my horse," she ordered.

"But what of yer bridegroom?" he asked, tightening his grip as she swung unaided onto her mount. "Did he cherish ye after a time in yer bed?"

Seated astride, she pulled a crop from beneath her saddle. "Release her," she said, and raised the whip.

The mare swung her haunches nervously sideways, her head tucked against her chest, her eyes rimmed white.

Killian scowled and tightened his grip. The animal was as bonny and fine-limbed as a doe, as fiery as hell, and not a suitable ride for such a delicate maid.

"Tell me, lass, is it by choice that ye ride alone, or is it yer temperament that dictates yer solitude?" he asked.

For one blessed moment she was speechless, then, "Do not make me call for Lord Gardner," she said, and set her heels to her mount.

If it was a threat, it was a poor one indeed, for the jovial baron had probably drunk himself into a stupor some time ago. God's bones, until Killian had stepped through his doorway, the other had been completely unaware of his guest's lingering presence. Did he not have knights to protect his property, to guard his holdings?

And what of this woman? Where was her champion? Tightening his grip, Killian scowled up at her. The mare tossed her head against the restraint. He drew her back down, and though he tried to hush the grating chivalry that seeped like old wine through his veins, he could not quite stop himself.

"If ye wish it," he suggested slowly, "we could change about."

The lady's brows raised slightly, but she didn't speak. Pride emanated from her in waves. Perhaps too much pride to allow her to admit her needs.

"Though the gelding is na so bonny as the mare, he will keep ye safe until ye reach—" he began, but suddenly she laughed out loud.

"Are you suggesting that I let you ride *Fille*?"

Killian felt the anger color his face, but he kept a tight rein on his emotions. "Pride can be a cruel mistress, lass," he said. "This I know."

"If I had any idea of what you spoke, I would respond scathingly. As it is, I must tell you, I wouldn't put that animal in my stew, much less in my stable."

He watched her carefully. Anger brewed in

her expression, but there was more, long-suppressed emotions hidden deep beneath the surface. "'Tis a strange thing," he said, "but some never learn to look beyond the flesh, no matter the past they've endured."

"Release me!" she demanded, and thumped hard against her mount's flanks. The mare lurched onto her hind legs. Caught off guard, Killian was yanked nearly off his feet before the bridle was snatched from his hand.

She leaned against the animal's mane, then straightened. The mare struck the earth with her footfeet, then lurched into a gallop.

Reaching forward, Lady Glendowne turned her about, drawing her into a tight circle.

"The land will be mine," she said struggling with her mount. "This I can guarantee."

Killian scowled and reached toward her. "Ease up on the bit," he ordered.

"So you may just as well crawl back into whatever cave you recently crept out of."

"Come down," he ordered, breath held. "Until she's settled."

"Leave. This is no place for you," she spat, and, loosening her inside rein, let the mare pivot onto the driveway and leap back into a gallop.

Killian cursed as they careened around the

corner, then, unable to resist urges older than time, he threw himself onto his own spavined steed and rushed after her.

Fleurette glanced behind her, saw the barbarian give chase and smiled as she leaned low over *Fille*'s gleaming neck. The mare's mane, black as night, blew against her face. Her hoofbeats thundered against the road, and her nostrils, stretched thin and wide with straining effort, blew like a roaring dragon. Fleurette turned again, and already the sorrel was dropping back. She laughed out loud and gave the mare her head. They all but flew over the hardpacked road, and it was that speed, that euphoric, liberating speed that eased the biting questions from her mind.

The barbarian's identity was insignificant, after all. Nor did it matter what he wanted, for she would make certain he did not get it. He was nothing more than a nettle in her saddle pad. An irritating nettle. An opinionated nettle. But a nettle nevertheless.

The road swung wide to the south, looping generously around Gardner's woods before winding back. *Fille* leaned into the northern turn. One more glance behind proved they had left Hiltsglen and his pigeon-toed gelding far behind, but Fleur let the mare run on, for they were both in the mood for a gallop.

All was well, Fleurette reminded herself. She was secure. Gardner would realize the wisdom of selling his woods to her. After all, Hiltsglen was not only a cretin, he was an unknown cretin, amongst the lowest ranks of the peerage. And there was nothing that irked the gentry more than dealing with underlings as if they were their equals. Of course, Gardner was a different sort. Maybe even a better sort, despite his affection for spirits. Still, she had created a good relationship with him and—

It was at that moment that something sprang from the woods. Seeing the thing from the corner of her eye, *Fille* lunged sideways, stumbling madly into the brush beside the road. Caught off guard, Fleurette tried to hold on, to keep her seat, to control her reins, but the mare was falling.

The earth spilled toward them. Panicked, Fleur kicked loose her stirrups and leapt. She hit the ground in time with the mare and lay absolutely still, staring through the branches at the sky overhead.

Moments passed with leisurely uncertainty, but finally the world settled slowly back into normality. She'd taken a foolish risk. Turning her head, Fleur saw that *Fille* had already scrambled to her feet. Her saddle was askew and her reins were broken, but she looked unscathed.

So luck had come through where Fleur's wits had failed. What was wrong with her? She wasn't some flighty debutante inclined to risk her mount or herself because of a few irritating words with an overbearing barbarian. She'd dealt with all types of men since taking up the reins of Eddings Carriages and had never acted so idiotically.

Scowling at her own foolishness, she braced her hands on the damp earth at her sides and tried to sit up.

"What the bloody hell do you think you're about?"

Fleur jerked around with a gasp, and there, not thirty feet away, stood the Scotsman.

"What . . ." She glanced side to side, searching for his mount, but he was the only animal in sight. "How did you get here?"

"Did I na tell ye to take me own steed instead?" he asked, and strode toward her. In a moment he was upon his knees beside her. "The mare was overwrought," he said, and reached for her.

She slapped his hand away and leapt to her feet. Pain ripped through her like a cannonball. She covered the agony with a snarl. "It was not *Fille*'s fault. Something spooked her."

"Nay. 'Twas na her fault, ye foolish twit. Did na one ever teach ye how to handle such a fine steed? I vow, if one of me squires mistreated such an animal so, I would make him polish me saddle each day for a—"

"It was you!" she gasped, and stumbled back a painful step.

He lowered his dark brows. A formidable man with a dark temper. "What in bloody hell do ye speak of?"

"You spooked my horse. You charged out of the woods like a . . ." She flipped her hand about. Even that hurt. "A demented warthog. What were you trying to do? Kill me? Do you want the land so much that you would resort to murder?" She took a truncated step forward, though he was still glaring. "Is that your plan, Hiltsglen?" she asked, her chin raised and her heart pounding. "Or did you simply hope to frighten me? For if that's the case, you'll soon find that I don't frighten easily. Indeed," she said and poked him in the chest with her crop. It had broken in half and dangled like a withered root. "I don't—"

"Listen, lassie," he snarled, and suddenly he grabbed the quirt, yanking her up against his body. It felt as unyielding as a boulder against her breasts. Planting a hand on his chest, she pushed herself backward, but he only advanced.

"I but came to make certain you did not break yer foolish neck, though I'll admit I'm tempted to wring it meself just about now. Ye've scared the poor mare senseless."

The world seemed to be slowing its pace. The first rush of anger was drifting away, and she found she was shaking. Still, it would hardly be wise to admit such a thing, so she narrowed her eyes. "Where's your mount?" she asked, her words slow and steady finally.

"What are you babbling on about now?"

"Your gelding," she said. "Where is he?"

"Ye needn't worry about what I've done with me own beast," he said. "Just be assured I would not treat him so thoughtlessly as—"

"You were furlongs behind at the very start," she interrupted. "You could not possibly have caught up on the road."

"As I told ye, lass, ye should not judge a thing on its looks alone."

"You cut through the woods," she reasoned.

He stared at her for a few seconds, then shifted his eyes away. "And what if I did?"

"The woods are thick and treacherous. Even *Fille* could not traverse them at such a pace."

He shrugged his gargantuan shoulders. "So ye are not so fine a judge of horseflesh as ye think yerself to be. Indeed—"

"You left him," she said, incredulous but certain. "You turned him loose and cut through the underbrush afoot." And he'd caught her. Good Lord, what kind of man could run down a blooded steed?

His brows lowered even more, a feat that seemed impossible, but she barely noticed.

"Who are you?" she asked.

He shifted slightly, his booted feet stirring centuries of undisturbed leaves. "Do ye disremember, lass? We've already met. I be Sir Killian of Hiltsglen and ye the greedy—"

"And why do you speak like that?"

He narrowed his eyes. The scar that bisected his eyebrow and nose had turned pale against his swarthy features.

"There is naught wrong with me speech," he assured her.

"*Naught* wrong?" she countered. "You talk like a suit of old armor."

"Men of the Highlands . . ." He paused and canted his head at her. His hair had come loose during his pursuit of her and hung nearly to the incredible width of his shoulders. "*True* men do not leave a maid to ride alone into danger."

She stared at him, her mind racing like a child's top. "So I was right," she murmured, awe

81

melding with a quiver of fear. "You caught up to me on foot."

He didn't answer.

"Because . . ." she said, and found that she could not, despite everything, control the tiny smile that lifted her lips. "Your gelding is no match for my mare."

Still, he only stared.

"Admit it," she said, and laughed out loud. "I was right."

"Aye," he said, and, turning away, marched over to *Fille*, who watched them with flickering ears. "Yer a wily one, ye are," he said, and, gently stroking the mare's neck, led her away.

"And don't you forget it. I know . . . Wait a moment. What are you doing?" she called and stepped forward, but pain shot through her knee and she winced. "Where are you going with my horse?"

"Think on it," he said, not deigning to do so much as glance over his shoulder. "A bright lass like ye is certain to sort it out," he said, and, striding onto the road, disappeared from sight.

Chapter 6

The mare snorted and danced sideways, swinging her haunches across the rutted road like a bonny dancer. Tucking her elegant head, she rolled dark eyes at Killian and champed the copper mouthpiece as if she scolded him.

"Well then," Killian rumbled, anger still roiling deep in his chest. "She should have been more careful with herself . . . and with ye. A spirited lass such as yerself should be coddled."

The mare shook her head, rattling the bit and prancing.

" 'Tisn't me own fault she took a fall," Killian

told her. "I warned her to be cautious. She has a firm seat and a soft hand, that I grant. But she's too stubborn by half. Stubborn and prideful."

The steed lifted her perfect forelimbs higher and flagged her kohl black tail.

"Na unlike yerself," he admitted, and straightened her heavy forelock with his free hand.

She flicked back her dark-tipped ears and bobbed her head. He scowled.

"And meself also, I suspect, but that does na mean she should risk ye on this road."

The mare glanced away, rolling her eyes toward the north. Briarburn was there, just around the bend, the ancient house crafted of chiseled stone, the stables just as old and equally venerable. It was a bonny spot, set against a backdrop of old forest and sweeping green fields.

Killian had seen it before. That he knew, though he could not remember when. The ragged memories seemed as old as time itself.

It was peacefully pastoral now, but had it always been so? He could not remember, for it seemed almost as if he had viewed this place with different eyes. Was it then, that he had changed so greatly, or the estate itself?

He could not say, and turned his mind irritably aside, lest his head begin to pound with questions. The answers would come if he let them. He would learn all he could of the willful lady he had left afoot. He would find the truth and learn why he was here in this time and place. And once that was accomplished, he would do what he must, as was his wont.

"'Tis na so verra far," he said, turning back toward the mare. "A furlong or two. Na more. Ye could run it in a matter of seconds. Yer mistress is well up to the task of walking it."

The dark eyes turned back with accusatory arrogance.

"She's na so delicate as she looks, I'll tell ye that," he said, and though he hated his own defensive tone, he continued on. "Maids." He shook his head. "They play on yer heart while they plan yer demise."

The mare snorted.

"Aye, very well then, I admit, 'twas mayhap a mistake for me to leave her afoot. Chivalry demands better." He drew a deep breath. Confusion rolled through him. Everything seemed wrong. But he dare not voice his uncertainty aloud. Confidence was everything. Weakness meant death. 'Twas as simple as that in his world. But was this his world? Since awakening alone beside the road some days ago, nothing was clear. Some things he remembered, but cast over it all was a fog of uncertainty. "Chivalry . . ." he mused, his mind churning as the mare danced onto Briarburn's sweeping drive, her hooves a staccato beat against the hard-packed clay. "It seems all but dead," he said, but at that moment a man burst from the house and hobbled rapidly down the path toward them, a furry, skewbald hound in his wake.

"My lady," he yelled when barely halfway to Killian. "Where is my lady?"

Killian deepened his scowl. It was bad enough confessing his sins to the mare. He did not care to share the news with this strangely dressed stranger. Though a few carefully phrased questions addressed to the miller's son had assured Killian the lady had no remaining relatives, he found it difficult to believe that this fellow was a servant, for his garments were of rare quality.

"Who might ye be?" he asked, striding toward the breathless gentleman.

"I am Lady Glendowne's butler," he said. The cur peeked uneasily from behind his legs. "Please, tell me where she is."

Now that it came to it, Killian felt some embarrassment for his actions, but he was not one to polish the truth.

"I left her down the road a wee bit," he rumbled guiltily.

The man stopped. His face paled. "She is not—"

Killian scowled. She must pay her servants well indeed for this kind of concern, for God knew she was far too imperious to gain it by other means. "She is well enough," he assured the other, "but ye'd best take a dray to fetch her home."

The manservant opened his mouth for a moment as if to inquire further, then closed his jaw with a snap and hobbled back toward the house.

By the time Killian reached the stable, a cob had already been hitched to a conveyance, the likes of which he had never seen. He watched in bemusement as the stout gray lurched into motion, with its driver bent furiously over the lines.

True, Killian thought, he had only been in London on rare occasions, but during his time there he had not noticed that the English were so very different from his kinsmen, or even from his French liege. The image of his master's face smote his mind like the edge of a dull sword, burning on contact.

There was no name to accompany the dark, impervious visage, only uncertainty and swirling emotions, but it seemed almost that his lord had sent him here, to this very place, and yet, not to this place at all.

He shook his head, trying to sort fact from impossibility. It seemed almost as if . . . But he did not let himself finish the thought. Instead, he strode into the stable and set his musings firmly aside.

There, the scents of hay and horses greeted him like age-old friends. Killian drew the fragrances slowly into his lungs just as a squire stepped out of a roomy stall.

"Fille!" he said, and rushed to the mare before stabbing Killian with his gaze. "Who are you?" he demanded, and snatched up the reins. "What are you doing with my lady's mount?"

Killian watched the boy run a quick hand down the mare's graceful limbs before straightening with brusque irritation. His skin was fair, his eyes brown, and his hair as red as sunset. He was not unlike Killian's own countrymen, but for the fact that by the ripe age of ten-and-five, most of Killian's companions had already been to battle, had earned their scars, or been long since buried. 'Twas doubtful the same could be said of the boy.

"I asked you a question, sir," the brash lad demanded. Killian watched him, fascinated by the boy's demeanor. Perhaps he was not a servant as he had first believed.

"How are ye called, lad?" Killian asked.

The boy shuffled his feet and narrowed his eyes slightly. 'Twas most probably true that he had not plied a sword on the field of battle, but he was wary now and belligerent. The expression reminded Killian of the baffling lady. Perhaps the information he had so carefully garnered regarding Briarburn's mistress was incorrect. Mayhap she yet had kinsman. Mayhap this lad was a cherished nephew or a coddled cousin. Or perhaps she was older than she appeared and had birthed the lad herself. If the English could erect the kind of awe-inspiring structures he had witnessed in the past few days, it was impossible to guess what other miracles they could have achieved. "Might ye be her bairn?"

The boy's brows nearly met when he scowled. The bay gave him an impatient nudge with her muzzle. "If you've hurt either the lady or the mare, you shall surely come to regret it."

"Ye've her infuriating attitude," Killian said. "Did ye share her womb?"

The boy blinked, then reddened dramatically. The shocking color reminded Killian of the wild poppies of the French countryside, though, if truth be told, he could not quite remember when he had seen them.

"How dare you!" gasped the lad. "How dare you speak of her ladyship as if she were . . ." He paused, looking winded.

Killian watched, more confused than irritated. More fascinated than confused. "So ye are not her progeny?"

"Her . . ." The blush seemed to deepen if such was possible. "Do you mean to ask if I am her son?"

" 'Tis what I said," Killian told him, then realizing the misunderstanding, almost laughed out loud. The boy had not been thinking of such an innocent relationship. Indeed, he was considering something far more lascivious, and not for the first time if Killian guessed rightly. "What else might I have meant?" he asked, and gave the lad a stern-faced stare from beneath lowered brows. It was the same expression that had quelled a score of battle-scarred soldiers near the low-lying marshes of Aigues-Mortes.

The lad turned jerkily away, throwing up the mare's near iron and fiddling with the girth. "I see you know little of my lady," he said.

"Aye," agreed Killian, "thus me question."

"She is not yet five-and-twenty, hardly old enough to wed, much less to bear . . . to have . . .

to . . ." He turned to glare over his shoulder. " 'Tis not a suitable subject."

Killian shrugged, watching the lad's progress. His hands were quick on the leathers but gentle when he touched the burnished mare. "In me own country a maid might have borne a half dozen bairns before reaching such a ripened age."

The boy gaped, his face still flushed. "Where the devil are you from?"

Where indeed? Killian wondered and watched the lad draw the tack from the mare's back. The saddle was small and light, crafted of dark, fine-grained leather, but it was the blanket that fascinated him most. 'Twas not made of rough woven fibers as his own stallions had worn, but of a soft, snowy white fabric that cushioned the mare's glossy back like a loving hand.

Where indeed? Killian questioned silently and wandered from the stables.

The sun still shone with friendly brilliance on the world through which he walked, but his mind was far away, lost in a land of shadows and war.

Where had he been? Why had he fought? Memories shrieked through his mind, the cries of his men, the screams of their mounts.

The sound came again. He glanced up and

found himself drawn from his reverie. 'Twas only a lark that called from a willow that shaded the lady's gardens. Only a lark, but as Killian scanned the greenery, his gaze fell on the towering statue of the Black Celt.

He felt the blood drain from his face, felt his limbs grow weak. God's bones, what devilry was in play?

Fleurette leaned back in her chair and rubbed her eyes. It was not yet ten in the morning, but she felt tired and worn. Perhaps Stanford was right. Perhaps she should hire someone to pay the bills and keep the books, but if the truth be told, there were few she would trust with the task. It was hardly unheard of for clerks to steal from their employers, and she had no wish to be amongst that foolish lot.

Pushing back her chair, she rose and paced to the window. Her knee had healed easily in the past three days. There was no swelling and little pain. The same could not be said for her pride. Bending her leg unconsciously, she scowled through the uneven glass to the street below, where two men squabbled and gestured. Farther to the east, where the thoroughfare was intersected by a rough side road, an old man sat alone with a bottle.

Perhaps Stanford was right about her company's location, too. Eddings Carriages was situated not two furlongs from London's hideous dungeons. Maybe it was time to move her business out of this deteriorating neighborhood to a more posh address.

She scowled, wondering if, in fact, Stanford was right about something else as well.

Leaning her forehead against the window, Fleur recalled his words about marriage. She remembered, too, the slobbering feel of Mr. Finnegan's lips against her knuckles, and the predatory look in Lord Lampor's eyes as he hunted her through the crowd of the ballroom. She was weary of the chase, was tired of being the prize plum in a public orchard. True, men might think it unseemly for her to manage her own business; but with the cost of living rising by the day, there were few who would turn aside her income. It seemed as if every snuff-toting gentleman in London was looking to increase his purse. But if she wed, she could surely curtail their harried pursuit.

She let the idea sink into her tired mind for a moment. If she wed, she would no longer have to suffer the advances of unwanted suitors. And if she wed *wisely*, she could still enjoy her freedom, could still manage her own affairs. There was no reason to think she couldn't make an amiable arrangement. Surely there were a few suitable gentlemen who would be happy to give her the title of wife without assuming the *rights* that the position assumed.

The memory of Madame Gravier's party returned with a vengeance. Was Mr. Kendrick truly Thomas's cousin? And if so, what had he hoped to gain by accosting her, she wondered, but in the back of her mind she realized her real concern.

Sir Killian of Hiltsglen.

The memory of him sent an untidy barrage of emotions sluicing through her. Where the devil had he come from? What did he want? Besides her land of course. The thought of his stealing the quarry out from under her nose irritated her no end. The memory of him taking her horse drove her mad. He'd been gone when she'd finally stormed into the stable in search of *Fille*. And she'd not heard from him since. Yet he'd haunted her dreams each night. Indeed, on one occasion she'd awakened with a start, certain she'd heard the deep burr of his voice. And though she disavowed it, she could not help but remember how his chest had felt beneath her fingertips. It was hard with muscle and sinew, as if sculpted from purest stone. He was unlike any of the titled gentlemen of her acquaintance, but as she would imagine a warrior of old. Hard and lean and unyielding, with—

"God's wrath!" she hissed, and yanked her mind to a halt. What the devil was she thinking? She had no wish to invite a man into her life. And she certainly wasn't interested in some overbearing barbarian who would dictate her actions, then steal her horse.

Oh very well—if she were going to be absolutely honest, he hadn't really stolen *la Fille de Vent*. And there was something about the way he had stroked the mare's neck that had caused a shiver to tingle up under her hairline. His hands were large and callused, but there had been a careful gentleness to them when he'd touched *Fille*'s burnished hide, and when Fleurette lay alone in her bed she could imagine how they would feel against—

"Damnation!" she snapped, and, snatching her reticule from beside her chair, stormed out of her office and onto the street.

She arrived at Lucille's home not ten minutes later.

"Flurry." The countess was still sleepy-eyed and dressed in a pink silk robe when she greeted Fleurette in the morning room. "Whatever are you doing here at such an ungodly hour? And wearing . . ." She let her gaze skim Fleurette's ensemble with deadpan distain. Fleur's shoes were decidedly ugly, her gown old and frayed and covered by the leather apron she had taken to wearing while at the shop. "What is that hideous garment?"

"I came here straight from the factory," Fleurette explained.

"And?" Lucille canted her head and took a cup of tea from the tray a prim-faced servant offered.

"I didn't have time to change into something suitable for your esteemed personage."

If Lucille recognized Fleur's sarcasm, she failed to show it.

"That hardly explains why you would choose to wear that disgusting thing at the outset," she said.

Fleurette took a cup also, though she hardly cared for it. Lucy's tea was as strong as her personality. "The truth is," she began, feeling fidgety and foolish now that it came to it, but wanting, nevertheless, to spill her newfound uncertainty, her doubts, her fears. Perhaps she no longer wished to live alone. Perhaps a husband would lighten her load. "I find that despite everything, I think I may want . . ." She paused, unable to go on.

"What is it you want, Flurry?" Lucy asked, peering at her over her teacup.

"I may need to find myself..." she began again, but old memories assailed her like banked storm clouds. She winced against the barrage. "A new hat," she said finally.

Lucille watched her for one elongated moment, then nodded thoughtfully. "Some say you have your priorities entirely askew," she said, and, setting her cup aside, headed for her dressing room. "But as of today I shall tell them that they are most certainly incorrect."

Chapter 7

~~~~∽◯◯∽~~~~

Killian's memory had cleared a bit, yet much lay beyond the shadows of his mind, still lost in the ragged mists of his past. He remembered the River Thames glimmering in the light of morn, and there was something hauntingly familiar about the catacombs that lay not far from Lady Glendowne's place of business. He had viewed the carriage company just the night before, for he must learn what he could of her as quickly as possible. Of that he was certain.

The structures he remembered from days past seemed strangely decrepit, while the new buildings . . . The new were bedazzling . . . huge, elaborate edifices that must surely have taken decades to build.

He scowled, unwilling or unable to believe the truth, to let himself dwell on the only possibility his mind could conceive.

Instead, he stood amongst a bevy of shops that boasted neatly painted signs and glass windows. Two young men walked down the cobbled street. But truth to tell, they wiggled more than walked. Ungodly tight pantaloons hugged their scrawny legs, and prissy white clothes throttled their throats, but it was the accessories that dumbfounded him most. One fellow carried a fan that he constantly burnished, while the other opened a small container shaped like a lady's bare leg. 'Twas outlandish, if not downright disgusting, and yet just the sight of that tiny, well-shaped limb made desire rumble through Killian like a roiling storm cloud.

Turning his head, he watched a gent in a pink waistcoat and green velvet jacket twirl an ivory-headed cane as he whistled past.

Nothing was as it should be. Ever since his awakening some days earlier, the world had been all turned about. He had been afoot, which was strange in itself. A knight was known by the steed he rode. But at least his garments had been familiar. He had been wearing his plaid and little else when first he came to consciousness. 'Twas what men of valor wore. But folk in the first village he'd passed had stared as if he'd been wearing nothing a'tall.

Having no wish to draw attention to himself until he'd sorted out his thoughts, he'd checked the leather sporran that hung about his waist. It was there that he had found a good deal of gold coin. Drawn to the sound of striking metal, he had made his way to a smithy's shop, and there he had found a man near as large as himself.

It had taken only one coin to persuade the aging blacksmith to part with his garments and his steed. Except for Killian's boots and the black blade that remained near his right knee, the attire had felt strange, but with his sword wrapped in a length of cloth and stowed on his mount, the English no longer eyed him quite so warily as before. Though, if truth be told, Killian doubted he would ever be mistaken for a Londonoy.

Another young man strolled past. He wore a tall black hat shaped like a brimmed cylinder and a tight-fitting coat with sleeves puffed nearly to his ears. But it was the lad's lower extremities that fascinated Killian most, for the boy's pantaloons were white with straps that fit beneath small black slippers and stockings with stripes of blue and yellow.

How could things have changed so in the few years since his last visit, Killian wondered? For he was certain it had been no longer than that since he had visited London.

True, seeing the statue in Briarburn's garden had shaken him, for at the sight of it, haunting, feral emotions had shaken him. But surely there was a sensible explanation. After all, he must surely have been struck on the head before falling into oblivion. And he knew firsthand that head wounds could cause a host of problems.

It had taken him some time simply to realize where he was. As to how he got there ... He winced against the pain of trying to remember.

Battle! He jerked at the clash of swords in his mind. Oh yes, he remembered warfare. Would never forget the slash of pain, the cries of the dying. But they seemed a world apart. As if a lifetime had passed since the battles that haunted him.

On the corner, an elderly man dumped a bit of powder onto his hand and inhaled it with a disdainful sniff and rapid jerk of his side-whiskered head.

London had ever been strange, but now ...

A movement to his right caught Killian's eye. He turned slightly only to watch a woman emerge from a shop. Her gown was the color of spring leaves. It had tiny sleeves that puffed over her shoulders but did little to hide the graceful fairness of her arms. A purple ribbon trilled down to each elbow, and the sides of her garment were split up to her tantalizing knees.

Killian couldn't take his eyes from her. He found, in fact, that his body felt as hard as granite. A trio of men strode past her, not seeming to notice, and Killian forced out a breath. Obviously, they were accustomed to such sights, or maybe . . . He watched another man prance into a nearby shop. Maybe they weren't men a'tall. Maybe they were the sort that preferred the company of their own sex. He'd heard of such things on more than one occasion. Indeed, O'Banyon had been propositioned . . .

O'Banyon! The Irishman's image rushed relentlessly into Killian's mind. Nairn O'Banyon. Was he friend or foe? And how had they known each other? Killian could remember so little, and still the man's face was as clear as sunrise, his eyes bright and blue, like a laughing window to a questionable soul. 'Twas little wonder men had been confused. He was as pretty as most . . .

Women! Another one sauntered toward him. Her hair, near as yellow as summer daisies, caressed her ivory skin like a lover's fingers. Killian's body all but quivered at the sight, and as she drew nearer, he realized the fragile fabric of her gown was wet. Indeed, it was soaked so that her nipples blushed through the sheer fabric and strained like cherries longing to be plucked. What had happened to her? Had she been doused, perhaps for her unacceptable attire? But then, surely, she would no longer be dressed so scandalously. He slid his gaze down her body and realized that through the pastel fabric, he could see the dark etching of her most private hair.

He felt himself grow tighter still as she entered a nearby shop. Turning her head, she glanced at him from beneath shadowy lashes. It wasn't until that moment that he realized he was staring like a farm lad at a magic show. But there was little else he could do. Indeed, staring was the least offensive act he wished to perform. Provocative possibilities rolled relentlessly through his lust-drenched mind, and he could not help but wonder again how others managed to control their baser instincts. And how, by God, did women dare wear such scanty garments when men like himself were only a few feet away, all but drooling as—

But just at that moment enlightenment dawned; she was a woman for hire. 'Twas obvious now that he realized the truth. Indeed, it seemed that every hamlet in every country in the world had such women, ladies unattached and needing to support themselves by whatever means necessary. He had never found reason to criticize such forthright financial endeavors. On the other hand, so far as he could recall, which, granted, was far from limitless, he had never sought out the company of such a woman either.

His crotch tightened painfully at the mere thought, for it had been a long while since he had eased his aching desires. How long he wasn't sure. But just now it seemed as if the dearth had begun well before the dawn of time.

Drawn toward her against his will and his better judgment, he stepped onto the shop's stoop, then turned the odd little sphere as he'd seen others do and pushed the door open.

Boxes and bags of endless merchandise lined the shelves, but Killian barely noticed, for the woman was there. She turned toward him immediately. Her cheeks were unnaturally red and her lashes black despite the paleness of her hair.

Stopping only a few feet away, Killian gave her

a nod and searched hopelessly for some small witticism. Nothing came to mind. O'Banyon had been the wit. Killian's strength lay only in his arm. "Good day to ye," he rumbled.

She smiled at him. "Good day to you, good sir," she responded, and let her gaze skim the open neck of his newly purchased tunic. The smithy had not been quite so broad across the chest as Killian, forcing him to leave the simple garment unfastened across his throat. "I noticed you earlier. Out shopping for cravats, are you?"

Killian didn't know what a cravat was, and didn't particularly care to be enlightened. But he gave her a nod. He was, after all, a civilized man and not one to fall on her person before the matter of money had been settled.

"It must be the very devil finding garments that fit." She skimmed her gaze downward, settling it for a prolonged moment on his crotch before lifting it back to his face. "What with your size."

His wick jerked spasmodically. He tightened his fist and remained very still, lest he change his mind about waiting to clear up money matters. "I would inquire about yer price," he said.

She raised her darkened eyebrows at him. Her mouth was as red as summer cherries and just as plump. "My price?" she said, and smiled a little as she glanced toward a gentleman near the door. He was busy with a purchase and did not turn toward them.

"For . . ." Killian paused momentarily, searching for diplomacy he'd rarely bothered to employ, "the pleasure of yer bonny company."

Her brows shot higher. She took an abrupt step to the rear. "I beg your pardon," she said, her voice rising.

"I've naught against the womanish fellow," he said, and jerked a nod toward the customer who conversed quite passionately with the clothier about fabrics and colors and fashions. "And I've na wish to hamper yer future dealings with him." He loosened his fist, reminding himself that this was naught but a matter of commerce. Still, it felt rather personal. "But I fear I will need the entirety of yer night."

Her carefully plucked brows were nestled somewhere in her hairline. She pressed splayed fingers against her exposed bosom. Killian could not help but notice how her pale flesh mounded between her digits like luscious, rising bread dough. "The entire . . ." She licked her lips and glanced rapidly toward the others again. Time seemed to stand still as she considered his proposal. "The whole night?" she murmured.

"Aye," he rumbled. "And well into the morning if ye're up to the task. But I'll na force—"

"My dear."

Killian lifted his gaze from the woman's bosom. The effeminate fellow had appeared at her side. He was as lean as a pig pole, his hips as narrow as a lance, his delicate hands flighty and bejeweled.

"You must introduce me to your . . ." The fop's smile was naught more than a sneer. "Gentleman friend."

"I'm sorry." The woman's voice was breathy, her eyes wide. "I fear I did not quite catch your name, sir."

"Killian," he said, and spread his feet slightly. He did not expect a fight from this fellow, but he'd found a bit of aggression early on could oft prevent further difficulties. "Of Hiltsglen."

"Killian," the man said, and laughed. The sound was light and strangely high. "Of Hiltsglen. How charming." Taking a small silver box from inside his coat, he opened the container, pinched out a bit of white powder, and applied it to his left nostril. His eyes watered immediately. He sniffed daintily and dabbed at his reddened nose with a frilly square of cloth. "And pray, what brings you to our fair city, good sir?"

Killian narrowed his eyes. He had never perfected the questionable art of making small talk, and now hardly seemed to be the perfect time to begin. "Are ye her keeper then?" he asked.

"Her . . ." The fop canted his head and sniffed again, his eyes still streaming. "Keeper?"

"Aye. The one what makes certain she is safe whilst she conducts her business."

"Ahh." The other laughed again. "How quaint. Yes, I suspect I am her keeper." He glanced at her, probably admiring her obvious charms. "Of course, I am also her husband."

The words struck Killian like a mallet. Her husband! The absolute wrongness of the situation overwhelmed him. Husbands were meant to protect their wives, to see to their needs, to cherish them, not to parade them about like pet parrots and sell them to the highest bidder.

The idea of such looming immorality was so overwhelming that his right arm swung without volition and suddenly the perverted wastrel was stretched out on the floor, his eyes rolled back into his head and his painted mouth ajar.

The woman squeaked, stared at her downed husband, then jerked her startled gaze back to Killian.

"If you wish," he rumbled, anger brewing like acid in his gut. "I will take ye from this place."

Her lips moved. No sound could be heard for a moment, but finally she whispered, "For the entire night?"

He scowled, trying to comprehend such odd goings-on. "I shall find ye a better protector if that be yer desire."

She blinked. "*You* wouldn't be my . . ." Her gazed skimmed him again. She cleared her throat and stopped her perusal on the bulge in his breeches. "Protector?"

Killian shuffled his feet uncomfortably. "Me apologies if I misrepresented meself. But I am na free to . . ." He shifted his gaze toward the door, wishing he had never approached her. He knew far better than to tangle with women. Although he didn't recall the circumstances exactly, he remembered betrayal with startling clarity. "I canna take on the task meself."

She took one step toward him. "I'm certain you're wrong there. Indeed—" she began, but in that moment the shopkeeper chimed in.

"My lady . . ." He was half-crouched behind his counter, the bushy plumes of his hat barely visible past a row of glass jars. "Is your husband quite well? Shall I call the watch?"

She continued as if she hadn't heard a word. "Indeed," she said again, "I think you would be more than adequate for the task at hand."

Killian realized with a belated blaze of awareness that there was much about this new London that he did not understand, much that could be his undoing.

"Me apologies," he said again, and, turning like a trained destrier, charged for the door.

Once outside, he strode rapidly down the street. Things were wrong, out of place, out of time. There was nothing that was as it should be. In fact—

But at that exact moment he saw the stallion and stopped in his tracks. The animal was tied to a post in front of a milliner's shop. Hale and restive, it blew out red-rimmed nostrils and cocked its hirsute head at the passing traffic. His crest was proud and heavy, his dark hide as sleek as a tiger's pelt. But it was his eyes that spoke volumes. For they were eyes filled with history. Eyes that had seen battle, had waged war, and won.

"Treun," Killian breathed, then noticed the women who paralleled his route as they traipsed toward the steed. Their backs were slim, their arms linked as they glanced toward each other and laughed together.

But in an instant, the fair-haired maid pulled the other to a halt. Even from a distance of several yards Killian could hear her intake of breath, and then, like one in a trance, she dropped her parcel and approached the dark stallion, her hand lifted wordlessly.

The animal rolled his black eyes. Beyond him, a high-stepping mare swished her tail and nickered. The stallion jerked his head and rumbled a response, but the maid seemed oblivious to danger. Indeed, she reached up to stroke the steed's brow. The mare moved on and the stallion, desperate to watch her retreat, slammed his body sideways.

The woman, seeming shocked from her idiotic trance, gasped and tumbled backward. The stallion reared in wild frustration, and Killian, without thought or any hint of good sense, leapt into the fray.

Chapter 8

Fleurette saw the stallion whip his head to the far side, saw him shift his weight and knew beyond a shadow of a doubt that she must move. In fact, she tried to leap out of harm's way, but before she could do so, his hoof struck her foot. She cried out in pain.

Startled by the noise and frustrated with his restraint, the animal snorted and reared. His knee struck her midsection, toppling her off balance. She twisted, trying to catch herself, but her head struck the earth, momentarily stunning her, and suddenly there was nothing she could do. Nothing but watch the giant hooves flail above her, watch the iron rims lower.

Then suddenly the world shifted. One moment she was prone and doomed. The next she was whisked off the ground like a bit of chaff in the wind. She hung suspended in midair, her toes barely touching the street as she hazily tried to sort fact from fiction. The stallion's hooves struck the street with resounding impact an instant later, and she shivered as if just waking from a hideous dream.

"Flurry! Oh, my good Lord!" Lucille rushed toward her, her face pale, her eyes wide with terror. "Are you all right? Are you hurt?"

"Yes. No." Fleurette shook her head numbly and found that it hurt. As did her elbows where they had struck the cobbles. "Yes, I'm fine." Her voice sounded shaky to her own ears. "It's just so embarrassing. I was . . ." Her feet settled magically onto the ground, but someone still held her arm, as if she might topple over like a toddler if left untended. ". . . so foolish. I didn't . . . I don't know what I was thinking exactly. I suppose I was not thinking at all. I just saw him and he reminded me so of the Black Celt's steed, like a fictional being that I—" She laughed breathlessly and motioned foolishly toward the stallion, her hand making a vague circular motion in the air.

"Sir," Lucy said, lifting her worried attention to the man behind Fleur. "You have our utmost appreciation."

"Yes. Yes." Fleurette turned shakily, feeling utterly idiotic. Good Lord, she knew better than to approach a fractious stallion. But he'd looked so majestic. Indeed, he'd looked quite magical, as if he had stepped out, real and alive, from the ancient past. His kohl black mane hung well past his muscular shoulders, and his crimped forelock half hid his otherworldly eyes. She'd felt herself drawn against her will just as she had been in Paris, just as she was every evening when she returned home to her own gardens. Still . . . "I must look like an absolute ninny. I'm afraid . . ." she began and turning, stopped in midsentence as her eyes widened and her jaw dropped. "You!" she hissed.

The Scot's dark brows lowered as he glared down at her "What the devil are ye about now, lassie?" he rumbled.

"What are you doing here?"

"Do ye na know better than to be bothering such a beast?"

"Are you . . ." She paused, breathless and stunned. It seemed almost as if he'd been conjured out of her restless dreams, drawn magically forth just as the stallion had been. Indeed, it seemed to her reeling mind as if he had come to snatch her from harm's way once again.

Which meant, of course, that she was going quite mad. She had never been the sort of woman to dream up foolish imaginings, nor believe herself the heroine of ridiculous tales, and the idea that she would become one now made her unmistakably angry. "Are you following me?"

"Following ye!" he snorted, and gave her arm a shake. "I am na yer nursemaid, ye silly flibbergib. Though 'tis clear ye need one. The beastie coulda killed ye soon as na."

"Flibbergib! What—You—He—Let go of me!" she sputtered, and jerked her arm from his grasp. The movement hurt like hell.

They faced off like spitting tigers.

"Tell me, lass," he growled, "might ye be trying to get yerself kilt, or are ye simply too daft to remain amongst the living?"

"Listen you!" she snarled back. "You are hardly the one to be slandering another's intellect, and I'm certain if you would cease bothering me, all would be perfectly fine. Indeed—"

"What happened?" An elderly man rushed onto the street. He wore an antiquated white wig, which hung askew around his ashen face. "My lady!" His hands were visibly shaking. "Are you well?"

Fleurette straightened her back and struggled for dignity, but her frock was rent near the elbow and soiled below the knee. Her shoes were ruined, her hair a wild mass, and her nose was running amuck, making it rather difficult to look perfectly turned out. Perhaps sane would be a reach, but she'd attempt that lofty goal. "I am quite well," she said, and brushed at her skirt as though she could sweep away any minuscule untidiness. "Thank you."

"My dear God! Did he . . ." The old man jerked his frantic eyes toward the stallion. The animal reared again, its narrow ears laid flat against its poll. "Did he attack you? Did he—" he began, and stumbled back a few shaky strides.

She shook her head. "You needn't worry," she said, though she felt irritable and foolish. "In truth it was entirely my own fault."

"No." The gentleman shook his head. "No, 'tis not. 'Twas vanity to purchase such an animal. My Betsy said as much. Buy a nice cob that the grandchildren can ride, she said but I . . ." He motioned weakly toward the black. "I feared this would happen." His shoulders slumped.

"He's been nothing but trouble since the day I purchased him. First the neighbor's mare. Now this. Well!" He straightened with a decisive snap. " 'Twill not do. 'Twill simply not do." He turned abruptly away, scanning the crowds that drew near to watch. "I'll see to the problem this very moment. I'll find someone to destroy him before—"

"No!" Fleur gasped, but her breathy denial was drowned by the Scot's angry objection.

She turned to glare at him, then jerked her attention back to the horse's owner. "I'll buy him—" she began, but the barbarian was saying the exact same thing.

Not taking time to argue with the irritating giant behind her, she stepped hastily toward the startled gentleman. "Good sir." She gathered her dignity carefully and gave him a practiced smile. "My apologies. I fear I did not have a chance to inquire about your name."

"Bayberry," he said, flitting his gaze from her to the horse. "Lord Bayberry of Kent."

"Of course." She strengthened her smile, hoping to hold his attention. "Lord Bayberry, I fear this bit of foolishness is entirely my doing. I was not thinking properly. Indeed, 'twas I who startled your poor mount," she said, and motioned toward the stallion. The steed tossed his lengthy forelock and bared yellow teeth. God above, what an animal! "I did not immediately realize his high spirits." The horse pawed angrily, his shod hoof striking the cobbles like a smithy's rounding hammer. Sparks scattered like falling stars. "Stallions can be troublesome, and perhaps you have no wish to deal with his moods. Indeed, maybe a quiet gelding would better fit your needs. I have several fine hacks I could trade for him if such—"

"I'll give you four gold coins," interrupted the barbarian.

The owner jerked his watery gaze from Fleurette to the Scotsman. "What?"

Fleur gritted her teeth.

"Four," Hiltsglen repeated.

"That is very—"

"Eight hundred pounds," Fleurette countered, jerking in front of the Scot, as if she had any hope of blocking the towering gargoyle from sight. "Payable here and now."

"'Tis solid gold, fair won and hard kept," vowed the Highlander.

Fleurette gaped, then spun her attention back to the aging gentleman. "Please, Lord Bayberry, you should know that I have the bloodstock to put your stallion's fine qualities to good use. While Hiltsglen here . . ." She tried not to snarl as she jerked her head in his direction. "He has not even a stable in which to house the poor animal. Surely you must take your horse's well-being into consideration and—"

"I'll give double what ye paid for him and deliver the sum to yer door at dawn's first light," Killian said.

"I'll not press charges," Fleurette rasped, suddenly cradling her arm and making her eyes go wide. A few tears would be a nice effect, but that kind of far-fetched dramatics took time and time was of the essence, for the towering Scot was all but breathing down her neck.

Still, the gentleman seemed convinced, for he gasped as if wounded himself. " 'Tis ever so kind of you to grant me forgiveness, madam. I am hideously sorry to have caused you such grievous distress when—"

"Then ye will na wish for it to happen again," Hiltsglen said.

The gentleman snapped his damp gaze back to Fleur's tormenter. "What?"

"The poor wee lass here be already wounded," Hiltsglen rumbled, and though he didn't shift his deadly dark eyes to Fleur's, she knew he was being cruelly sarcastic. "What worse might happen if she took such a braw animal to her own estate?"

119

Bayberry opened his mouth as if at a loss for words. His eyes went round in abject terror.

"You've no need to worry on my account," Fleur hissed, then unclenched her jaw and gave him another smile. "I've a good deal of experience with horses. Indeed, I have been astride more than afoot since the day I was born. You must not judge my skills by this one silly mistake. 'Tis simply that I was not thinking properly, and—"

"And there lies the truth of it," said Hiltsglen, stepping around her and taking Bayberry by the arm. He loomed over the aging gentleman like a giant over a midget and only spared Fleur one dark glance. "She is naught but a poor simple maid and *oft* does na think proper." He canted his head. Bayberry glanced at Fleur wide-eyed. "The next time she may na be so fortunate as to have someone close to hand what can snatch her from harm's way."

"Damn you, you conniving son of a—" Fleur snarled, but Bayberry already seemed to be imaging the worst.

The merest hint of a smile played around the corners of the barbarian's lips. "Ye dunna want such a wee gentle maid's blood on yer hands, do ye now?" he asked.

"Lord Bayberry—" Fleur began, but it was already too late. He was shaking his head and waving his hands frantically in front of him of if to wash away the entire situation.

"Take him, sir! Take him straightaway," he insisted, gazing up at Hiltsglen. "Before someone else gets hurt."

The barbarian growled some sort of idiotic response, then it was over.

Bayberry mumbled a disjointed apology and disappeared like a shaky wraith into the crowd.

Fleurette dropped her hand away from her injured arm and tightened her fists. Hiltsglen stared down at her, and though his lips no longer quirked upward the slightest whit, she realized he was smiling, in his own barbaric way.

"Are ye na going to congratulate me, lass?" he asked. His eyes were gleaming and his right brow, bisected as it was by some fool with a damnably faulty aim, lifted the slightest degree. "On me own new purchase?"

"Well, I would of course," Fleur said, and primly brushed at the mud that stained her skirt. "But I find I would much rather stab you in the eye with my hatpin."

For one elongated moment, he continued to stare at her; and then he laughed. The sound was like the distant rumble of thunder. Something coiled up tight in her belly. She scowled at

121

him. Hate, she thought. It must be hate she was feeling.

"Well, I'll say this about ye, lassie," he said, still grinning like a fool. "Ye may be as snooty as a prize sow at spring festival, but I'd na care to face ye in a pitched battle."

She gave him an arch look, the same one that had set the duke of York back on his heels. "Had I any idea what you were babbling about I would respond in kind," she said.

"He means you're a lively opponent," Lucy explained, and stepping forward, lifted her hand toward the barbarian. "Lady Anglehill," she said. He swallowed her fingers with his own and bowed shallowly, his damned eyes still gleaming. "My friends call me Lucille."

"And the high-and-mighty lass there . . ." he said, canting his head toward Fleur but not shifting his gaze from Lucille's. "Might she be a friend to ye?"

"Generally," said the other. "But I dare not cross her."

He nodded solemnly. "What might a hatpin be?"

Lucy watched him for a moment, then smiled. "I am having a modest gathering at my estate a week from this Friday," she said. "I would very much enjoy your presence."

He shook his head a little, so that the cords in his broad throat shifted slightly. "I fear I am na the sort to do well in genteel crowds, me lady."

"Truly?" Lucille's eyes were narrowed now, her expression thoughtful. "What sort are you, sir?"

He shifted his gaze to Fleur.

"Mayhap I be the sort to be speared in the eye by a wee lassie's hatpin."

"Aye, well," Lucy said, and smiled as she turned away. "Seven o'clock at my estate then. I shall make certain our little Fleurette comes bareheaded."

Chapter 9

❦

"**W**hat the devil were you thinking?" Fleurette demanded.

They'd returned in utter silence to Lucille's spacious home, and though Fleur's growling anger had lost a bit of its biting edge, it continued to gnaw at her guts. Damn the barbarian to utter darkness!

"Thinking?" Lucy asked, and, handing her newest chapeau to a maid, sauntered into the parlor.

"You know exactly what I mean," Fleur hissed, following testily in the other's perfumed wake. "Why in heaven's name would you invite him to your house?"

"Who?"

Fleurette gritted her teeth and counted to ten. This was exactly why she was so fond of hounds and horses. They weren't so convincing when they acted dumb. "The barbarian," she hissed. "The damned . . ." She tried to continue but ran out of words and found herself waving wildly as she searched.

"The Scotsman?"

"Yes the Scotsman! Why did you invite him here?"

Lucille shrugged lazily. "I find him intriguing."

"Have you lost your mind?" Fleur stormed, and found to her consternation that she was pacing the room like a caged cat.

"You don't find him the least bit fascinating?"

"I find him rude, overbearing, irritating, and damnably egotistical."

Lucy canted her head and took one of the tiny raspberry tarts offered to her by a blank-faced manservant. "I fear I shall have to assume that is a no."

Fleur abandoned her pacing, coming to a shuddering halt. "Have I done something to upset you, Lucille? Have I wronged you in some unfathomable way?"

"As a matter of fact you have," Lucy said.

Fleurette felt her jaw drop. "Truly?" She was immediately sorry. Lucille was an anchor in the turbulent sea of life. A friend when troubles rained down on her like volcanic ash. "What have I done?"

"You refuse to wed."

"What?" Fleur asked, drawing back abruptly. "What are you talking about? You've been widowed longer than I, and you've yet to do so much as consider matrimony."

Lucille took a delicate bite of the tart and set it aside. "But I remain alone for entirely different reasons."

"That is neither here nor there, Lucille, and you demmed well know it. I am a grown woman, well able to make my own decisions, and if I decide to—"

"Yes, you are able to make your own decisions, but when you make a foolish one I shall ever be irritated by it."

"Foolish!" Fleurette spat "You can't be suggesting . . ." She hacked a laugh. "You *can't* be suggesting that you think that . . ." She waved her hand rather wildly in the general direction of her latest confrontation. "That odiferous cretin might be marriage material."

"Well," Lucy said, her tone agreeable. She shook her carefully coifed head. Tightly curled ringlets danced against her neck. "He is not very fashionable. I shall grant you that."

"Fashionable!" Fleur snorted. "He's barely human."

"His clothing is a bit rustic."

"Rustic! Rustic!" For a moment Fleur could think of nothing else to say. "The man looks as if he stepped out of the Middle Ages. I'll wager he doesn't even own a cravat."

"Not at all like Thomas then," Lucy commented. "Remember how fastidious he was about his stocks? Each one embroidered with his initials and guarded like the crown jewels."

Fleurette fell silent.

"I imagine our Scotsman would look rather out of place at one of Prinny's garden parties."

"Absolutely," Fleur said, but thoughts of her deceased husband had blasted the wind from her sails. "Like a bear at a tea party."

"More concerned for that abominable beast of a stallion than the fit of his breeches." Lucy sighed. "I imagine you're right, Flurry, he is neither shallow enough nor effeminate enough to be a fine gentleman of the *ton*. But he would be quite perfect for a few hours alone in the dark."

Fleur glared at her.

"Admit it," Lucille said. "He is rather appealing in a baser instincts sort of way."

"He couldn't be less appealing if you doused him in pig manure and dressed him in cornstalks. He's an irritating, overbearing—"

"I believe you said as much earlier."

"Oversized, egotistical—"

"Oversized is new."

"Daft—"

"Yes well . . ." Lucy interrupted and yawned as she waved a perfectly manicured hand. "That's all very interesting, but I must ask you to excuse me now. I am really quite exhausted. You don't mind seeing yourself out do you?"

Fleurette knew exactly what Lucy was trying to do. Sitting in stony silence, she stared at the brocade seat opposite her as her phaeton rolled smoothly toward Briarburn.

Oh yes, she knew. Lucy spoke of independence and personal freedom, but perhaps when it came down to it, she was the same as any halfwitted ninny who felt a woman needed a man to make her complete. To make her whole.

Well, Fleurette had had a man, and she was in

no great rush to have another. Especially one who would feel it was his God-given right to order her about from morning till night.

The carriage slowed and bumped. Beneath her, the springs moaned. Fleurette scowled. Such a heavy vehicle might well benefit from a hardier suspension system, she mused. She must see what could be done to hasten the arrival of the new Cadway springs. And perhaps she would try them in the viceroy model as well.

She continued her ride home and finally descended from the carriage with some relief. She, too, was tired, and yet, as Horace turned the grays toward the stable, she wandered down the cobbled path toward the gardens.

Once past the rose-shrouded arbor, the world seemed a different place. A better place. The scent of warm earth and ripe blossoms filled the air, but it was the Celt that drew her.

He loomed in the misty moonlight. She glanced up at his face, wishing almost that she could see his eyes, that she could know his thoughts. And then she laughed at herself. He had no thoughts, of course. He was nothing but a statue. And yet . . . Reaching up, she placed a hand on his knee. The stone still retained the heat of the sun, and the rock was smooth from years of wear. It almost felt real, almost alive, as if he had charged through the centuries to be at her side.

Fleurette all but rolled her eyes at her own fanciful musings, but though she reminded herself of the penalties of such girlish foolishness, she could not quite leave the Celt alone, and so she sat in the quiet darkness, letting the solace of the garden soothe her soul.

It was sometime later that she entered her house. Henri rose from his place near the door and trotted over, tail wagging. It seemed dark inside, despite the lamp Mr. Smith had lit in the entry. Handing her shawl to him, she finally ascended the stairs to her bedchamber. Candlelight flickered across the pictures on the walls. She stepped into her room, feeling the quiet of the place, the hominess.

"My lady." Tessa bobbed as she hustled through the doorway. "You've had a successful day I hope."

"What? Oh. Yes." Fleur felt better now, soothed, despite her ridiculous confrontation with the towering Scot. "Successful enough I suppose."

" 'Tis late," said the maid, unclasping her mistress's gown in the back. "You must be exhausted."

Fleur glanced over her shoulder at the young

woman's cheery face. " 'Tis no later for me than for you," she said.

"Well, I never have thought of it in just that light," Tess said, her quick hands pausing on the endless row of wooden buttons. "God's truth, *I* must be exhausted."

Fleurette laughed, feeling the last of her tension slip away. "How many years have you been here at Briarburn, Tessa?"

"Near eight I suspect." Bending, she retrieved the shoes Fleur had just abandoned. "Why might you be—" she began, then stopped and turned suddenly, her eyes huge in the flickering light. "You're not thinking to be rid of me are you, my lady?"

"Don't be ridiculous," Fleur scoffed, surprised at the maid's unfounded fears. "You're the wife I've never had."

Tessa chuckled, relaxing visibly. She was plump and comely, with a ready laugh and a kind soul. "Well," she said, setting the shoes on the floor in the wardrobe before straightening. "Better you than some man what beats me morning and—" She stopped, gasping suddenly. "My lady! Your frock!"

"Oh." Fleurette felt immediately embarrassed, remembering the scene she'd made over the stallion. "I had a bit of a mishap is all. I imagine the garment is beyond repair. 'Tis good it was just my work—"

"No," Tessa breathed. "Not that gown. This one."

Fleurette turned rapidly toward her, premonition tightening her throat.

And when Tessa drew out the delicate garment, she saw that it had been slashed from the bodice to the hem. A hole began just where it would have rested on her left breast and continued down in a shuddering line toward the floor.

"However did this happen?" Tessa asked, but Fleur could not talk. She was frozen in time and place, shuddering on the ragged edge of terror.

"My lady?" Tessa said, her voice shaky. "Are you well?"

"Oh. Yes. Of course." Fleur forced herself to speak, to breathe, to act as if all were well, for she'd learned that trick long ago. "I'm fine. 'Tis just a garment, after all."

"But who would have done such a thing to your lovely frock? And why?"

Who? The answer slipped into Fleur's mind like a dark dream, but she dare not loose the name. "I'm sure 'twas not apurpose," she said instead.

"But—"

"It must have happened during laundering."

"But it has not been washed since last you used it, my lady. Remember? It has been some years now. You wore it to Lady Gravier's soirée though Lord Glendowne did not much care for—"

"Yes, I remember," Fleur interrupted. Her voice sounded harsh, but she could not quite seem to soothe it. She should have thrown the gown out long ago. Should have burned it with a host of old memories. "It has been a long day, Tessa. Be rid of the gown, please. Both of them, in fact."

"But—"

"Tessa!" Her voice shuddered with sudden exhaustion. She forced a wavering smile. "Please."

"Yes, my lady. My apologies. I shall hurry them down to the cook fire and come back straightaway to help you with your hair."

Fleurette pulled on her night rail and carefully kept her hands from shaking. "You needn't return this night. I can see to my hair myself."

"Are you certain?" The maid's pretty face wrinkled with worry. "Would you—"

"Leave me," Fleur insisted, then shut her eyes, feeling immediately guilty. "My apologies," she said. "Please forgive me. I simply need to sleep this night."

"Yes, my lady," said the maid, who gathered both gowns to her plump chest and hustled from the room.

The night was long and dark. Even in the sanctuary of Fleur's private chambers, it seemed as though she were not alone. As if there was another there, watching her, reading her very thoughts, spying on her.

A noise rustled in the darkness. Jerking upright, Fleurette held her breath, listening, but all was quiet. Still, someone had breached the security of her chambers. Someone had crept into her wardrobe and ripped her gown. Why? The questions plagued her, keeping her awake and restless. Thus, long past midnight, she gathered her childhood coverlet and crept down the stairs to the quiet solace of her gardens. Peace lay quiet there, and the Celt, ever diligent, watched over her as she drifted into dreams.

It was sometime before dawn when she awoke. Feeling strangely limber and rested, she allowed herself a brief glance at the Celt before she threw herself into her work.

It rained for the next two days, keeping Fleur irritably confined and drawing down her mood. She was accustomed to riding astride, to strolling through her gardens and feeling the peace of fresh air against her face.

By the time she left Eddings Carriages that Wednesday, her head felt tight. There was an ache in her lower back, and her eyes were gritty.

The street outside was dark and drear. Murky puddles dotted the dirt and splashed onto her skirts. Cursing silently, Fleur edged the worst of the mud and headed for her waiting carriage.

"My lady."

She nearly screamed as she swung toward the sound of the voice.

Kendrick stood watching her. She swallowed and raised her chin, careful to show no fear. Had he been the one to creep into her bedchamber? And if so why? What did he want from her?

"Forgive me. I did not mean to frighten you," he said, but her heart was already racing. The street was empty but for her own carriage. "I fear I may have given you the wrong impression when last we met."

"What do you want?" she asked, and was pleased to find that despite her foolish fear, her voice was steady. The rain was spitting from the north, and her nerves were rattling, but she stood her ground.

"I only want the truth," he said, and spread

his hands with placatory earnestness between them as he took a step toward her.

"Oh?" She glanced toward her carriage. Horace was most likely huddled inside as she had told him to do when the weather was inclement. She would not be so foolish as to make that suggestion again. "And is that why you invaded the privacy of my home, Mr. Kendrick?" It was a desperate guess. But she felt desperate. Desperate and alone and afraid. "To learn the truth?"

"I did not say that I wished to *learn* the truth, my lady. Oh no. I know the truth," he said, and took a step toward her. "I merely wish to hear it from your pretty lips."

She watched him approach and felt her breath come faster. "Then why were you in my bedchamber?"

"Your bedchamber," he said, and laughed. "My dear lady, do you suppose that someone else knows the truth? That someone else longs to hear you repent?"

"I don't know what you're talking about. What do you want?" She tried to keep her tone businesslike, but her heart was hammering against her ribs, and her throat felt tight with terror.

"I'd hear the facts about my dear cousin's

death," he said, and took another step toward her.

It took all her floundering courage to remain as she was.

"How do I even know he was your cousin? He never mentioned you."

"Strange. He never mentioned you either," he said, and laughed. "But then we were distant relatives, in terms of geography as well as lineage. Surely you know how it can be, my lady; you wish to be close to someone, to form a relationship filled with respect and caring, but you cannot seem to make it so, no matter how hard you try."

How much did he know? And how much did he guess? Her hands felt shaky, but she clasped them together, careful not to let him see. Fear had never done her a whit of good. Not in all her life. "Fascinating as this topic is, Mr. Kendrick, it is quite late, and I must be returning home."

He smiled. The expression looked grim in the settling darkness. "You are a strong woman aren't you, Lady Glendowne?"

Her knees felt wooden, her muscles frozen. "If you'll excuse me," she said, and turned away.

"It's said you've made yourself quite a fortune since your husband's death."

She turned stiffly back. Her heart was still thumping nervously, but anger was beginning to brew slow and steady in her tightly wound system. "I've been fortunate," she said.

"I think you are being modest, my lady. I hear it is your own clever managing that has made your businesses such a smashing success."

"I am flattered. But I fear I cannot take credit for my good fortune. God and London have been good to me, as I am certain you know. Now I really must be leaving," she said, and turned away, but he grabbed her arm.

"I know what you are," he rasped.

"Leave me be."

"Some think it improper for a lady to spend her days in the company of men."

She tried to jerk her arm away, but he tightened his grip.

"What do you do with all those clever carriage blokes?" he gritted.

"Release me."

"Not until—"

"Who goes there?"

"Horace," Fleur yelled, but her voice was no longer steady.

"My lady!" Her driver's footsteps rushed through the darkness.

Kendrick released her arm. Backing cautiously away, he gave her a blistering smile. "Some other time then, my lady," he said, and disappeared into the night.

"My apologies," Horace rasped, breathless from worry or haste. "God's truth, I should be horsewhipped. I was blanketing Lily and didn't see you come out. What happened? Are you well?" He turned his head to scowl into the swirling raindrops, fists tightening belligerently. "Shall I go after him?"

"No!" she said, then, realizing the panic in her tone, closed her eyes and soothed herself. "No. Let him go. I am unhurt."

He glared into the distance, his brows beetled beneath his top hat. "Who—"

"'Tis nothing to trouble yourself about," she said. "Please, I just want to return to Briarburn."

"Of course, my lady," he said, and hustling to the carriage, lifted down the step, and handed her in.

Fleurette drew the blanket over her lap and gave him a smile as she tucked it under her legs, but as soon as the door closed, she dropped her head against the upholstered cushion behind her and drew a shuddering breath.

God almighty! What did Kendrick want with her? Where had he come from? She had been led to believe that Thomas had no living relatives. But a distant cousin or two would hardly have been his greatest secret. She closed her eyes to the thought. She had always believed she would have a marriage such as her parents'. Indeed, she had been determined to make that happen. Kendrick was right; she knew what it was like to try to form a good relationship and be stymied at every turn.

Despite Thomas's fine attributes, he had often seemed more fond of his clubs than of her. At least that was certainly the case after the courtship ended and the marriage began. Before that, during the lovely evenings of dancing and dining, he had found no fault with her. He was unconcerned that she was not as curvaceous as some. Indeed, he had often said she was the very picture of perfection.

Fleurette swallowed the lump in her throat and attempted to turn her mind aside, but it was not to be. Her thoughts were on a runaway course, spurred on by Kendrick's terrifying appearances and her own sleepless imaginings.

Things had seemed so right for some time. Indeed, she had believed she would be happy with Thomas. Lonely no more. They would have a family. Children's laughter would echo in their home. But children never came. And perhaps that had been the crux of their problems. Perhaps that was why he had found fault with her. Every man wanted sons.

Age-worn thoughts tormented her. Outside her phaeton's bevel-paned windows, London rolled past, dark and dank.

There were times when she considered buying a house in the city, but she was glad now to leave that place behind and return to her own bucolic estate. The carriage bumped to a halt. The garden called to her, but the rain had begun in earnest again. Mr. Smith appeared with a lantern and an umbrella. Stepping beneath the shelter he offered, she entered her house, wished him good night, then hurried up to her private chambers, where she changed quickly.

Climbing into bed, she turned her back to her looming wardrobe, refusing to imagine someone pawing through her dresses, touching her things. Closing her eyes, she willed herself to sleep. Henri pressed close to her side, but dark dreams still haunted her.

She was riding alone in the meadow. The sky was clear and crystalline blue. From a verdant hillside, an orchestra played a haunting waltz. The musicians wore knee breeches and sparkling white stockings. Their full, formal wigs were just as pristine.

Smiling, she pressed *Fille* nearer, but when the exuberant maestro turned toward her, she saw that he had no face.

He stared at her from empty eye sockets.

She jerked her mount away. The mare stumbled and fell, screaming as they tumbled downward. And suddenly bony hands were reaching for them, snatching them down into the fetid depths of the earth.

Fleur awoke with a start, her heart pounding.

Beside her, Henri whimpered and leapt to the floor.

The night was silent, the room dark and close. She couldn't breathe. Couldn't think. Rolling hastily out of bed, she stumbled to the window. It opened grudgingly beneath her sweaty hands.

Fleur steadied herself on the sill, closed her eyes, and drew a deep breath.

It was then that she smelled the smoke. She snapped to full consciousness, sweeping the darkness with her gaze. A horse shrieked from the stable.

She was bolting for the door even as she screamed for help. She stumbled on the steps, nearly fell, then caught the railing and lurched downstairs.

"My lady! What is it?" Smith rasped from the darkness.

"Fire!" she breathed.

"Nay!" Someone hissed, but she was already outside, already racing toward the barn.

The latch stuck beneath her fumbling fingers, then swung open. Flames licked a pile of fodder near the door and was reaching hungry fingers up a supporting beam.

Fleur leapt toward the nearest stall. Swinging the door wide, she jolted toward the next. Across the aisle, Horace was freeing the others. Someone yelled from outside. At the end of the stable, *Fille* circled her stall in a panic. Fleur jumped toward her. "Get the others! The others!" she screamed, and threw open *Fille's* door.

The mare reared, thrashing the air with frantic hooves. Fleur flattened herself against the wall, then scooted around the side. "Out! Get out!" she yelled, waving wildly. But the mare wheeled back toward her, knocking her aside. She crashed against the wall.

In the aisle, a yearling skittered wildly from its stall, lost its footing, and skidded on its side for several yards before scrambling to its feet and lurching into the mob at the far end of the barn. The horses milled frantically there, loose and crazed as they stared at the crackling flames.

Fleur screamed at them, her voice melding

with the sound of thrashing hooves and her servants' harsh cries.

Firelight flickered at ancient beams. A weanling lunged out of a nearby stall, flames dancing in her white limned eyes as she pivoted away from the door to circle with the others.

The flames spewed higher, consuming the chaff. *Fille* quivered against the wall, her legs never still as she danced in frantic terror.

Fleur turned back toward her. "Run!" she croaked and lifting her night rail, flapped it madly in the mare's face. Terrified by the fluttering fabric, the horse plunged for the door. Fleur leapt after, but at the last instant, *Fille* wheeled back into the stall.

Her shoulder struck Fleur, spinning her sideways. She tried to catch her fall, tried to yell, to stay afoot, but the wall rushed toward her. Her head struck something solid.

Someone yelled her name. Sparks seemed to fly in her head. Noise clattered around her, disjointed and chaotic, then darkness fell, deep and quiet and unforgiving.

Chapter 10

Killian sat atop the hillock and gazed out over the land below. The night was as black and silent as the days of yore. But even now there was a difference, a newness. Beneath him, the dark stallion arched his tremendous neck and gazed out over the moon-shadowed valley.

There was no way of knowing how they had come together once again, no way to be sure if it was fate or foolish luck that had brought Killian to Treun at that precise moment on the strange streets of London. But they were now reunited.

The dark knight and his devil's steed as they had once been called.

Oh yes, he remembered that much and more, but each wee tidbit of information was slow in coming, slow and wrapped in misty uncertainty. For naught made sense. It seemed that he had come to this place from another time. But that was certainly foolishness. More likely by far was that he had simply been riding from Hiltsglen to London and during the journey had been attacked by brigands. They had knocked him unconscious, and when he came to all seemed addled and strange.

He scowled. But if such was the case, why was his sporran still filled with coin? Why were there no bruises on his skull? How had Treun ended up in the hands of an aging lord who failed to realize the value of a renowned destrier, and—

A crackle of noise sounded in the forest behind him. Killian jerked about, sword in hand, but Treun only arched his great neck. He flickered his ears toward the noise but remained unmoved. Even when the wolf trotted from the underbrush, he stood immobile.

Killian narrowed his eyes, tightening his grip, and the wolf, tawny and large, lifted his snout, testing the scents before moving forward to sit not far from Treun's iron-shod hooves.

"What's this then?" Killian murmured, but memories were already streaming in, dark and ancient and unchecked.

"Good Christ," he breathed, for the reminiscences struck him like a blow to the chest. Hard and ferocious and unyielding, they came, like a dark horde on tireless horses. He winced as they rolled over him, then closed his eyes, but the thoughts remained. There was no logic, just facts, and he would accept them, for there was naught else to do. Still, it took some time to do even that. Thus he sat very still, letting the memories envelop him, letting the truth be felt in the very marrow of his ancient bones.

The wolf stirred restlessly. Killian looked down at him, scowling at the force of his own memories.

"So," he rumbled, "we are gathered once again, the three of us."

The wolf glanced up at the sound of his voice, almost grinning, but in an instant he was distracted and rose nervously to all fours. His ears strained forward and he lifted his muzzle, catching unknown mysteries on the slightest breeze. A growl rumbled in his chest.

"What is it?" Killian asked, tensing.

The animal trotted forward a half dozen

steps, then halted again, nose raised. Beneath Killian, Treun flared his wide nostrils, shaking his heavy crest and mincing nervously.

Then suddenly the wolf bounded forward.

For a moment Killian tried to deny, tried to disbelieve, but the stallion was pulling at the bit, and there was nothing he could do but live the life before him.

Loosening the destrier's reins, he leaned over the heavy mane and gave the animal his head.

The stallion charged forward, his dark hooves churning up moldering leaves. Branches whipped past Killian's face. From deep in the woods, a stag leapt away. The forest floor slanted downward, but neither the wolf nor the stallion slowed.

They hit the road at a dead run, then careened to the right; and then Killian smelled it.

Smoke. He cursed in silence and urged Treun forward, but the stallion was already running flat out, his hooves pounding like battering rams against the curving road. Briarburn's lane appeared as nothing more than a glimmer of gray in the darkness. They sped around the corner. Killian could hear the shouts, the frantic screams of panicked horses.

The doors of the stable were thrown open, spewing forth smoke and the harsh crackle of flames, but Killian pressed Treun straight for the entrance.

A white-gowned servant rushed from the barn, nearly colliding with the stallion. Treun reared in the doorway, then landed, his feet striking the earth with a crash of power.

Inside, the fire had spread nearly the width of the aisle. Horses milled frantically at the far end. Off to their right, a servant yelled at the fractious herd, but it was the sight of a woman that speared Killian's attention. She was in a stall, just now staggering to her feet, her face as pale as the filthy night rail that fluttered around her. And though Killian could not see her clearly, there was no doubt about her identity, not a shadow of a question.

"Get out!" he roared, but even as he said it he knew his words were wasted, for she was already reaching for the mare's head.

He swore in earnest and spurred Treun past the flames and into the bay's stall. The mare pivoted away, nearly colliding with Fleurette, but Killian was already reaching for her. She screamed when he snatched her off the ground, but he dragged her facedown over the pommel, and she was not so foolish as to remain there. Instead, she scrambled upright, straddling the saddle in front of him. Her legs, bare to midthigh, gripped the stallion, and her face, smeared with grime, turned frantically toward him.

"Drive her out!" she ordered, waving at the mare. "Get them out!"

But he was already turning Treun toward the door, toward fresh air, toward safety. Reaching down, Fleurette grabbed a rein and hauled the stallion about.

"Save the horses!" she gritted, eyes ablaze in the firelight. "Or leave the task to me."

He almost argued, almost yanked the rein from her hand, but every moment lost was a life compromised, thus he turned Treun toward the milling mob at the back of the stable.

The horses crowded aside, scrambling to escape both the fire and the charging stallion, but there was nowhere to go, and the huge destrier was already amongst them, squeezing them aside, breaking a path in their midst. Turning on his haunches he bared his teeth and struck. A chestnut squealed and bolted away, but another careened frantically into her hip, throwing her off-balance. She stumbled to her knees.

"Juliet!" Fleur screamed, but the mare was already struggling to her feet. A gelding bolted forward, trampling her. She skidded onto her side and into the flames. Fleur screamed again. The smell of burning hair stung Killian's nostrils. The mare scrambled shakily to her feet and tried to return to the others, but the wolf had arrived.

Legs spread wide, it stood between the chestnut and the others, teeth bared as it snarled a warning. The mare trembled in terror and braced herself to leap, but the hound sprang first, flying at the mare's head. She spun about, quivered in uncertainty, then leapt the fire and raced through the open door.

The herd flinched and quivered as it watched. Treun tore at the nearest steed's haunches. It tucked its tail and bolted through the melee. Flames shimmered on its hide as it leapt the burning fodder and disappeared after the mare.

Ears flickered as the others watched, and suddenly they were moving as a herd, bumping and straining as they broke for the door. Nostrils flared, hooves skittered in panic, but they were galloping, careening toward safety.

Fille watched them go, then, in the last second, dashed after them, firelight dancing in her terrified eyes as she joined the herd outside.

Killian felt Fleur sob with relief as Treun leapt after the others. Curling his arm across her face, he felt the heat of the flame sear his elbow and thigh, but in a moment they were safely outside the confines of the smoke-clouded stable.

Beneath them, Treun pranced with manic energy. His ears flickered, his nostrils flared as he searched the breeze for scents and sounds of the escaping herd.

The lady coughed and tugged at Killian's arm.

He turned his attention irritably toward her.

"What the devil are ye about now?" he growled.

"Let me go."

He tightened his grip. "What foolishness have ye got planned?"

Somewhere in the dark a horse whinnied. The noise sounded frantic and lonely in the night.

"Foolishness!" she hissed and twisted toward him. Flames danced like madness in her devil's eyes.

"Aye, foolishness," he growled. "What the hell are ye planning? To run them down in yer bare feet and bed clothes? Ye've servants to tek care of such—" he began, but suddenly she was scrambling to free herself.

He tried to hold her, but she was like water in his hands, slipping relentlessly away. Her night rail caught on Treun's pommel. The sound of tearing fabric rent the night. She struck the ground with an audible grunt.

Temporarily stunned, she sat for a second, but

by the time Killian had dismounted beside her, she had bounced to her feet and spun toward the herd.

Barely thinking, he grabbed a fistful of her gown and reeled her back. She twisted toward him like a cat. Perhaps he should have realized she was about to strike. Perhaps he should have been able to prevent the blow, but pain exploded in his eye, nevertheless.

Shocked and blinded, he stumbled backward; but battle instincts honed long ago flared up. He was reaching for her even before his vision cleared. His fingers closed on something soft and he yanked her back.

Through one functioning eye, he saw her glare at him.

"Who are you?" she rasped.

Damn it to Hades! He had forgotten pain. "I am vengeance," he rumbled, and, loosing her hair, grabbed her arm.

She stumbled back a step.

"What do you want?" Her voice was little more than a hiss in the darkness. Her eyes were as bright and round as an autumn moon in her soot-streaked face. "Why have you come?"

He said nothing, but watched her. Fear and caution glowed in her eyes, but suddenly she threw herself at him.

"What do you know?" she shrieked.

He caught her arms. She gasped at the bite of his fingers. Her gaze lifted to his, then she was falling.

Stunned and uncertain, he swept her into his arms and drew her against his chest. Her breasts were as soft as down pillows against his flesh. Her eyes were as wide as a doe's.

"My . . . my lady?" someone stammered. She glanced in that direction, seeming dazed, but Killian turned to the servant with a snarl, and the man stumbled back.

"Yer lady has all but been kilt," he growled. "What is yer purpose if na to protect her?"

The manservant's lips moved, but no sound came.

"Fetch the steeds," Killian snapped. "I will see to yer lady's well-being."

The other muttered something, but Killian took a single step toward him, and he bolted away, nightshirt fluttering.

"You've no right to speak to my manservant in that . . ." Fleur began, but he lowered his gaze to hers with a snarl.

"Manservant!" he mocked. " 'Tis na man a'tall what would let a wee maid fend for herself while the stable burns down about her—"

"I am no wee maid!" she snapped, but she

was suspended like a swallow's nest in his arms, and there seemed little need to point out the foolishness of her words.

Instead, he strode across the courtyard toward the house. Her breast pressed more firmly against his chest. He gritted his teeth against the velvet impact and managed to skim his arm beneath the soft curve of her bottom and open the door.

"I am the baroness of Briarburn," she insisted, as if she were lecturing a green lad instead of lying, weak and exhausted, in his arms. "Lady of these—"

"My lady!" gasped a maid, wide-eyed and wild-haired. "My lady, are you—"

"Why did ye na keep her safely inside?" Killian snarled.

The maid's jaw dropped. "I . . . We . . ." she began, but Killian had no time for foolish stuttering.

"Where is her bedchamber?"

The maid bent backward, her eyes wide with terror. "Up. Up the . . ." she began, but he was already moving, taking the steps three at a time as he bore her to the top. The first door stood open. An ornate lantern of sorts was lit and suspended by a brass rod that protruded from the cloth-covered wall. Its light glowed on polished wood and gilt mirrors.

He felt Fleurette's tension even before he looked into her eyes. Anger was there, and pride. But there was something more. Something he could not quite fathom. He jerked out of the massive chamber and bore her away to the end of the hall. The door was open there also. Stepping inside, he glanced about. Light from the hallway issued softly into the room, illuminating rich oils and simple fabrics. A hound peeked out from beneath the mattress.

Killian glanced down at the woman in his arms. Uncertainty danced like flames in her unearthly eyes. "If I leave ye here, will you stay?" he asked.

The fear was gone from her face, replaced by a dozen swirling emotions he could not define. "Who are you?" she asked again, but her voice was quiet now, and low.

His own emotions filtered down a little. All was well. The stable would need repair, but no lives had been lost.

He paced toward her bed as the dog scooted backward. Its nose disappeared just as he seated himself on the edge of the mattress. Fleurette's buttocks, barely contained by the sheer weight of her night rail, pressed with fresh intimacy against his balls. He gritted his teeth and tried to swallow, but his mouth had gone dry with longing. The very thought made him angry.

"Tell me, lady," he growled, "do ye disdesire to live?"

"Disde—"

"Could ye na think a simpler way to kill yerself?"

She shifted slightly. Through the fragile fabric of her night rail, he could feel the bulb of her nipple brush his chest, but her eyes never flickered away, as if she were completely unaware of her compromised position. "Did you destroy my gown?" she breathed. "Did you set the fire?"

He scowled, taken aback, then shook his head, trying to comprehend her words. "The fire I only just drew ye from?"

She watched him in silence as if she could read his mind, but he hoped desperately that she could not, for even now his body was wreaking havoc with his roiling thoughts. How long had it been since he'd held a bonny maid in his arms? How long since he'd felt the softness of her skin against his flesh.

"Who sent you?" she asked.

His mind sprinted back to the matter at hand. He had troubles far deeper than simple lust. He was in a time and place he did not know, for reasons he could not quite fathom.

"Mayhap 'tis ye who should answer that question," he said.

She reared back slightly, pressing her hip against his groaning erection. "No one sent me. This is my home."

He watched her narrowly. "Ye are na a fool," he said, "though ye sometimes act it."

"Why thank you, Sir Killian. And you are not an overbearing warthog though—"

"I but meant that mayhap ye could tell me why I have been called here."

"What?" She reared back even farther.

He gritted his teeth against the torturous feel of her movement against his ancient desire. "I believe ye know much ye are na saying."

Her face was pale and perfect in the flickering half-light, her eyes round and innocent, but he had learned long ago to distrust a woman's softness. Even now he remembered silvery eyes and a bewitching smile. Even now he felt the pain though he could not quite identify it. Oh, yes, women knew the weakness they wrought in men. They knew, and they used the effects against them.

"About what?" she breathed. Her lips remained slightly parted. They looked as red as poppy petals and just as soft. The muscles in his arms bunched helplessly against her back. Beneath her half-naked legs, his thighs ached with tension.

"Sir Killian?" she murmured.

He came to with a start.

"I think ye ken why I am here," he managed.

She blinked and tilted her head slightly. The smooth length of her elegant throat shifted slightly, making a sweeping V down beneath her gown. The laces had come undone and lay loose against her breasts. Even in the uncertain candlelight, he could see the intoxicating bulbs of her nipples through the pale fabric.

"You don't know why you've come?" she asked.

He swallowed, trying to think, to relax, but she shifted again, and his erection danced frantically against his belly. He could feel his face redden. Women had been an anomaly in his world, a rare and delicate hallucination in the midst of battle-ready warriors.

"Then why are you here?" She was watching him closely. He could not help but wonder if she could see the blush on his cheeks. He squirmed slightly and found that the movement only made matters worse, for now her hip pressed up hard against his shaft. "What do you want?" she asked.

Well now, finally a question he could answer,

he thought frantically. He wanted her. Her softness, her toughness, her sassy tongue, her sunny laughter. Oh aye, he wanted her desperately. But he would not say so to her. Never to her. So he deepened his scowl.

Intimidation had rarely failed him in the past.

"Methinks ye know what I want." He was breathing hard, and his head felt light. "Ye are na a nidget, despite evidence to the contrary."

Her lips tilted slightly, as if she almost smiled. "Are you ..." She paused, watching him. His erection bucked. He shifted again, trying to push her farther away ... maybe. She reached up, steadying herself with a hand against his arm.

He froze like a startled stag beneath the touch of her fingers.

"Might you be trying to compliment me in your own incomprehensible manner?" she asked.

He deepened his scowl and hoped quite desperately he wouldn't pass out. God's truth, if he passed out, he would fall on his own sword and be done with it. "I am na the sort of man to spew foolish flattery, lass," he rumbled.

And then she laughed. The sound was like magic, light and clear and as bonny as a skylark's song. "No," she said, "you do not seem like the flirtatious sort." She tilted her chin down. Tiny, nearly indiscernible freckles were sprinkled across the bridge of her upturned nose, and diffused candlelight shone like stars in the evergreen innocence of her eyes. "Indeed . . ." She paused, and her expression grew serious. "You do not seem like any sort ever I've met."

He scowled. He was not a bonny man, and he well knew it. Long ago, his nose had been smashed by a Frenchman wielding an ax. He remembered the man's face as if it had been yesterday. Killian's nose had never healed properly. Neither had the Frenchman, but he'd left his mark, and the scar that split Killian's brow could not be considered handsome.

Yet she stared at him from nerve-wracking closeness and did not seem repulsed. His wick danced beneath the unnatural confines of his trews. Why would grown men wear such foolish garb? It was far easier to hide one's appreciation for the fairer sex beneath a rough plaid and horsehide sporran. But maybe men in this time and place were not so easily moved. Indeed, that must be the case, for this irresistible maid moved freely among them with little seeming concern that she might be accosted at any moment. Indeed, women were constantly parading the streets in little more than a sheet to cover them from their nipples down.

And now the thought of nipples made his mind go numb and his wick dance like a sapling in the wind.

"Where do you come from?" she asked.

Another age, another time, another truth. But he could not tell her. Indeed, he could not understand it himself.

"I am Scot," he said simply.

She still watched him. Still no repulsion, and why was that? The English had long detested the Scots, and round about, if the truth be told. "I had guessed as much," she said, and gave him the flicker of a smile that made his breath catch tight in his throat. "I but wonder where Hiltsglen might be."

" 'Tis well up in the high lands," he said, and tried to continue to breathe, though desire was like a hot brand within him.

"Is that where you obtained this?" she asked, and, lifting a hand, ran her finger ever so slowly along the scar that marred his brow and nose.

The touch of her fingers felt like magic, like the caress of a fairy's wand.

"Sir Hiltsglen?" she asked.

He jerked back to reality with a snarl, bolted to his feet, and dumped her onto the bed.

Her night rail, displaced by the sudden motion, slipped past her knees to her thighs and pooled like forbidden waters around her barely hidden womanhood.

He stood transfixed, bunching his fists and trying to breathe.

"Wha—" she began, but he took a shaky step to the rear.

"Dunna light the wick, if ye've no means to douse the flame," he snarled, and, hardening his faltering resolve, turned on his heel and marched down the stairs.

Chapter 11

❦

What the devil was the matter with her?

Fleurette sat at her desk, staring numbly out the window. From below, the sound of a hammer striking steel mingled with the hum of men's voices as they worked. They would be producing the first Eddings vis à vis today, but she couldn't quite seem to dredge up her usual enthusiasm.

Closing her eyes, she rubbed them wearily, and in the back of her head, she saw Killian's face. He was not pretty, not flashy. Indeed, he was wholly unlike the elegant men of the *ton*, for there seemed to be no subterfuge to him, no sly cleverness. He was what he was. Solid and honest and—

Good Lord, what was she thinking? She didn't know if he was honest. She didn't even know why he kept appearing at the most unlikely times. Was he attracted to her? Did he find her unforgettable just as—

Dammit! Why the hell would she care? Didn't she have enough problems as it was? Someone had breached the privacy of her home and destroyed her clothing. And though she had questioned the servants, none had given her any clues to the perpetrator. Thus, she had merely warned them to be on their guard. But there was no guarantee that that same someone couldn't do something just as disturbing again. Or something far worse.

Indeed, her stable had nearly burned to the ground. Her beloved horses had almost been killed. And for all she knew it might well have been the barbarian himself who was the source of all her problems.

"Dunna ignite the wick, if ye've na means to douse the flame."

For heaven's sakes. What did that mean? She tried to chuckle at the idiocy of his statement, but her laughter emerged as a stifled groan. Her head made a clunking sound as she dropped it onto her desktop. She knew exactly what he'd meant, despite his archaic speech. She was, after all, no blushing virgin. She was a widow, for pity's sake, experienced, seasoned, practical.

So why the hell had she been sitting on his lap? On his lap, for God's sake! She felt the blush burn her ears. Oh yes, she'd like to believe he'd held her there by force, that he had overpowered her, and maybe for a time he had. Indeed, he was certainly capable of such a feat.

Without the least bit of trouble she could remember the strength of his arms as he'd crushed her to his chest. Holy heaven, he'd snatched her onto his stallion as if she weighed no more than a summer shawl. And still, several days later, she could easily recall the shift of his muscular thighs against hers. The entire episode had been like a dream, like an ancient, romantic vignette from times long past. The beleaguered maiden, fighting against all odds, and the chivalrous knight, charging up on his black destrier to save her. The determination of his granite expression as he sat the rearing stallion, his face illumined by the flickering blaze. The deep rumble of his voice. The flare of flame in his narrowed eyes. The glisten of his charger's black hide. The sheer drama of it was breathtaking. As if—

Damn it all! She jerked to her feet and roamed her office like a caged hound.

And that was another thing! The hound. Where the deuce had that unearthly animal emerged from? In the uncertain light and the roaring fear of the blaze, it had looked as big as a stag and ungodly feral.

She snorted at her own foolishness. Obviously, her idiotically girlish fantasies were driving her mad.

Still . . . She paused by the window to gaze down at the street below. Barbarian or no barbarian, Hiltsglen had saved her horses. Indeed, it might well be that he had saved her very life.

For just a moment, Fleur let herself dwell on the panic, allowed herself to remember the pealing terror of her cherished herd.

Aye, he may have saved them all.

On the other hand, perhaps it was he who started the flame at the outset. How had he known about the blaze unless he had ignited it himself? And why had he been close enough to be aware of it? Was he watching her? Was he lingering in the woods nearby? Was it he who had snuck into her home? She had oft felt that she was being observed, but that had hardly begun just since his arrival. Indeed, it had often seemed that she was not alone, even in the absence of others. But try as she might, she could not imagine the Scotsman skulking about her house. If he wanted to come in, it seemed likely that he would tear down the door and enter at will. In fact—

"My lady."

She almost screamed as she jerked toward the door of her office.

Mr. Benson stood in the opening, one hand on the door latch, the other fearfully clutching his hat. "My apologies," he said, bobbing his balding head. "I did not mean to startle you."

"No. No." It was all but impossible to draw her breath, but she managed it, then paced fretfully back to her chair and seated herself. "I was lost in thought is all. What can I do for you, Mr. Benson?"

His eyes shifted toward the window and back. She tensed. Stanley Benson was a fine overseer and a wise advisor, but he had never been entirely comfortable about working for a woman, and he had never quite determined how best to deliver bad news. In fact, he tended to look exactly as he did now when there was a less-than-favorable turn of events.

"What is it?" she asked.

He cleared his throat. "'Tis regarding Lord Gardner's quarry, my lady."

"His quarry?" She felt somewhat relieved. After the goings-on of the past few days, she found it quite simple to imagine much worse. Indeed, if nothing had caught on fire and no one was threatening her life, all seemed quite perfect.

"You asked me to purchase the stonery and the land that surrounds it," he said, and nodded jerkily as if he feared she may have forgotten.

"Oh, yes. Of course." She gave him an encouraging smile. "Is Lord Gardner being stubborn?"

Benson cleared his throat again. His Adam's apple bobbed like a drinking chicken's. "I'm afraid he ahhh . . . I'm afraid he offered the land to another."

"To . . ." She half rose, then settled back into her chair and drew a deep breath. "To whom?"

He blinked. His eyes were watery and pale. A tic winked in his left cheek. "I believe the gentleman's name is Sir Hiltsglen."

She leapt to her feet. Her chair exploded to the floor behind her. "What?"

He actually took a step backward, as if he half expected her to fly across the room and attack him. Mrs. Benson was said to have a quick temper.

"I am sorry," he said, and, judging by his expression, he truly was. "But I fear—"

"Well, that's unacceptable," she said, and

paced the room once again. "You shall return to Lord Gardner and convince him to accept our offer."

"But—"

"It does not matter what is required."

"I fear—"

"Mr. Benson." She straightened her back and looked him in the eye, not a simple task, since his tended to stray rather wildly. "That land once belonged to my dear husband's estate."

"I realize that, my lady, but—"

"It shall again. Now, you must return to Lord Gardner posthaste and offer whatever is necessary to secure the purchase of that property."

" 'Tis not so—"

"Try to obtain it as inexpensively as possible, of course. But pay what you must."

"It's—"

"Mr. Benson," she said. "I shall see my husband's estate returned to its former grandeur. The cost matters—"

"Hiltsglen already holds the deed," Benson said in a rush.

She drew a sharp breath, held it for a moment, and forced herself to be calm. "What?"

Benson turned his hat fretfully about in his hands. Its tattered rim suggested it might have made the same nervous circuit on more than one occasion. "Sir Hiltsglen," he said. "I fear he already holds the deed to the property."

"That's impossible," she breathed, but she knew that it was not, knew Hiltsglen was just the sort of man to steal the land from under her grasp even as he pretended to come to her aid. She pursed her lips, glanced at her desk, and carefully closed her account books. "Mr. Benson," she said, her tone carefully clipped now, "please ask Horace to bring my carriage around."

"Yes, my lady," he said, and turned away thankfully.

"And Mr. Benson."

He twisted back with an undisguised grimace.

"Do you happen to know any investigators?"

His eyes widened marginally. "Investigators, my lady?"

"Yes."

"No, my lady, I fear I do not. But I . . . I imagine I could find one if you so desired."

"I do," she said, and gave him a curt nod. "I do indeed."

Killian rubbed the ancient wound beneath the plaid cloth that crossed his bare torso, then bent and heaved a pair of stones into his makeshift dray. It had taken him most of the morning to fashion the thing out of rough timber, still longer to rig a harness so that it might be pulled by a horse.

He looked at his sorry handiwork and sighed. He was hardly an accomplished wainwright, he thought, and glanced toward the north. A furlong in that direction, the River Nettle hustled along in its fertile bed. From the surrounding trees a pipit sang to the setting sun. 'Twas a bonny spot there by the quarry, pastoral and quiet. Mayhap a man could find peace there. But did he deserve peace?

He turned his gaze to Caraid. The sword of his ancestors leaned against the stone wall, its upturned hilt etched with intricate knotwork. His dark memories assured him that it had served him well in the past, but mayhap those days were far behind him. Mayhap he had come to this place to start anew. He glanced at the tumbled cottage. Then, lifting another pair of displaced stones, he tossed them into the wagon behind the spavined gelding. The chestnut remained absolutely unmoved when the rocks hit the growing cairn.

Treun, on the other hand, flickered back his foxy ears and issued a snort of disgust.

Killian gave him a glare. "You'd best be keeping yer comments to yerself, laddie, lest ye wish to carry yon load upon yer own back." They had had something of a disagreement hours before about whether or not handsome destriers were meant to pull homemade drays filled with rocks from tumbledown cottages. Killian was fairly sure he himself had lost the argument.

The stallion shook his hirsute head. Lifting his heavily feathered foreleg, he struck the oaken trunk to which he was tied.

"And ye'll stay where yer put," Killian added, "if ye dunna wish to spend the remainder of yer days as a gelding."

The stallion swung his great head toward the east and trumpeted like a battle horn.

"Aye," Killian agreed grumpily. "And that's where the fiery lass will be staying. Well out of the reach of the likes of ye." The bay mare was no less dangerous than her mistress, who could hit with surprising strength when moved to violence. Killian's eye still ached like the devil where she'd struck him.

Treun snorted as if laughing and thumped the tree with irritating repetition.

"Ye may well think it funny now, but ye were na so merry when I found ye with yer bonny mare."

Treun pawed again, more aggressively still, and Killian snorted.

"Oh aye, she be a lovely sight to behold, but she is na so delicate as she seems, aye?" When Killian had discovered the two in the woods beside the smothering stable, his charger's shoulder had already sprouted a swelling the size of his fist. "Ye cross her again, and she'll have ye seeing double or na a' tall."

The stallion half reared, restive and angry.

"Ye think yerself a bleeding hero just now, but ye'd best na forget, she would have beat the living tar out of ye had I na dragged ye away. 'Tis a blessing to ye she caught ye in the shoulder where she can do ye na damage instead of in the balls where—"

Treun jerked his head to the east and screamed again. Killian turned with a start.

Just stepping from the woods, was the bay mare. And upon her back sat Lady Glendowne.

Killian's breath caught as if he'd been struck with a battering ram.

Fleurette rode as straight and true as a conquering queen. Her strawberry hair shone like rosy gold in the waning sun, and her eyes, as green as the Highland hills, scanned him with regal disdain.

And despite himself, Killian felt himself flush. If the truth be known, he preferred to be dressed in full armor in the presence of the fairer sex. But at least she had not heard him discussing nether parts with his randy steed like a demented stable lad.

The lady drew her mount to a halt. The mare tucked her delicate head to her chest and rolled white-framed eyes at Treun.

"Sir Hiltsglen." Her voice was dulcet, her velvet-clothed shoulders drawn back like a wee, battle-ready soldier.

"My lady," he said, and felt strangely naked in naught but his belted plaid. Which was strange, since he'd spent most of his life in naught else.

Her eyes skimmed him again, as if he were some strange phenomenon she'd found beneath a rock on the river bank. "I've a matter I would speak of with you . . . if you are not too busy discussing delicate matters with your steed."

Chapter 12

$\sim\!\!\!\curvearrowright\!\!\!O\!\!\!O\!\!\!\curvearrowleft\!\!\!\sim$

God's breath, she'd heard him. Killian scowled, hoping to control his blush. But it was no use. So he glared at her and straightened his back. It ached dully. A warrior was not meant for menial labor. But times had changed with confusing abruptness. And he must change with them or fall. "What would ye discuss?" he asked.

She remained silent, staring at him. He resisted the urge to shuffle his feet like a callow lad.

"Did ye come here apurpose, my lady?" he asked. "Or have ye lost yer way?"

Anger sparked in her eyes as she raised them

to his, and Killian was glad to see it, for it was good to remember that she was no fragile blossom. Indeed, despite her touchable skin and delicious fragrance, she was no more tractable than the fiery mare she controlled with such cool aplomb.

Turning deliberately away, he bent and lifted another stone from the tumbled pile. It met its mates with a clatter. Killian raised his scowl to her lowered gaze and found that she had fixed a careful smile on her perfectly sculpted face. Her skin, he noticed, was as fair as a windflower, with just the slightest blush of pink on her bonny cheeks.

"Would it not make more sense to use the stallion for that task?" she asked, nodding toward the gelding, who stood with one hind resting lazily and his bottom lip drooping.

Killian turned his gaze toward Treun. The black charger reared again. His cock had already gone hard and jerked like a long dark arm against his taut belly. God's balls!

Killian cleared his throat and snapped his gaze back to the lady's.

"Treun thinks himself better suited for other tasks," he grumbled.

"Such as—" she began, then paused as the steed swung his haunches about, affording her a better view of his opinion of his value. "Oh." It was her turn to clear her throat. Indeed, it was her turn to blush. Killian watched in fascination. Mayhap she was not so worldly as he had thought. "I just . . . I . . ." She cleared her throat again and straightened her back even more, though he would have thought it impossible. "Treun?" she asked, and refused to glance at the stallion again.

Killian almost smiled at her obvious discomfort. Indeed, if he had not throbbed with such impatient lust himself, he might well have laughed out loud.

" 'Tis the beastie's name," he said, but she did not respond. In the past, he had rarely been uncomfortable with silence. Indeed, he was not the sort to care for idle blather. But he shuffled his feet, feeling lost in her wordless presence. "It means brave . . ." he said, "in the Gaelic."

"Oh."

"Aye." God's nuts, he was like an unwashed boar at the sight of a prize sow.

"Well . . ." Her mare danced a slow-cadenced *rondeau* beneath her, but the lady's lithe body only swayed the slightest degree while her hands were as steady as the earth. "He is that," she said, and pursed her lips. They looked as succulent as elderberries, as bright and lush as spring flowers. "He seemed quite fearless . . . despite the fire." She cleared her throat and glanced down momentarily. "I do not deny that I would like to have him amongst my own stock, but just now I am quite grateful he was in your care."

Killian stood transfixed as her lips moved. How soft they would feel beneath his. How plump and warm and—

"Sir Hiltsglen."

"Oh! Aye!" he rumbled. What the devil had she been saying? He jerked his gaze from her mouth to glare at Treun. The stallion kicked out behind and trumpeted again. "He is na usually so rank as all this."

"Not usually?" Her brows dipped toward her ever-bright eyes. "You speak as if you've owned him for a decade."

Damnation! He had to keep his wits about him, but her luscious lips kept moving, drawing his attention, tightening his body. And now she was staring at him, and he had no idea what to say, and—

"Sir Hiltsglen?"

He swore in silence and tried not to sweat. God's truth, 'twould be safer to face a troop of his own wild clansmen than spend ten minutes in her dangerous company. "He . . . reminds me of a steed I once rode."

"Truly?" She eyed the stallion, her lips slightly quirked. "I've not seen his ilk. Not in all of England."

Treun strained at his tether, his erection snatched up tight against his barrel, his teeth bared.

"Aye, well, they're a breed apart in the Highlands."

She turned her gaze back to him. He felt the impact like a direct blow. As if she had reached in and struck his heart.

"Did he . . ." She paused and Killian realized he was rubbing the aching bruise Treun had left on his biceps. "Did he bite you?"

The slightest suggestion of a smile was tilting her rose petal lips, calling to him, begging for him. He took a step toward her, then caught himself with taut impatience and perfected a glare. "I've a task to do," he snarled. Rampaging lust rarely put him in a good mood. Being laughed at by a maid who smelled like heaven and hit like the devil made him downright nasty. His eye twitched, reminding him she had surprising strength in her foolishly tiny fist. "And I cannot dringle me time away on foolish blather. What be yer purpose here?"

A muscle jumped in her jaw. Her mood could change like the weather, a good thing to remember, considering his eye. "My purpose," she said, "is of a business nature."

He clenched his jaw and held himself steady. Damn it all, didn't she know that some men still acted like men? Some men could not hear her speak without wanting to kiss her, to pull her into his arms and—

And he was daydreaming like a green lad again. "State yer business," he snarled.

"A gentleman . . . indeed, a *civilized* man," she said, and raked his bare chest with her hot gaze, "would not wish to discuss business like two badgers over a fresh kill."

He tightened his fists and willed himself not to blush again. 'Twas no surprise to learn she did consider him to be one of the preening peacocks she called gentlemen.

"And what would a gentleman do, my lady?" he asked, refusing to be quelled.

"He might . . ." She glanced toward his tumbledown cottage as if suddenly uncertain. "Invite me in to . . . discuss matters over tea and . . . crumpets."

He almost laughed out loud at the idea. Tea! He was lucky to have water and a cup to put it in, but he bowed, then motioned to the hovel with sincere sarcasm. "Me apologies, me lady," he said. "Would ye care to view me grand estate?"

She gritted him a smile. "No," she said, and brushed a speck of dust from her immaculate frock. "But thank you ever so much for asking."

Maybe it was her tone that irked him. Maybe it was her baiting. Or maybe, God damn it, it was just her. He returned her taut smile. " 'Tis a strange thing," he said, and took a step toward her. The mare tucked her handsome head and retreated. "I did na think ye the type to be afeared of a barbarian such as meself."

"Afeared?" she asked, and brought the mare to an abrupt halt. "I am hardly afeared . . . afraid," she corrected, "of the likes of you."

He gave her a smile, the one O'Banyon had once compared to an irritable bear's snarl.

"Then please . . ." he said, and swept his arm toward the moldering abode. The movement burned through his biceps like fire. Damned horse. 'Twould serve him right and well to spend the rest of his days as a hapless stag. "Will ye na join me in me . . ." He paused. "Solar?"

She glanced toward the house. Had the building been fully restored to its former, dubious glory, its entirety would have fit into Briarburn's master bedchamber. But that wasn't where she spent her nights was it, he thought, and wondered about her reasons.

Their gazes met. She scowled, then hid away the expression and lifted her chin. "Very well," she said, and, kicking an iron free, balanced momentarily on her left foot before jumping to the ground.

The mare swung her hips wide and rolled her eyes at Treun. As for the stallion, he was sweating as if battle-ready. A lazy beam of fading sunlight found its way through the new spring leaves and shone on his hide with blue-black luster.

The lady smiled. "Where shall I house my mount?" she asked, then glanced about as if surprised. "Oh, but I see you've got no stable."

Killian gritted his teeth. "Bring her 'bout back," he said, and led the way around the cottage.

He was somewhat surprised to find her following.

Behind them, Treun's demanding trumpet had turned into a pleading whicker.

Killian snorted. Damned pathetic was what it was. 'Twould be a cold day in hell before he would lower himself to those depths.

"Ye can put her up in there," he rumbled, and motioned toward the remains of a stone stable.

By the looks of things, it had once been a fine structure, but time and neglect had taken their toll. Still, he had managed to repair the walls of a small portion and replace the timbers to keep the rain at bay. Unfortunately, a door was sadly lacking. A single tree trunk, denuded and crooked, served as a gate between the enclosure and freedom.

Leading the mare inside, Fleurette removed the bridle while Killian lifted the timber. She left the saddle in place and stepped through the opening before he slid the plank into place behind her.

She turned. He glared at her, completely uncertain what to do next. She stared back, her brows slightly raised and her nose in the air.

"Shall we go in out of the rain?" she asked.

He glanced up and realized somewhat belatedly that it had indeed begun to sprinkle. Turning toward his tilted door, he pushed it open.

She stepped through like a reigning princess, then stood to the side, surveying the room.

There wasn't a great deal to see. Indeed, he had accomplished little more than clearing the rubble. His nooning fire still smoldered. Desperate for something to do with his hands, he squatted by the hearth and stoked the embers with a half-burned branch. They sparked to life.

He nudged in a bit of kindling, blew up the flames, and added a few split logs. The fire was crackling gently when he straightened and turned.

Lady Glendowne's gaze snapped upward, and he wondered idly where she'd been looking. Surely she wasn't interested in the likes of him. And yet he could not deny the feelings that swarmed through him at the sight of *her*. It did little to improve his mood.

"Are ye about to tell me why ye've come?" he asked.

"You don't know?"

"I'll admit I'm pitchkettled."

She raised her brows at his choice of words, but didn't ask for an explanation. Instead, she scanned the room again. "I am told this cottage was once a fine hunting lodge."

He watched her roam to the window and glance out. Perhaps a pelt had been scraped to transparency and placed over the opening at one time, but nay. Animal hides were no longer used for such things. Instead, the English had windows that were covered with glass not unlike that of a fine bottle. The strangeness of it made his head hurt.

"My husband's grandfather enjoyed it a great deal."

He watched her, and she turned finally to look at him.

"Perhaps you were unaware that this was one of several pieces of property that once belonged to Lord Glendowne."

He didn't respond, but checked a black kettle for water, then placed it over the fire.

"Briarburn was a fine estate, stretching from Lord Gardner's property to the Nettle and beyond."

He lifted his gaze to hers.

"The manor house was crafted from the very stones found in the quarry here."

She was a relatively small woman, he realized, though she somehow managed to seem quite tall. Her spine was as straight as a spear, her gloved hands clasped in front of her pleated skirt as if in silent supplication.

"Indeed, the house was built more than a hundred years ago. Thomas resided at Glendowne for the most part, but he and his family very much enjoyed Briarburn." She drew a careful breath. "Surely you can see why—"

"So ye cherished him?"

Her lips remained slightly parted, her eyes wide as she stared at him. "He was my husband, Sir Hiltsglen. Indeed, he was a respected—"

" 'Tis na what I asked," he said, walking to the window and leaning his shoulder against the stone wall. It felt cool against his bare flesh, reminding him of his state of undress. But he would not show his discomfort, not to this cool maid. "I but wondered if ye cared for him."

She held his gaze for a moment longer, then flitted it away. "Of course."

"Then he was good to ye? Kind?"

Did her face go pale? Did her eyes look haunted?

She pursed her lips. "Are ye a married man, Sir Hiltsglen?" she asked.

Memories assaulted him. Memories of a maid with golden hair and quicksilver eyes. But his thoughts were torn asunder by pain. He winced at the tearing reminder. "Nay," he said, and locked the shattered memories carefully away for further inspection.

"Nay?" she asked. "Nothing else? No explanations? No regrets?"

"Nay."

For a moment her eyes narrowed as if in thought, but she smiled in a moment and took a careful breath. "Sir Hiltsglen," she said, "I have been a widow for some years now."

Seven. That much he knew, but little else. And even that bit of information was difficult to believe, for she looked as young as a coddled child. Unless one looked into the depths of her evergreen eyes.

"My husband was taken from me quite tragically. Indeed—"

"Why do ye avoid me questions?"

"I do no such—"

"I would but know if he was kind. If ye were content as his wife."

"Why?"

Why indeed? He would like to think he only meant to learn what he could, to find his reason for being drawn to this place and fulfill his duty, but he feared there was more, something deeper. Yet he could not admit it. But when he looked into her eyes, he could not wholly deny it either, for her softness and strength drew at him like velvet cords. He lifted his shoulders, as if attempting to shrug off the bonds. "I . . . 'Twould ease me mind to know."

Her lips parted slightly. "Why would you care, Scotsman?"

He would not. He dare not. And yet he did. "A lass such as yourself . . ." He tried to stop the words, but he had ever been a man who spoke the truth. "I would that ye be happy."

Some emotion crossed her face. It seemed almost like pain.

"But I dunna think ye are," he added.

She brightened immediately, but the expression was slightly askew. "You are entirely wrong. I have much for which to be thankful."

He watched her in silence.

"My business is doing well." The words were rushed. "My stable . . . Well, you have seen my horses."

He nodded slowly. "They are a handsome lot."

"Aren't they?" She seemed to relax a mite. "My Juliet shall bear her first foal in quite some time. And *Fille* . . ." Her eyes were bright again. There were secrets she was hiding. As well as pain, but she was woman who could adjust, who could find her stride and make the best of things. "I thought, perhaps, when she is a bit older I might mate her with your Treun."

He said nothing, for she was entrancing.

"I'll pay you," she added quickly. "Even though he should have been mine at the outset." Something shone in her eyes. Humor maybe. Teasing, and he found he wanted nothing more than to fan it into a smile. To hear her laugh, but there were things he must do, or he himself would be lost.

"Did ye have yer steeds when yer husband yet lived?"

"I . . ." The light in her eyes was abruptly

doused. She cleared her throat. "Thomas was not particularly interested in horses."

"Where then did his interests lie?"

"With his clubs," she said, then closed her mouth tightly, as if she'd not meant to loose the words.

"His clubs?"

She shrugged as if it was of little interest. "I did not begrudge him his time away. Indeed I was glad—" she said, and stopped abruptly.

The silence felt heavy.

"I am sorry," Killian said, "that he was not what ye wished for."

She blinked, lost, but in a moment, she rallied and laughed. "You're entirely wrong."

"Often," he said, "but not this time, I think."

"You're wrong," she repeated, and her voice was brittle.

"Why did he na get ye with child?"

Her eyes widened, and she hissed a tiny intake of breath as if startled. Mayhap 'twas not proper to speak of such things, he realized, but he could not help but wonder. Surely her childlessness was not for lack of effort on her husband's part, for no man could help but long to see a child at her breast.

"I hardly think that any affair of yours," she said. Her voice was cold, cold enough to spur him back to the matter at hand, his reason for being there, his mission, which he must not fail.

Killian narrowed his eyes, watching her, remembering that women were dangerous, no matter how fragile they seemed. "A landed gentleman like yer husband would have longed for an heir," he said.

Did she seem unusually pale suddenly? Did her eyes seem as wide as the moors in her stunning face?

"Perhaps he did," she said. "But—"

"Did he blame ye for yer empty womb?"

Her lips moved again, then, "I want this land back, Hiltsglen," she said, straightening her shoulders with a snap. "I shall give you a fair price. Indeed, you will make a fine profit."

" 'Tis said he drowned in yon river," he said.

Her lover's lips were pursed. "Yes," she said. "That is true."

He watched her. "Could he na swim?"

She shifted her eyes to the window and back. "I am not entirely certain whether—"

"Ye never swam together?"

"No."

"Did he na wish to?"

"Whyever would he?"

"Because ye would feel like heaven—" He stopped his words and fisted his hands. God's truth, he was a dolt. "The river is neither wide nor deep," he finished lamely.

She blinked. " 'Twas a rainy season."

"And yet ye were upon a boat with him."

"I . . ." she began, then drew a deep breath, her eyes still wide, her hands still clasped. "Have you been spying on me, Sir Hiltsglen?"

" 'Tis said he was fond of spirits."

Her nostrils flared as if she were angry, but did her hands tremble slightly? "Why have you come here?" she asked.

He shrugged as he pushed himself slowly away from the wall. Not toward her. God no. He had enough troubles as things were. " 'Tis a bonny spot and as good a place as any. Why do ye stay?"

"This is my home," she said. "I've little reason to leave."

"I thought mayhap the memories would be too harsh for ye to bare. With yer beloved gone." He watched her closely. " 'Twould it na be simpler to find a place in London? A place where the memories dunna haunt ye. Somewhere more manageable for a wee lass such as yerself?"

"A wee lass such as myself," she said, and narrowed her eyes at him.

Perhaps he should be warned by her tone, he thought. Perhaps he should retract the statement before he found her wee fist firmly planted in his as of yet unmolested eye, but there was something about her expression that intrigued him.

"Might you think me incapable of managing Briarburn on my own?" she asked.

He stared at her. If the truth be told, he doubted there was much that was beyond her ability. "Na a'tall," he said. "I but thought ye might tire of being alone on that grand estate."

"I am hardly alone," she reminded him. "Unless you think a woman is bereft until she is duly wedded and bedded."

"Did ye share his bed then?"

"What?" she asked, and all but stumbled backward.

"Yer husband," he said. "Did ye share his bed, or did ye always sleep in the wee chamber at the end of the hall?"

She licked her lips. Killian watched her tongue dart out and in. Something curled up tight in his gut. Damn it to hell. There had been a time when he'd considered himself strong. But perhaps a few centuries of celibacy weakened a man's resolve.

"'Tis none of your affair where I choose to sleep," she hissed.

"So ye share yer bed with others?"

193

She snapped upright. "How dare you?"

"I would but know," he rumbled, and knew he should back away, should hold his tongue, but emotions stormed through him like an angry wind. "Are ye yet true to yer husband's memory, or do ye favor one of the preening fools ye call men?"

"And I suppose you think yourself a true model of manhood," she snarled, and stepped forward.

He watched her come. "Mayhap na a model, but a man for certain."

"True manhood is not determined by the size of his . . ." She skimmed his bare torso and jerked her head toward him. "Chest. Or the . . . the . . . strength of his arms."

"Nay?"

"Nay!" she spat. " 'Tis decided by a man's wit. His education. His good taste."

He scowled. "Ye are looking for a man what tastes good?"

"Don't play daft with me," she hissed, and grabbed the plaid where it crossed his bare chest. "I've known your sort in the past, and I've no wish to know one again."

Her knuckles were pressed against his chest. His heart beat like a hammer against her hand. "And what sort is that, lass?" he asked.

Her face was lifted toward his, her eyes gleamed and her small teeth gritted. "The kind that needs to overpower. To possess. To control," she said, and shook her fist in his plaid.

He stared into her eyes. "So 'tis ye who wishes to tek control?" he asked.

Her lips parted. "Perhaps I do," she whispered, and forced her fingers to open on his woolen. Battle waged in her eyes, but she took a deep breath and struggled for calm. Her hand trembled slightly against his skin. "Would that be so wrong, Scotsman?"

He tried to think, but she was so damnably close, so fair, so horribly alluring. "Mayhap that answer is determined by what ye would do with that control, lass."

Her lips parted again. Her gaze slipped to his chest, and her fingers opened fully against his flesh. Beneath her hand, his skin burned on contact.

"I just want . . ." she began, then stopped. She was breathing hard, and her fingers, soft as the morning air, slipped over his nipple.

He jerked, but managed to think, to breathe, to function. "What is it ye want?" he gritted.

"I just want," she began again, but suddenly she was rising on her toes. Her lips brushed his, and then there was no longer any hope for coherent thought.

He yanked her up against him. She came with a growl, her fingers hard against the back of his skull, her other hand raking the plaid from his chest. He pressed her backward. Where the hell was the bed? He stumbled a few feet. She was struggling with his belt. Her hand brushed his erection.

Damn the bed! The floor would do. He caught their weight on his shoulder.

But a shriek tore through the house, jerking them apart. They stared at each other, eyes wide, almost coherent.

Something crashed outside the window, and the mare screamed.

"Fille!" she cried, yanking herself from Killian's arms and racing to the door. He stumbled to his feet, disoriented and hapless.

She was outside before he'd even marshaled his senses, but Treun's deep-throated call, brought him around.

"Nay!" he yelled. "Stay back." He stormed through the doorway, but one glance outside told him she was already in harm's way, already planted like a willowy sapling between the rearing horses. The impromptu gate was on the ground. A tattered rope swung from the stallion's head collar. The mare's teeth were bared, her eyes rolling. "Stay back!" he yelled again, but in that instant, Treun lunged. He struck Fleurette with his shoulder as he leapt past. She was tossed aside like autumn chaff.

The mare pivoted away. Treun gave chase, trumpeting as he went.

"God's teeth!" Killian lunged to the baroness and dropped to his knees. "Me lady, are ye well? Are ye whole?"

She struggled to sit up. He slipped an arm behind her back, supporting her. "I'm . . ." she began, but her words failed as their gazes melded. He leaned toward her, drawn against his will, then Treun screamed again.

"Stop him," Fleur insisted.

But when they looked up they saw that the mare was standing perfectly still. Treun shook his head and reared, ready to mount her, but she let her heels fly. Iron-shod hooves caught him square between his hind legs.

Even from that distance, they could hear the impact, his grunt of pain. He dropped to his forefeet, nearly falling to his knees.

Fleurette yanked from Killian's arms and leapt to her feet, but the mare had already cocked up her tail and was prancing back toward the cottage.

Killian hurried up to Treun, but the stallion barely raised his head. Instead, he merely turned tortured eyes on his scowling master.

"Aye," Killian growled, feeling the pain in his own nether parts as he watched the baroness catch her mount. "I tried to warn ye, lad." The maid turned toward them, her cheeks flushed and her eyes wide in her perfect face. "But 'tis bloody hard to think in the heat of battle."

Chapter 13

⌒◯◯◯⌒

"**M**r. Johnson," Fleurette said, rising from her desk and giving her newest employee a prim nod. He was two inches shorter than she, pudgy around the middle, and, judging by his gold-rimmed spectacles, severely nearsighted. The Doderty Agency definitely knew how to pick their men. "What have you learned?"

The little man's mustache twitched as he removed his top hat. As it turned out, he had more hair beneath his nose than atop his head. "Regarding one Sir Killian Hiltsglen of Scotland," he said as he opened a leather-bound book and pushed up his spectacles to study his notes. "On the third day of July in the year of our lord 1817, Killian, Sir Hiltsglen, purchased one stallion of unknown lineage from a Lord Bayberry. Later that same week, he bought an acreage consisting of woodland and a small quarry. Formerly, it belonged to one Lord Gardner. Sir Hiltsglen is currently residing in the original cottage that was built upon said property some centuries past."

He glanced up. Fleurette blinked. "Continue."

Mr. Johnson pursed his lips. Perhaps his cheeks were the slightest bit flushed. "I fear that's all the information I've been able to obtain thus far, my lady."

She stared at him agog. "Mr. Johnson, I knew more about him at the outset." For instance, he was a barbarian and a lout, an overgrown, overpowering cretin and a veritable thief. He also had arms the size of tree trunks and a chest like a boulder. He was as strong as a stallion, able to lift her without thought. A woman would never be safe around him, and yet, somehow, inexplicably, she had felt . . .

"My apologies, my lady," Johnson said, and gave her a prim, insulted bow. "But as I told you at the start, this sort of investigation takes time."

"I realize that, Mr. Johnson," Fleur said. "But I don't have much time. He has already stolen a steed and a valuable piece of property right out from—"

"Stolen?" Johnson asked, his tone clipped. "If it's a matter of theft, you should contact the proper authorities posthaste." He blinked, looking nervous. "As I've said before, I'm uncomfortable dealing with the criminal element. In point of fact—"

"I was not being literal," she said, and resisted the urge to give him a sound knock on the side of his head. "Just . . . please, find out what you can as soon as humanly possible. Anything at all regarding his past . . . where he was born, his family life, his business enterprises, what he's been doing these past few years."

Mr. Johnson sighed heavily, as if he weren't being paid handsomely to do the very things she'd just outlined, "I'll see what I can do, my lady," he said, and left her office.

The remainder of the day went no better, and the rest of the week was singularly unspectacular. Friday arrived with alarming haste.

Fleurette stood in her dressing room, trying again to think of a plausible reason to avoid Lucille's party. She was tired, after all, and the weather was unpleasant. The roads were in poor traveling condition after days of endless rain, and . . .

And Lucy would undoubtedly accuse her of cowardice if she didn't make an appearance and face down the barbarian Lucille had so cruelly invited. The countess had sent round a note, in fact, reminding her to arrive at six o'clock sharp.

A rap on the door interrupted Fleur's reverie.

"My lady, might I assist you with your costume?" Tessa inquired, and since Fleurette could think of no sound reason to stay home and hide in her bedchamber, she bid her maid enter.

"Oh, my lady, you look a sight you do." Tessa sighed.

"Do you think so?" Fleur gazed at herself in the walnut-framed mirror. Her gown was made of pale yellow linen. It boasted small cap sleeves, a gathered bodice, and tiny bows strewn about the high waist. She had purchased it with summer in mind. But now—"Are you certain I'm not too . . ." She canted her head. "Old for such a—"

But Tessa was already shushing her. "Too old! Don't be silly. You look lovely, so slim and elegant."

Slim. She scowled at herself in the mirror. She had long thought slim to be a defining euphemism for underdeveloped. Turning sideways, she looked at her breasts. They were decidedly unimpressive. "Fetch the green taffeta, will you, Tessa?" she asked, and began her toilet anew.

"Fleurette." Lucille located Fleur seconds after she entered Anglehill's towering ballroom. "I cannot tell you how flattered I am that you were able to tear yourself away from your busy day just for my little gathering."

Fleur took a glass from a passing servant and waved to Antoinette. Newly arrived from Paris, the *comtesse* was, regardless of travel and fatigue, perfectly groomed and impeccably coifed. Dressed in pristine, glowing white, she was surrounded by suitors. Fleurette turned her gaze back to her hostess.

"I'm sorry I'm tardy."

In fact, Fleur was well over an hour late owing to her own idiotic uncertainties. As it turned out, the taffeta hadn't seemed quite right either.

"I hadn't noticed. I'm certain it's well before midnight."

Fleurette took a sip of punch. It was sharp and crisp, suiting Lucille's personality perfectly. "You could simply chastise me and have done with," she suggested.

"Chastise you," Lucy said, grasping Fleur's elbow and steering her into the crowd. "Why-ever would I do such a pedestrian thing? You're my best and dearest friend. I am certain you would have arrived on my doorstep precisely at six to ease my tattered nerves if you could possibly have managed it."

Fleurette gave her a look. Lady Anglehill didn't have nerves.

"You look delightful by the by," Lucy continued, and glanced at the tiny rosebuds that edged the bodice of Fleur's lilac-colored frock. It was gathered snug at the bust, which had the desired effect on her bosom, but did hideous things to her ability to breathe. It also made it difficult to look anyone in the eye without blushing. It had taken her two hours and fifteen minutes to choose this gown. The idea appalled her. She had spent less time on business acquisitions. "Is this a new purchase? It's lovely. So delicate. Oh, and look, it has matching ivy at the hem. How charming. You must—"

"Lucy," Fleur said, and drew the other woman to a halt. "I'm sorry I'm late."

Lucy stood with her mouth open for a moment, then, "Well, you demmed well should be," she said. "I'm your best friend. In fact," she said and scowled dramatically, "I may be the only person in London who doesn't think you're sleeping with your accountant."

"My accountant is a woman."

"It only makes the gossip that much more delicious. They also think you've propositioned your overseer."

"Benson is seventy years old and married to the most cantankerous woman in all of England. I'd have to be daft or suicidal to—"

"There's Lord Gardner, of course—but that's acceptable, since he's a peer of the realm," Lucy said, and steered Fleurette toward the refreshment tables. They spread the length of the ballroom and, as far as Fleur could decipher, contained every delicacy known to the civilized world. She chose a glazed apricot and nibbled at it. The taste was perfect, sweet but tangy. "But it's the idea that you're sleeping with your little redheaded stableboy that has the *pink of the ton* absolutely agog."

Fleur slanted a jaded glance in Lucille's direction. "Gannon O'Malley is not yet fifteen years of age. No one could possibly believe I'm sleeping with him."

"That's because I haven't yet started the rumor," Lucy said, and Fleur laughed, but her amusement was cut short, for through the crowd she caught her first glance of Killian.

Her breath stopped in her throat. Gone were the rough plaid and battered belt. In their place was a black cutaway jacket and breeches that hugged his bulging thighs like a second skin. His snow-white shirt seemed to gleam against the contrast of his broad, dark-skinned throat, and the shoulders of the jacket looked endless. His cravat was tied just so and his hair almost restrained by a silver clasp. And yet, despite all the polish, he did not manage to look quite tamed. His fingers appeared broad and ridiculously capable against the cut crystal of the glass he held, and his eyes, dark and deadly, scanned the crowd with something akin to feral wariness.

"And now I think I shall not have to," Lucy said.

Dear God, he looked like an untamed wolf amongst panting lapdogs. Like a—

Lucille's laughter cut her thoughts short.

"What's that?" Fleur said, forcing a smile and turning, heart thumping, toward her friend.

"I've just now thought of a worse punishment for you," Lucy replied, her words low and her eyes gleaming as she steered Fleurette toward the towering Scotsman.

In a moment, they were standing before

Hiltsglen, and just as suddenly, Fleur felt ridiculously undressed.

His gaze, dark as midnight, fell to her breasts, and his nostrils flared the slightest degree, like an untamed stallion testing the breeze.

"I assume you remember each other," Lucy said. She couldn't have sounded happier had she just been declared queen.

"My lady." Hiltsglen's voice rumbled through her soul.

Fleurette remembered the feel of his chest against hers, but it was the memory of his words that burned brightest in her mind; *"I would that ye be happy."* Why did he wish for her happiness? Not everyone did, of that she was certain, and yet she was sure he had not lied. Indeed, he might not even be capable of such a thing.

The idea made her nervous, for she herself could never be so honest. It was difficult to resist the aching urge to look away, but she managed it and gave him a prim nod. "Sir Hiltsglen."

Lucille laughed as though she'd just been privy to a most amusing jest. "Well, this is absolutely magnificent. I hear the two of you are neighbors now."

Fleur gritted a smile and shone it with malevolent distaste in Lucy's direction. "Good news travels quickly I see."

"Indeed, yes. Are you truly living in that ramshackle cottage near the ancient quarry, Sir Hiltsglen?" Lucille asked, apparently unimpressed by Fleur's rising wrath.

He nodded, but didn't quite manage to force his gaze from Fleur's. "I am na accustomed to such luxurious conditions as ye have here, Lady Anglehill. 'Tis na hardship living as I do."

"Lord Gardner says you are single-handedly putting the cottage back to order."

He didn't respond. Lucy pulled her gaze from his with a seeming effort. "Fleurette, have you yet seen his progress?"

Memories stormed in on Fleur. Gentle words, strong arms . . . She could feel her face flush with hot embarrassment, but she refused to glance away. She was certain Lucille knew nothing about the debacle in the woods, but she fully intended to flog her to death at the first possible opportunity anyway. "In fact, I visited Sir Hiltsglen some days ago," she said.

"Oh?" If Lucille got any happier, she would certainly die of the condition.

As for the Scotsman, he was watching her like a hunting hawk, his dark brows low over brooding eyes.

Fleurette cleared her throat. "I thought it only . . . civilized . . . that I welcome him to the area," she said, and took another sip of punch.

"Is that what ye were about?" Hiltsglen asked.

Fleur's heart thumped to a halt. Her cup froze halfway down from her parted lips. "What's that?"

"Did ye plan to welcome me?" he asked. "For if that be the case, our methods are a bit different in me own part of the world."

Although she desperately tried to lock away the shameful memories, she could not forget how her lips had clashed against his. How her hands had trembled against his belt buckle. Like a stag in rut. Like a mare in season. But no. Much worse, for at least *Fille* had had the good sense to maim and flee. The only way Fleur could have wounded the towering Scot would have been if she'd thrown him to the ground with too much force when she was having her way with him. And—Oh God, they were waiting for her to respond, waiting for her to come up with some kind of coherent rejoinder. She could literally feel her heart pound in her breasts. Could feel a flush heat them to their peaks. Damn him for his unchivalrous ways! She was going to have to come up with a response before . . . "And what do they do in the caves where you crawled from, Sir Hiltsglen?" she asked, preening a smile.

Lucille was absolutely silent, but turned with glowing eyes on the gigantic Scot. His smile was as predatory as a wolf's.

"Ladies of quality . . ." he paused and bowed slightly . . . "such as yer ladyship, dunna usually lower themselves to visit a mere knight such as meself. 'Twas a great honor for me to welcome ye to me humble abode."

Damn him to hell. Damn him. Damn him. Damn him.

Lucille was laughing again, the sound low and quiet. "Why, Sir Hiltsglen" she said, "I do believe I owe you an apology."

He turned slowly toward her. "I am certain ye are wrong," he said. "For ye have shown naught but good manners and fine breeding." A muscle ticked in his lean jaw. "Indeed, the same canna be said of all present."

He didn't turn an accusatory glance on Fleurette, but it was not difficult to catch his meaning. Damn him.

"'Tis ever so nice of you to say," Lucy twittered, "but you are a guest in my home, and I fear you've been abused." She, on the other hand, did cast an accusatory glance at Fleurette. Damn her. "Whatever can I do to make amends?"

He bowed and extended a hand. It was the approximate size of a draught horse shoe. "Might I accompany ye to your tables, Lady Anglehill?"

"Most certainly." Lucille had once complained that her hands would dwarf a blacksmith's, but her fingers looked as delicate as a fairy's in the Scot's gigantic paw. " 'Twould be my pleasure." She lifted her chin. "If you'll excuse us, Lady Glendowne."

Fleurette watched them go. Lucille was cackling like a demented laying hen. The Highlander was silent, possibly because he hadn't yet mastered the nuances of the spoken language. But he leaned close to Lucy's ear finally, causing the countess to laugh again, and despite Fleur's venomous mood, she could not quite manage to deny that they looked rather handsome together. Damn them. They were both tall and stately, both masterful, yet oddly elegant in their finery. Lucille's gown flared from an unseen draft, brushing delicately against the Highlander's muscular legs. Even with Lucy, he looked unreasonably tall. Ridiculous even, Fleur thought uncharitably, and watched as they swept through the crowd like hawks in a flock of pigeons.

"They look quite grand together."

Fleur turned with a guilty start, smoothing the frown from her face. The man who stood at her elbow was tall and lean. His hair was the color of autumn wheat. Long as a horse's mane, it boasted a braid at each side of his face and hung loose against the golden skin of his throat. He wore no cravat, but it was difficult to fault him for such a faux pas, for his eyes were all entrancing, as blue and enchanting as a summer sky. "I . . . I'm sorry," she said, realizing she was staring like a flummoxed milkmaid. "I don't believe we've been introduced."

"Nay," he said and bowing with graceful panache, reached for her hand. Her breath caught as his thumb brushed her knuckles with intimate tenderness.

"The fault is entirely me own," he said, and pressed his lips to the back of her hand. Sensations scurried up her arm like fluttering butterflies. "I am Sir O'Banyon of the Northern Celts. But me friends call me naught but Nairn."

"Nairn," she breathed.

"Banyon," someone rumbled.

Fleur glanced up to find Hiltsglen and Lucille had returned.

O'Banyon brushed his thumb across Fleurette's knuckles once again and raised his gaze to Hiltsglen's. "Killian," he said. " 'Tis good to see ye fit and . . ." He shifted his summer blue eyes to Lucille. A smile flickered across his stunning face. "Well occupied." Abandoning Fleur's hand with seeming regret, he bowed to Lucy. "Me lady," he said, "I fear I owe ye me apologies."

Lucille seemed to be speechless for the first time in her life. Indeed, her lips moved, but no sharp witticisms came forth. For a moment, Fleur wondered if the world might actually be coming to an end.

But the Irishman bowed and flashed a smile as he kissed Lucille's hand. Had the countess been made of softer stuff, she might very well have hit her knees.

"Good Christ," she murmured to Fleurette, then, slightly louder, "an apology?"

"Aye." He had a dimple in his left cheek that curved with rapscallion grace around his satyr's mouth. "I fear I have taken the opportunity to enter yer home uninvited."

When Lucille failed to answer, Fleur gave her friend a nudge.

"I'm certain you had good reason," said the countess finally.

O'Banyon's smile brightened like the sun. "I was na told that London women be so understanding," he said. "Nor so bonny."

Did she blush? Did Lucille Bevre, the reigning countess of Anglehill, who had carelessly brushed off kings and dignitaries, blush? "I'm happy we could enlighten you, Sir—"

"Nairn," he corrected and stepping forward, pulled her hand into the crook of his arm. "Might I beg a favor of ye, me lady?"

Lucille shifted her eyes momentarily to Fleurette's. Lust shone as bright as a promise there before she dulled the flare and turned back to the Irishman. "I'm afraid my firstborn is already spoken for."

His laugh was a low rumble of pleasure. "Might ye honor me with a dance then?"

They were gone in a moment. Fleurette stood breathlessly watching them, until she realized the Scotsman was doing the same. She turned, reminding herself to breathe. "A friend of yours?" she asked.

"Friend?" His voice echoed from the depths of his Herculean chest, and his eyes were deep and dark as they followed the couple onto the floor. "Aye. As the wolf is friend to the lambkin."

"Oh?" Fleur raised her brows. "And tell me, Hiltsglen, which of you is the wolf and which is the innocent?"

Chapter 14

⟨ ∽∽ ⟩

Lady Glendowne lifted her gaze to Killian's. He clenched his fists and held himself at bay. He was not such a fool as to tempt fate again. Aye, she'd nearly been his undoing when she'd visited his cottage some days before, and though he would like to think it was naught but lust that drove him, he feared it was more. There had been a vulnerability to her that day, a sadness that haunted him, and he'd wanted nothing more than to put things right, to see her smile, to hold her close.

But he had no way of knowing if it was all a ploy. So, he would be more careful henceforth.

He would not stand so dangerously close, would not let himself breathe her garden-fresh scent, and would not, under any circumstances, allow himself to be alone with her. Still, even with a roomful of strangers, he found he wanted nothing more than to pull her to his chest and demand favors he had no right to demand. Or perhaps, if the truth be told, he might very well whimper and beg for her attention just as Treun had at the departing swish of the bay mare's tail. Pride was a slippery thing when one's wick was up. He glanced down into the warm, smiling face of cleavage. God's balls. He clenched his teeth and tightened his hand on his cup.

"Well?" she said, and he just managed to raise his gaze to hers. There was nothing coquettish about this lass, at least not with him. She met his eyes full on. A challenge of sorts. A call to battle. And God help him, he'd been born to fight.

She had the face of an angel, the body of a goddess, as slim and sculpted as a statuette's. Mayhap the fashion of the day leaned toward plump women, but Killian favored a firmer form. And this one was as sweetly curved as a Grecian urn. But there was steel to her, like the hard-edged blade of Caraid.

"Sir Hiltsglen?"

He snapped his attention back to the conversation at hand, though he was not a man for idle banter. Nay, he was a man of deeds and little else. "Killian," he rumbled, and held her gaze in a hard clasp.

"I beg your pardon?" She tilted her head slightly so that a curled tendril of hair caressed her kitten-soft throat. His body yanked up hard at the sight, though he could not begin to guess why.

"Me name," he said, and though he knew better, he took a step toward her, drawn like a trained destrier to the cry of the battle horn. "'Tis Killian. Not Scotsman. Not Hiltsglen. Killian."

She raised one brow as if amused. "Killian," she repeated. Her eyes were as green as the valleys of his homeland. Her throat was as long and slim as a royal swan's. "You've not answered my question. And now I wonder, might you be the proverbial wolf in sheep's clothing?"

"I think it should be clear enough that I am na a wolf. Indeed, I am naught but what ye see."

"And what might that be, good sir?"

"A man na overfond of foolish questions."

"'Twas not I who made the reference at the outset," she reminded him. "But never mind. Perhaps you can answer this query. Where is

217

this Hiltsglen from which you hail? I've not heard of such a place."

Aye, she was bonny, but like many bonny things, she was also deadly. Even now, she laid a trap for him. He could smell it though it was diffused by the wild scent of her. The scent that curled like sweet opium into his mind.

"Hiltsglen would hold no magic for ye, lass," he said, and watched her with narrowed eyes. "For 'tis a plain place. Without the gilt ye are accustomed to."

The corner of her lips twitched up the slightest degree. A single brow rose with it. "Do you presume to know what I find magical and what I find mundane, Sir—?"

"Killian," he finished. She held his gaze with steady interest, as if his every word was somehow important. Why? Might she find him the least bit appealing? But nay. He dare not hope for that. Indeed, he dare not forget how she had looked at Banyon only moments before. How every woman looked at Banyon. He forced his gaze away, finding the man who was sometimes his friend, often his adversary. He was laughing, as was the maid with whom he danced. Indeed, there seems to be a gaggle of women gossiping together as they watched the pair.

The Irishman lifted his gaze, catching the attention of the ethereal woman dressed all in white. For a moment the maid's eyes widened, then she disappeared into her crowd of admirers. Killian almost grinned. Women were rarely discerning enough to escape O'Banyon's questionable charms. Indeed, if Lady Anglehill had the brains of a peahen, she would pelt the damned Irishman with rocks and bolt for the hills. Although it would probably do her little good. O'Banyon could run like a spurred charger if he put his heart into it. And for a bonny lass, he would do just that. His heart and a number of other body parts.

"Is that where you met the wolf there?"

"What?" He snapped his gaze to hers.

Her brows rose sharply. "If you are the innocent, then I must assume your friend there is the wolf," she said.

Killian drew a careful breath, calming himself. She was no fool, that much was certain, but she was, as of yet, unaware of the unearthly forces at work. "Ye speak of the Irishman," he said.

"O'Banyon wasn't it?"

Indeed it was. And who else might she be considering? Even the Golden Lady of Inglewaer had been intrigued with him, though she had been careful to prove her interest in none but Killian himself. Oh yes, he remembered her now. She had come to him in a dream just three nights before, as lovely and melancholy as when he'd first met her. Her fingers were like satin against his fevered skin. Her voice had been that of an angel.

He'd awakened in a cold sweat.

From across the cavernous room, Killian heard O'Banyon laugh. He turned toward the couple that swayed about the dance floor. Ironically, it had been the Irishman himself who had warned against trusting the golden lady. A strange thing, since Banyon had forever been besotted by one maid or another. He'd always been as discriminating as a hound, or so Killian had thought, and yet the other had seen through the lady's deception. But by then it had been too late. Far too late for either of them.

And Lady Glendowne was still watching him, as though she could discern secrets best left hid.

"Or do you call him something else?" she asked.

"He's been called a host of names," Killian said, remembering back to a distant time, before the darkness, before his fatal mistake. "In an assortment of languages."

"Truly? He seems quite charming."

How many times had Killian heard those words, or a variation of the same? He felt irritation tickle the back of his neck as he watched the other glide past. Lady Anglehill was still laughing. The Irishman had once partnered the princess of Teleere. She had begged him to run away with her the very same night, "As can a serpent," he said, turning back toward Fleurette. "But it is rarely wise to befriend one."

She was watching him again, though Banyon was still visible through the crowd. Which was strange. But for the delicate maid dressed all in white, every other woman present seemed transfixed.

How many moments would pass until the baroness turned back toward the Irishman? Not that Killian cared, of course. She could be besotted by whomever she chose, even if he was a womanizing hound.

"Shall I assume you do not care for him?" she asked.

" 'Tis the maids what are ever agog when he is near."

She nodded, but frowned a little, as if puzzled. "Maids . . . women . . ." she corrected, "are often fools."

He could not have been more surprised if she had spat in his eye. Indeed, he would have hardly been surprised at that a' tall. But to think she did not find O'Banyon appealing, was beyond belief. "Are ye saying he holds no allure for ye?" he asked.

She laughed a little, making him wonder if his expression proved his disbelief. "He has a pretty face," she said. "I'll grant you that."

"And a smooth tongue."

She shrugged and took a sip of punch.

"He dances well. The lassies adore him."

She laughed out loud. " 'Tis little wonder with you singing his praises as if he were a champion roadster."

He deepened his scowl. "I but wonder if ye lie, or if he truly holds no charm for ye."

She looked him in the eye. "The truth is this, I've little use for flowery speech or fools who dance divinely. Indeed, I've had both and found them of little value."

He was momentarily speechless, then, "Ye jest."

Anger flashed in her eyes like summer lightning. "Is it so difficult to believe that I would value honesty and strength of character over a pretty face, Scotsman?"

He was astounded. And flattered, and dangerously hopeful, which made him as irritated as hell, for he had no way of knowing if she spoke the truth. If, perhaps, there was a chance that she could cherish him despite his homely face and distinct lack of panache. "Is there some reason ye canna use me proper name, lass?" he asked. " 'Tis Killian, God damn it. Killian."

She raised an imperious brow at him, completely nonplussed by either his scowl or the fact that he outweighed her by a good five stone. He could lift her with one hand, could carry her from the room that very moment whether she wished to go or nay. Why did that not occur to her? Why the devil did that not concern her? He'd once faced a dozen brigands unaided. They'd been armed to the skin and in no mood for defeat, but in the end, they'd turned tail like a pack of cowed curs. What the hell was wrong with her?

"Killian then," she corrected evenly. "Are you hoping to change the subject?"

"Now why would I be wanting to turn the peat?" he asked, and darkened his glower. She raised her chin a notch. Hmph. "Surely ye are not the sort of maid to use a man's words against him."

"Turn the peat," she said, and laughed. The sound was sweet and quiet, like the soft ripple of water in a friendly garden fountain. "Tell, me Sir . . ."

He darkened his glare.

She brightened her smile, her anger seeming to be all but completely spent. "Killian," she said. "Do you invent these quaint phrases on the moment, or do you lie awake at night thinking them up?"

He watched her, though there were a host of other things he longed to do. "Me nights are spent in naught but sleep," he said, but it was a lie, and he was certain it showed on his face, for many long hours passed while he did nothing but grind his teeth and think of her.

She watched him, her lips parted silently and the barest blush of color brushing her cheeks. But in a moment she cleared her throat and spoke again, as her lashes fluttered downward.

"So you still have not answered my question. What is this O'Banyon to you? A relative? Or perhaps someone with whom you do business?"

"Tell me, lass, is it common amongst ladies of your ilk to consider business and naught else?"

"Ladies of my ilk?" She gave him another smile, but there was some steel to it now. If it was a true expression of happiness, he would eat his sword, hilt and all.

"In me own time, lassies such as yerself would have had other things to occupy their days."

"Your time," she said, tilting her head slightly. "And when was that, sir?"

Caution coiled in his gut. Damn him. He knew better than to spar with the likes of her.

He did not have the Irishman's gift of gab, nor was he accustomed to idle banter with a bonny lass who could twist a man's guts about like sailors' knots.

"I meant me *place*," he lied. "Me homeland."

"The ungilded Hiltsglen," she said.

He forced himself to hold her gaze, to refrain from shuffling his feet. Though they hurt, bound as they were in the foolish shoes he had purchased some days ago. Was there not a man in all of London who knew the value of a well-worn pair of boots? "Aye, Hiltsglen," he said.

"And how do the fair lassies of Hiltsglen spend their days?" she asked. She'd put a wee bit of a brogue into her speech, and though he knew she mocked him, the sound was yet sweet to his ears.

"The maids of me homeland are a gentle, bonny lot," he said. "Quiet and respectful to the men to whom they pledge their—"

"Respect!" Her eyes sparked with sudden anger. "I would be respectful, too, if I found a man who deserved such a thing."

He watched her in surprised silence, his brows raised in wonder.

She held his gaze for some seconds, then cleared her throat and shifted her eyes rapidly away. "What I meant to say . . ." she began, and

225

cleared her throat again as if embarrassed by her sudden outburst, "is that some of us are not so fortunate as to have a man to see to such mundane details as putting bread on the table."

Was that what she had meant, he wondered. She lifted her gaze back to his, but if there had been any embarrassment there, it was gone. Replaced with a spark of challenge.

He almost smiled as he nodded toward the crowd that milled about them. "Surely there is one man amongst them willing to take on the likes of ye." But would any man survive the wedding night? If their time together in his cottage was any indication, she would be no docile kitten in the bedchamber, but more a wildcat, clawed and untamed and dangerous. The image drove him to new pangs of agony, but he refrained from shifting uncomfortably. "Even in this weak-kneed crowd of will-gills," he added.

She stared at him for a moment, then fluttered her eyes in mock flirtation. "I am ever so flattered that you think me capable of snaring myself a gentleman, good sir, but perhaps you overestimate me."

He shrugged one shoulder and watched her eyes spark. "Ye managed to find yerself a husband in the past."

"Perhaps he was terribly desperate."

Desperation he could understand, he thought, and felt his cock buck insistently against his belly.

"Dunna sell yerself short, lass," he said, and let his gaze skim to her bosom. " 'Tis certain you have something to offer a man."

She gritted her teeth for an instant, then forced a sugary smile. "Oh, Sir Hiltsglen." Her eyelashes fluttered again. His erection ached in retaliation. "I fear I owe you my sincerest apologies. When first I met you I thought you quite crass." She brightened her smile, though he would have been quite certain she could not. "But I see now that I was entirely mistaken. However did the fair ladies of Hiltsglen allow you to escape their clutches?"

" 'Tis interesting," he said, nearly laughing aloud at her fine performance. "Ye can say one thing with yer mouth and another thing entirely with yer eyes."

"There you go again, sir, flattering me. I fear I am blushing."

And actually, she was, though he doubted it was from embarrassment. Anger snapped blue-green in her eyes.

"Tell me, me lady," he said, "did ye give yer husband a moment's peace whilst ye shared his home?"

She took a step toward him, teeth bared. "Are

you suggesting I was less than the quiet little lass you are accustomed to?"

" 'Tis said there is no hell like an unhappy wife."

"Tell me, Hiltsglen," she snarled, "do you consider yourself an expert on wives, too, or just on desperate men?"

"Neither," he said, and felt the pain of her closeness like a blade in his heart. "Merely an expert on hell."

Her lips parted, but for a moment she did not speak, as if she contemplated his every thought.

"Since Hiltsglen seems like heaven in your eyes, I can only assume 'tis London and my company you find offensive," she said, and, visibly calming herself, took a sip of punch. A droplet remained on her lips. She swiped it away with her tongue.

God balls, she was driving him mad. She kept talking, baiting him, laughing at him, and yet he could not forget those moments at his cottage, when she had had better things to do with her lips. He watched them move, watched them part, watched the quick dart of her tongue against her tidy teeth.

"Hiltsglen!" she snapped, and he jerked himself from his trance.

Bowing jerkily, he straightened and backed

away. "I must leave," he said, though he knew he was a coward.

"Leave?" she said. "I didn't mean . . . I don't want you to . . ." She paused, her eyes wide, and began again. "You've not answered a single question."

"Mayhap another time," he said, and turned away.

She caught his sleeve and scurried around him. "Who are you?" she breathed.

"I am what ye see," he said, gazing into her bonny eyes and wishing it were not true. "A man hard used and far from all he is accustomed to."

For a moment something flared in her eyes, but she hid it away. "Why have you come here? What do you want? Who is this O'Banyon?"

He turned sharply toward her, emotion sparking in his gut. "He is not for ye," he said.

Her jaw dropped, showing ivory teeth and a rose pink tongue. She shook her head, but when she spoke, her tone was stunned. "Do you presume to tell me whom I should choose?"

He had gone too far. This he knew, and yet he could not seem to stop himself and took a step toward her, so that their bodies all but touched. Still, she didn't back away. "He will neither improve your bank account nor increase the purity of yer blood. That much I know."

She stared at him for some seconds, then shrugged as if she had not a care in the world, as if the universe lay at her bonny feet. "Perhaps not. But as I said, he has a pretty face and might well improve the look of my future children."

Killian tightened his fist about the punch cup and held himself carefully still.

She watched him with ungodly bright eyes, and her lips perked up at the corners as she weighed his reaction. So she was toying with him, and yet he could not quite disavow the hot spur of emotion that jabbed through his very soul.

"If I cannot have integrity, I may as well settle for handsome, don't you agree?" Her tone was perfectly innocent, her verdant eyes as wide as the hillocks, and yet, miraculous as it seemed, he refrained from tossing her over his shoulder and carrying her to the nearest bedchamber as his heated dreams insisted.

"If the truth be known," he said, employing every ounce of his strained self-control, "I dunna much care whether a man is pretty or homely."

"Don't you?" she asked and laughed again. "Well, you will certainly not fit in well with the *ton* then."

"The *ton*?"

She looked puzzled for a moment, as if he were an interesting new specimen found amidst the muck. "The gentry," she said, and waved her spread hand across the gay crowd. "The peerage. They spend most of their time considering looks—their own as well as others.'"

He glanced about the room. It was crowded with a sea of brightly dressed couples, laughing and dancing. Eating and drinking.

"Do they na have better things to do with their time?" he asked.

"What would you suggest, sir? Surely you do not think they should concern themselves with . . ." She paused, and her eyes gleamed. "Putting bread on their tables."

So he had been caught in his own words. He did not like to be bested, and yet there was almost a spark of satisfaction with her jab.

"Tell me, lass," he rumbled, and stepped closer still, so that her half-bare breasts just touched his foolishly clad chest, "is there na a man amongst yer *ton* with stones enough to claim ye for his own?"

Her eyes widened. Her lips parted and moved, then . . .

"My apologies," someone said from behind. "But I must insist upon a dance with Lady Glendowne."

Killian turned slowly toward the newcomer. He was tall, bowed like a grapple, and smelled distinctly of fish oil. Killian lowered his brows.

"What say you, my lady? Might . . ." he began, but when his gaze darted to Killian's he stopped in midsentence. "I . . . ahhh . . . I am Lord Lampor. And . . . you?"

"I am speaking with the lass," Killian growled.

"Oh! Ahh . . . Certainly. The lass. My apologies," stuttered the narrow lord, and bumbled back into the anonymity of the crowd.

Killian watched him go.

"That was . . ." Lady Glendowne began. He turned back toward her. Her lips moved prettily with no sound for a moment. "That was amaz. . . ." She blinked, looking lost, then straightened her shoulders and hurried on. "Indescribably rude."

"Not him then," Killian said.

She reared back. "Not him what?"

"He would na be the one with the stones to claim ye."

"Claim me!" she snarled, and suddenly she was grasping his jacket in one tiny fist. He glanced down, spellbound by the sight of it. Even her fist was pretty. "Might you think I am some . . ." Her teeth were gritted, her bonny bosom heaving. "Some broodmare, meant to be stabled and claimed and . . ."

"Well." Lady Anglehill's voice sounded perfectly thrilled when she appeared beside them. "I am so glad to see that the two of you are getting better acquainted." She shifted her happy gaze from Fleurette to Killian and back. "You make a lovely couple. Don't you agree, Sir O'Banyon?"

"Aye." The Irishman's tone was as dry as the dust of Israel. "But 'tis a known fact that our Killian has a way of bringing out the best in the lassies."

"And I can certainly see why. What with his manly demeanor and chivalrous airs. Don't you agree, Flurry?"

Killian turned back to Lady Glendowne. Her lips moved, and he was quite certain she spoke, but for the life of him, he couldn't understand what she said, for it sounded like nothing more than a feral growl.

"What's that?" Lucille asked, leaning closer, but in a moment the lass had forced her fingers from his jacket and pivoted stiffly into the crowd. They watched her being swallowed up by the milling mob.

"Well, that went well," said Lady Anglehill, but at that precise moment the cup shattered in Killian's clenched fist.

Chapter 15

❧

"**L**ady Glendowne. Fleurette."

Fleur stopped her mad dash toward Lucille's front door. She saw that the Comtesse de Colline watched her from the corner farthest from the irritating Celt, but she would not explain her hasty retreat, not to a woman who understood neither troubles nor emotions. And certainly not to a woman who was drowning in hopeful suitors, Frederick Deacon amongst them.

"Wherever are you going in such a rush?" Stanford asked, hurrying up to her. "I just now realized you'd arrived."

234

Fleur tried to calm her straining heart, to settle her breathing, but rage stormed through her like roiling thunder. Damn the barbarian and his oversized . . . everything.

"Stanford." She tried to smile, but turned instead to stare through the crowd in the direction she'd just come. It almost seemed that she could hear Lucille's laughter even now. But that was fine. The countess deserved the overblown cretin. Indeed, she probably deserved the cretin *and* his Irish friend. Although the one called O'Banyon looked to be tolerably well mannered. At least in comparison to—

"Fleurette?"

"Oh, Stanford." Reaching out, Fleur guiltily touched the baron's arm. His coat was made of finest serge and was snug against his narrow biceps. "I'm so sorry. I just . . . My mind was wandering." She glanced again in the direction of the trio she had just left. "What did you say?"

He laughed and took her arms in both hands. "Are you quite well? You look terribly flushed."

Flushed? She was about to combust. Damned overbearing Highlander with his rumbling brogue and his endless shoulders. Who the hell did he think he was, treating her like a soppy milkmaid with no more brains—

"Fleur?"

She closed her eyes and shook her head. "I must return to Briarburn, Stan. I'm sorry."

"Briarburn. You jest. You've only just arrived. You've not yet spoken to Antoinette or—"

"I know. I—" she began, but through the crowd she thought she heard a rumble of laughter. Was it he? Was it the Highlander? Was he laughing at her? She could imagine how his chest would feel beneath her hand as he . . . "I must go," she breathed, and, pulling from Stanford's grasp, rushed out the door.

Taking a deep breath, Fleurette closed her account book and rose to her feet. On the street below, a pair of carriages rumbled past each other, barely leaving so much as a wisp of air between their spinning hubs. A small boy with a dog cart sold an orange to a passerby and happily pocketed the coin. An old man with a limp and a cane turned the corner toward Tooley Street.

In other words, nothing had changed. All was well. Pulling her cloak from its peg near the door, Fleur exited the factory, gave Horace a nod, and stepped into her favorite cabriolet.

Rumbling along on the velvet-covered seat, she dropped her head back against the upholstery and refused to allow herself to think of anything more irritating than a warm bath and a hot meal.

She would have both within the hour.

The stairs to her bedchamber seemed unreasonably steep, but she managed to reach her room. Closing the door behind her, she turned with a sigh toward her bed, and felt the breath freeze in her throat. For there, upon her tattered coverlet, was a man's cravat embroidered with the letters TME.

"Tessa! Tessa!" She screamed the girl's name even before she thought, and suddenly the maid was beside her, white-faced and gasping in her doorway.

"What is it, m' lady? What's wrong?"

Fleur pointed shakily toward the bed. "Thomas's . . ." She tried to calm herself, to breathe, to think, but it was no use. "His cravat. What's it doing there?"

Tessa turned wide-eyed toward the bed. "I don't . . . I'm sure I don't know, m' lady. I haven't seen it for years."

"Was someone here? Did Benson borrow it? Was it recently laundered. Did—"

"M' lady." Tessa reached out, grasping Fleur's hand. " 'Tis just a neck stock."

Fleurette tried to relax, but terror crowded in like darkness. "Who left it there?" she breathed.

Tessa blinked, pale and befuddled. "I don't know. I was tending your—"

"Well find out!" Fleur snapped, then drew a deep breath and quieted her voice. "Please, Tessa, if you could . . ." Everything was fine. All was well. It was the simply the strange events of the past few days taking their toll on her nerves. "My apologies. Please forgive me. I am just . . ." Her gaze strayed back to the bed. It was just a tie. A scrap of cloth. Nothing more. "It has been a difficult day. Could you please find out who put the cravat on my bed?"

"Certainly, m' lady. Right away," said the maid, and scurried from the room.

Fleurette closed her eyes to calm herself, but her chamber suddenly seemed overheated and airless.

Through the north window, the gardens looked calm and peaceful, overlooked by the towering Celt. She delayed only a moment, then hurried down the steps and out the front door. Drawing a deep breath, she steadied her hands against her skirt and slowed her pace though her mind skittered ahead, imaging the comfort of the dark statue.

But that was ridiculous, of course. It wasn't as if she needed to be near it. It wasn't as if she could not manage alone. But passing under the arched arbor, she instantly felt better. Striding past the hedges, she assured herself that all was well. A lark sang from the heights of the bay willow as a chipmunk chattered to its companion and scurried for cover.

Fleurette closed her eyes and drew a deep breath. The air was pungent and sweet and . . .

She snapped her eyes open, every nerve suddenly taut, for the smell of tobacco filled the evening air. She turned woodenly, searching the lengthening shadows, half-expecting to see Thomas lounging on the bench beneath a laughing cherub. Half-expecting to see smoke curl from his favorite pipe.

And suddenly she couldn't breathe. Couldn't think.

Thomas was dead. He'd drowned. Not far from where she stood. Not so very far. Just through the woods, where the Nettle bent to the south. And suddenly she was running, racing through the garden and into the forest. Branches slapped at her face, but she slapped back, flailing wildly. Her breath came hard. Darkness poured into the forest behind her. Mist curled up in cloudy waves, but she raced on. She had to see the spot, remember the past.

A sound moaned from her right. She snapped her gaze in that direction, but there was nothing. Up ahead, something rustled. She started, but it was only a field mouse, scurrying for cover. She stumbled, then slowed to a rapid walk and calmed her racing heart. All was well. She was being ridiculous. Acting like a frightened schoolgirl, when there was nothing to fear, but in her mind's eye she saw Thomas's face. He was dead, long dead and lost on the river's bottom, and yet he stared at her from empty eye sockets as if accusing her of his death.

A branch crackled behind her. She jerked about. Mists curled in silver waves from a nearby bog. She skimmed her eyes side to side, but there was nothing unusual, nothing but the gnarled trunks of ancient trees and the soft scrape of branch against branch.

She turned back to the west and moved on. But the woods seemed eerily silent. Every creaking branch sounded sinister. Every hiss suggested a threat. And then she heard the hoofbeats.

Her breath caught in her throat and though she knew she should turn about, she could not seem to do so. She cranked her eyes to the right. A branch snapped.

She spun about.

Nothing. But she was shaking now, and breathless. She swallowed and closed her eyes. All was well. She was being foolish. Chiding herself for her weaknesses, she turned.

Someone grabbed her. She screamed, but her mouth was covered. She tried to spin away. To flee, but it was too late. She cranked her eyes upward, finding her captor's face.

"Hush," he murmured.

Her eyes widened. Her heart stopped. 'Twas Killian who loomed over her, his hand pressed over her mouth.

"Stay put," he whispered, and released her.

"What?" she breathed.

But he only raised his hand to his own lips and disappeared.

Perhaps she would have followed him, or perhaps she would have mounted the dark stallion that stood not far away. But her legs seemed strangely incapable of supporting her. Thus, she grasped a nearby branch and sank to a boulder to wait.

Minutes ticked endlessly past. A modicum of courage returned, assuring Fleur that she had been ridiculous. She'd been frightened for no reason. The woods were perfectly safe.

"Why are ye here?"

She shrieked as she spun about.

Killian jerked to a halt, his looming form filling her vision.

Fleurette swallowed hard, clasped her chest and tried to breathe. "What are you doing here?"

241

"Me?" He advanced a couple of careful steps. " 'Tis me own woods ye be in, lass."

Reality settled slowly in. She nodded, then shook her head, fighting her own shuddering reason. "That hardly gives you the right to sneak up on a person."

"A warrior does na sneak," he said.

"Then you should—"

" 'Twas someone else."

Her heart stopped dead in her chest. "What?"

Even in the darkness, she could see his scowl. Or maybe she could feel it, bearing down on her like a dark cloud. "Did ye na ken ye were being followed?"

She stared at him, then forced a laugh, though her imagination ran wild. Who could it have been? Kendrick? A business competitor? Or was it someone with a grudge of a more personal nature? Her throat felt dry, barely able to utter a sound. "That's ridiculous. I . . . That's ridiculous."

"If ye did na ken there was someone behind ye, why were ye running?"

The world seemed surreal. Terrifying. Dark and unknown here deep in the woods. But he looked as solid as granite, as unmoved as the earth itself. Fear was not something he would understand. And hers had been a foolish terror, brought on by a discarded necktie and a wisp of tobacco smoke. Hadn't it?

He remained watching her, his eyes hawkish, his body unmoved. "Do ye oft venture into these woods?" he asked.

She refused to allow herself to glance about, for even now, old memories were crowding in. Memories of happiness and fear, of hope and hopelessness. "This was a favorite spot of mine once," she said, and dug deep for some hint of backbone. Surely she was not such a wilted flower that she would allow a few eerie events to quell her spirit. "Before you stole it from me," she added.

But he didn't rise to the bait. "In the dark?" he asked.

"What's that?"

"Do ye oft wander here alone in the dark?"

"Oh, well, no," she admitted, and straightened her skirt, as if she were preparing for a ball. "Not on a regular basis."

His gaze bored into her. She shifted hers away.

"Why now?"

She cleared her throat and forced herself to take a seat on the boulder again. "What?"

His brows lowered as he strode forward. "Why have ye come here, alone and in the dark? Have ye no sense whatsoever?"

She straightened her back with an effort. "I am perfectly safe in the woods." Memories roared in. She shoved them back. "Or would be, were it not for you."

"Ye think me a threat, lass?" he asked, and, reaching up, grasped a branch in his oversized hand. He loomed over her, as powerful as a force of nature.

She swallowed and forced herself to refrain from scrambling off the rock and away. "Tell me, Sir Hiltsglen, are you trying to frighten me?"

The woods seemed absolutely silent, and he laughed. The sound was quiet, rumbling softly through the night, like a part of the darkness itself. "Mayhap I would," he said, "but I fear 'twould do little good in the end."

She tilted her head in agreement, though her chest still felt tight with the gnawing terror. " 'Tis true," she said. "I do not care to be afraid. What good would it do me?"

"It might keep ye alive," he said, and leaned aggressively forward, "had ye the good sense to know danger when ye see it."

She jumped to her feet, knees knocking. "Are you threatening me now?"

"I would na be the first," he rumbled, then, "Why are ye here?"

"As I said—"

He stepped forward, crowding her back. "I dunna care for lies, lassie."

She almost scrambled away, almost gave in to the towering fear, but some foolish instinct made her step forward instead. "And I dunna care to be threatened, Scotsman. Not by the likes of you."

"Oh?" They stood toe to toe, facing each other in the misty darkness. "Then who do you prefer for the task?"

"Don't be idiotic. I've no desire to be terrorized."

"And yet ye are."

Her breath caught in her throat.

"What happened, lass?"

She wanted to skirt the truth, to hide the facts, to lie outright, but his expression was so dark and earnest that she found she could not. "'Twas nothing really. Just a . . ." She took a steadying breath. "Just a cravat left upon my bed."

"A cravat?"

"A man's stock. A tie." She tried to force a laugh, but the sound was weak. "As I said—"

"And ye dunna ken whose it was?"

She would like to have lied, but she could not quite manage it. "'Twas my husband's."

Silence echoed in the woods.

"And this frightens ye?"

"I just . . ." She tried to find her balance, her nerve. "I was spooked. I acted the fool. Forgive me."

"But ye are na a fool, thus I wonder why ye fled."

"Because he's not dead." The words rushed out. She covered her mouth with an unsteady hand and shook her head. "I didn't mean that. 'Tis simply that his body was never found."

"Ye think yer husband yet lives?"

"No. No. I mean, I wish it were true, of course. I would give anything. But he drowned. And yet, his body was not found. Thus I have nowhere to mourn his loss, and sometimes the nightmares—"

She trembled, and suddenly she was wrapped in his arms, held gently against the hard thrum of his heart.

"There now," he rumbled. "Ye needn't fear. Ye are safe here."

And she was. Despite the terror, despite her past, she felt, suddenly, as safe and cherished as a babe. He stroked her hair, and she closed her eyes to the shivering feelings. How long had it been since she'd been held with tender caring?

"Have ye reason to believe he survived?" he asked quietly.

She shook her head against his chest. "No. Not logically at any rate."

"Do ye believe in specters?"

"I . . ." Leaning back, she glanced into his face. No, I . . . No."

"Then mayhap someone is playing tricks with yer mind. Have there been other such instances?"

She wanted to deny, but again, the truth came unbidden to her lips. "Someone slashed my gown. And tonight, in the garden, I could smell his tobacco."

"So someone means to make ye believe yer husband yet lives."

She swallowed hard, and her words, when they came, were no more than a whisper. "Do you think so?"

"Aye lass, I do," he said, "I but wonder why his return would frighten ye?"

"It doesn't. 'Tis—"

"It does," he countered.

They stared at each other in the darkness.

"Tell me true, lass, what did he do to make a woman like yerself afeared?"

"Nothing."

"Did he threaten ye?"

"No."

"Did he—"

"I said no," she insisted, and ripped herself from the shelter of his arms.

"If it were so, 'twould na be yer shame, but his." He said the words softly, but she was already shaking her head. "Ye can admit the truth."

"I've told you the truth."

"Then who is bedeviling ye?"

"I don't know."

The world was quiet for a heartbeat. "Ye can tell me true, lass," he said finally. His words were slow and steady, filled with an old-world solidity that was his alone.

She felt her knees buckle as if the earth were melting beneath her feet, but she braced her legs against the weakness, for she could not afford the cost.

"I do not need your help, Scotsman."

He watched her carefully, his expression stony, his gaze the same. "Methinks ye do."

"Well you're wrong." Fear as sharp as a blade pierced her. She had believed before. Had believed in love, in happily ever after. Yet here she was. Alone. Fighting her own battles. But she had survived. "I don't need anyone. Indeed, I do not trust anyone."

But just then a twig snapped off to her right. She leapt forward.

A wolf stood not thirty feet away. Its hide shone tawny bright in the moonlight. It was tall, its shoulders well past her knees, its head dropped slightly. But it was its eyes that held her captive. They gleamed like living coals in the darkness. And they were trained, unblinking and yellow as a giant cat's, on her throat.

Chapter 16

Fleurette gasped and it was that sound, that small whimper of fear that set Killian instantly into motion. Instincts as old as time itself ripped through him. Snatching a branch from the ground, he leapt forward and turned, legs spread, arms outstretched, unconsciously shielding the maid behind him. And there in the darkness, he saw his adversary. It growled low in its throat. The sound rumbled like an ominous challenge through the woods, but Killian steeled himself against its onslaught and stood his ground.

The wee lass would not be hurt, not so long as

he drew breath. But the beast's golden eyes gleamed like fiery faggots. It lowered its head and advanced.

"Come then, beastie. Come if ye dare," Killian snarled, but in that moment Treun snorted from a few yards away. The wolf turned its head toward the sound, and it was then, with the moon gleaming like gold upon the gilded fur, that Killian recognized the beast.

The animal grinned, blinked its unearthly eyes, and disappeared like a wraith into the darkness.

"All is well," Killian said, and turned toward the lady, only to find her directly behind, so close her tender breasts brushed his chest.

There was little he could do but wrap his arm about her.

"Is it gone?" Her voice shook the slightest degree, and against his chest, he felt her wee body shiver.

He must tell her, of course, that the beast was naught more than his occasional companion.

"Was that a wolf?" she breathed.

He winced. "Aye." Well it was. In a manner of speaking. "But yer safe now, lass."

"Safe?" she whispered, and lifted her gaze to his. Her eyes were wide with fear and something more. Something horribly akin to trust.

A trust he longed for but knew he could not claim.

Emotions coiled up tight inside him, galvanizing his body, steeling his fist about his rough weapon. He did not want these feelings, had no use for such weakness, and yet they were there, wrapped about his innards like a wily serpent.

"The beast'll na harm ye," he vowed.

She pulled her attention from his face to skim the darkened woods once again, and he scowled down at the top of her head. It was gilded by the moonlight, caressed by the mist.

Silence echoed around them.

"Are you sure . . ." She drew a careful breath, as if gathering strength. "Are you certain it is gone?"

"Aye," Killian rumbled. He felt her ease away a quarter of an inch, and though he tried, he could not help but add, "though it might return soon enough."

Her eyes flashed quickly to his again. He knew he should be ashamed, and yet, with her lithe body pressed against him, he found it was beyond his capabilities. She felt like magic in his arms, like a small bit of heaven sent to warm his soul.

"Was it he that was following me?" she asked.

Mayhap 'twould be in his best interest to assure her it was, but the lie was too much.

"Nay," he said. " 'Twas na."

She glanced into the darkness again. "How can you be sure?"

" 'Tis me own task to ken such things, lass."

"You've seen the beast before?"

He almost cleared his throat. "Aye, I believe I have."

Her gaze flitted hopefully to his. "Perhaps your hound will keep it at bay."

He winced, but forced himself to remember that chivalry was long dead. 'Twas hardly his job to try to revive it. "Mayhap."

She straightened slightly as though gathering her courage. But truth be told, Killian did not miss it. Still, 'twas bound to be hard for a maid of her ilk to accept her own fear. She moved away slightly, and though his body groaned at the premature separation, there was little he could do but let her go.

"You spoke to it," she said, her voice small, but strengthening. "You spoke to the wolf."

" 'Twas naught but a warning of sorts."

Her lips parted. He yanked his gaze from them, tightening his resolve.

"So you speak to wolves and horses."

The memory of his words to Treun sparked

a bout of unwanted embarrassment. "Aye, well, yonder steed understands meself quite well."

Her lips lifted a fraction of an inch. "Then I would think he would have listened when you warned him to stay clear of *Fille*."

He lowered his brows and found he was grateful for the darkness. "I but said he understands, na that he heeds me warning."

"How is he faring?"

Her mare had hit the poor fellow like a battering ram. Indeed, his balls had swelled up like a sheep's bladder. But Killian found it impossible to say as much. "Well enough," he said instead.

"I hope the injury will not impair his ability to . . ." She paused. He watched her. He could all but feel her heartbeat, they stood so close. "That is to say . . ." She skimmed his chest with fretful eyes, then planted her gaze firmly on the dark shape of Treun. "Such strength and courage . . . 'Tis a rare thing."

God's truth, he wanted her with an aching need.

" 'Twould seem a shame to waste such outstanding . . ." Her gaze flitted back to him. Her lips remained parted, but her words whispered to a halt.

He couldn't resist. 'Twas too much to ask of

him. He was only a man. In truth, he was barely that.

Still, he leaned toward her. Their lips almost met, but he stopped himself at the last instant, remembering his resolve. "I thought ye said ye did na trust me," he snarled, and gave her a moment to realize she was still pressed up against him, her breast a bonny weight against his arm. "And yet here ye are."

It took her a second to marshal her senses, but he knew the instant she understood his meaning, for her back straightened, lifting her breast ever so slightly against his chest. Breasts and pride all in one bonny parcel. 'Twas surely more temptation than a warrior could withstand. Lust spurred through him in a fresh wave, but he fought through it.

"I would not be too flattered, Highlander," she said, and though she tried to step away, he found it impossible to allow it. His arm, it seemed, was intent on keeping her where she was. She lifted one brow at him and gave him a cool stare. "As my choices were between you and the wolf."

His erection danced against her belly, and though he hoped she could not feel its movement, he knew better, for her eyes widened the slightest degree, and her body stiffened once again.

"Mayhap ye would have been safer with the beast," he rumbled. Perhaps he had meant the words as an apology, or maybe it was a warning of sorts, but whatever the case, she did not draw herself immediately from his embrace.

"Who are you?" she whispered, and he wanted nothing more than to tell her that it did not matter. That she felt like heaven in his arms, that she was a light in the darkness, a song in the wilderness. But he was not a man of pretty words. Nay, he was a knight of the most basic truth.

"I am but a man," he said, and felt the burn of her nearness like a flame against his chest.

"And men can't be trusted," she whispered.

He nodded once. "Ye must be more careful with yerself, lass. Ye should na have come here."

She tilted her head, studying him in the moon-shadowed darkness. "I do not care to be told where I can and cannot go, Highlander," she said, and though he tried to stop himself, he tightened his arm around her, pulling her closer still.

"Do ye na ken what I long to do to ye?" he groaned.

He watched fear flash in her eyes and waited for her to draw away, but instead, she raised her hand to his chest. He gritted his teeth against the aching impact. "In truth," she said, "I am not entirely sure."

He scowled. "Surely a widow would know."

"Forgive me," she said, her voice but a whisper in the night, "but you are a difficult man to understand."

"Nay, I—"

"You stand even now with your weapon in hand, snarling down at me as if I were Satan's own spawn. Is that what you think of me?"

He deepened his scowl. Damn it all, he was a man of action, not meant for pretty smiles and mincing words, "I . . . dunna think ye are Satan."

Her lips twitched, then, "Tell me, Scotsman, what is it you believe I am?"

She turned slightly. Her breasts brushed his chest. He winced at the sharp hiss of feeling.

"Ye are beauty itself," he rasped.

She stopped, going abruptly still, then she lifted her hand to his face. He closed his eyes and quivered against the gentle caress.

"What do you long to do to me, Scotsman?" she asked.

He fought the weakness like an ancient foe, but he had lost before and he lost again. Curling his fist into the back of her gown, he drew her closer still. "If I but dared, I would lay ye back against the mosses and kiss the sweet petals of yer lips. I would unclothe ye one breathless inch at a time." She smelled of sweet lavender. Like an ancient garden where lovers laughed and flirted and kissed. The scent was driving him mad, taking his mind, weakening his body. "I would stroke yer bonny skin until the morning sun paints ye gold. And when finally ye shiver with unbridled passion beneath me, I would surrender to ye body and soul."

Her lips were parted. She blinked, then swallowed. "If you dared?"

He drew a careful breath and kept himself absolutely still, lest he lose control and burst into flame. "I canna trust ye, na more than ye can trust yerself to the likes of me."

Her head was tilted back as she gazed up at him. Her lashes shadowed her delicate cheeks, and her heart beat a rapid song against his chest. "You do not trust me?"

Her surprise tormented him, and he chuckled manically. "Nay, lass, I dunna."

She scowled as if thinking, then lowered her hand, and slowly, ever so slowly, ran her fingers down his corded throat and onto his chest. He gritted his teeth and shivered like a bairn beneath her touch.

"Forgive me," she whispered, her tiny palm

lying flat between his tensed pectorals. "But I do not think I could hurt you."

He chuckled at the ridiculousness of her words, for he hurt already, ached with an intensity that burned him alive. "Surely ye canna be so naïve."

"Naïve?" she whispered, and slipping his helpless buttons from their holes, skimmed her hand downward. His muscles danced in unison, shivering beneath her touch, begging for more. "No, I do not think myself naïve."

"Then ye ken the power ye possess," he said, and grabbed her hand, stopping its motion. "Ye know the power ye wield in these wee fingers," he said, and kissed her palm.

She blinked up at him, her eyes wide with innocence. Though he knew better than to believe. "No," she whispered breathlessly. "I do not know."

He could not help but kiss her wrist. "Methinks ye lie," he said, but when he looked at her, he saw that her eyes had fallen closed. He kissed her arm, just where it bent and the skin was as soft as a rose petal. "For maids have wielded the same power since the dawn of time," he said, and, weakening, bent and kissed her neck.

Her head fell back. "What maids?" Her whisper was a mere breath in the darkness. "Surely not I."

"Aye," he said, reaching up and skimming his thumb across her cheek. It felt like living velvet, like the blush of magic against his skin. "Ye are every maid what ever bewitched a hapless lad. Every lass what has left a man shaken and weak."

Her gaze stroked him. He slipped his fingers into her hair. It had fallen loose during her flight and lay like spun gold against her narrow back. The soft weight of it drew him up hard, and her lavender fragrance bound him. He moved closer, feeling her heat against his chest.

"I believe you're thinking of someone else," she murmured.

"I could na even if I wished to."

"I'm not the bewitching sort."

"Ye are Delilah."

He could feel her breath against his skin and closed his eyes to the heady impact.

"Delilah. Cleopatra." Somehow, she had slipped her hand loose and pressed it now against the taut muscles of his abdomen. "Lady Waer."

She shook her head. Her hair danced like a fairy's wand against his arm. "Who?"

He tightened his jaw and tried to think. But it

didn't go well, for she was far too close, too warm, too soft.

"The Golden Lady of Inglewaer," he said, hardening his resolve, forcing himself to remember the pain of wanting. "Surely ye've heard of her."

"No. I . . . ." she began, then raised her moon-bright eyes to his. "Was she your lover?" she whispered.

"Nay! Nay. Never a lover," he said, and forced a chuckle, though the sound hurt his throat. "She is . . . was . . . She lived many long years since in the land of the French." She smoothed her fingers over the hard ripples of his belly. He gritted his teeth and wished to hell he was not so very weak. "There was a great army amassed against her."

"An army," she repeated and slipped her hand around to his back. He arched away from it, into her softness.

"Aye. For she was the Dark Master's sworn enemy."

She skimmed her fingers up his spine, easing along the indentation between his aching muscles. God's truth, he couldn't take much more of this delicious torture.

"The Dark Master?" she whispered.

"Aye. He had a hardened battalion of warriors, and at their head rode the Black Celt."

"The Celt!" She drew suddenly back, drawing her hand with her, but now it lay against his hip, tormenting him, teasing him.

"Aye," he said. "The Celt was a powerful knight, but he had no soul." He winced at the memory. "Indeed, he would hire his arm to the highest bidder with na regard to good or evil, and the Dark Master..." He drew a deep breath and continued. "He was verra evil, but verra wealthy."

She shivered against him. "And the lady?"

"She was all that is beautiful, with hair like living sunlight and eyes like the cloudless sky."

"The Celt knew her."

"Knew her?" He chuckled mirthlessly. "Mayhap none knew her. But he had seen her, had caught a glimpse of her now and again. And each time he wanted her more, for she could entrance a man with a glance, with the merest flicker of her lashes. But the golden lady..." He said the name softly, for despite the countless years of darkness, he could not manage to despise her. "She possessed an army of her own."

"And so they were joined in battle?" she guessed. "The Dark Master and the lady."

"'Twas to be," he said. "The armies drew nigh to each other. Indeed, they were so close that ye could smell the sweat of the lady's men, could taste their fear and battle lust on yer tongue like aged ale. But in the darkness before the dawn, she sent a messenger to the Celt.

"Except for his steed and a comrade of sorts, he kept himself apart from the others as was his wont. And in the silence of the night, she sent an emissary to him." He shook his head, still regretting the foolishness, the weakness. "Even his besotted companion knew better than to trust her, but the Celt could not be gainsaid. Thus he journeyed to her tent. And she was there." He whispered the words with shivering reverence. "Her very scent was intoxicating. Like a dream." He drew a breath, smelling the rich fragrance that teased his nostrils. "Like a prayer. And her skin . . ."

Reaching up, he touched Fleurette's face. "She was as bonny as a summer's morning, as sweet as old wine." He almost smiled at the memory, though it stung like hell. "And much stronger than she looked. Indeed, she put a *sgian dubh* to his throat."

"A *sgian dubh*?"

"A black blade," he whispered. "Slim and sharp and deadly." He paused for a moment, thinking back.

"Mayhap he could have disarmed her before she took his life. Mayhap he could have bested her, for he had his hand about her throat." He closed his eyes. "But she began to cry, and her tears . . . They were like droplets of silver, like rain in the deepest desert, melting his heart. She did na wish for battle," she said. "She wanted naught more than peace for her peoples."

The lady's eyes were wide in the moonlight. "So she convinced him to stay the battle?"

"Aye," he rumbled. "She said that if the Celt would but join her army, they could convince the Dark Master to cease his aggressions, for he was more powerful than all the others combined, more forceful than the pull of the tides." He made a fist, then shook his head and let his hand fall lax.

"He would na longer be hated and feared. Instead, he would be revered and cherished, for he would be an ambassador of sorts. Without him the Master could na win the day and would be made to see the value of peace. No more lives need be lost. No more blood need be spilled."

"So he agreed," she whispered.

"Na readily, for he was a hardened man," Killian said. "Hard and well paid. But she kissed him." He shook his head and felt the sweet curve of the lady's waist beneath his fingers. "And he was weak. By morning's first light, he was entranced. Indeed, he gladly took the white flag she gave him. Just as the sun found its way over the eastern horizon, he rode his destrier up the hillock to wave the banner of truce between the armies, to put an end to the battles, to . . ." He drew a deep breath and let his eyes fall closed. "But he should have known better."

"Why? What should he have known?"

"During the night, even while she moaned in me arms, even while she vowed her love, she had sent her army about her adversaries' flank. The Master's battalion was surrounded. Her men attacked even as the Celt unfurled his shameful flag. Mayhap 'twas the screams of me comrades what brought him from his trance, but by the time their cries dried in the morning air 'twas far too late, for the Lord had realized the betrayal. He realized his black sergeant had joined his greatest enemy, and in his wrath, he cast forth a terrible curse. I—" he began, but she thrust herself suddenly out of his arms.

Treun snorted and tossed his head.

"*Your* comrades?" she said.

Reality smote him like a broadsword. "*His,*" he corrected. "The Celt's."

She stared at him for one breathless moment, then shook her head. "You said, *me.* You said *I.*"

"Lass—"

"No!" she rasped and stumbled backward. "What are you trying to achieve? Do you hope to drive me mad? Is that your ploy? Were you sent by Kendrick?"

"Kendrick!" he snarled. "Ye would put me in league with his sniveling ilk?"

"Are you?"

"Nay."

"You lie," she hissed. "Why have you come here?"

"I have come because I must."

"Why? For money?"

"I na longer care for coin."

"For revenge then?"

He opened his mouth for a denial, but he could not speak, for he did not have the answer.

"God save me," she breathed, and suddenly she twisted about and bolted away.

"Lass, come back," he called, but she was already catching Treun's reins and swinging into the saddle.

"Wait!" he demanded, and leapt forward, but the stallion charged past him.

Killian stood alone, his fists curled in frustration, his breath heavy in his chest.

A scrape of noise sounded behind him, and he turned.

The wolf stood there, watching, waiting, his

eyes gleaming with unearthly knowledge. Their gazes met in the darkness.

"Go then," Killian said.

The animal dropped its muzzle to the earth, tested the scents for one brief instant, and darted away. Killian followed, running through the forest, following the wolf that followed the maid, but she knew the woods well and Treun was fleet. In a matter of moments, he had lost them all. His foot found a rut and he fell to his knees.

Cursing, he reached for the nearest tree and pulled himself upright, but even as he did so, he saw a scrap of white tied about the tree's trunk. Bending, he undid the cloth and straightened. It was frayed and weathered and damp with mist, but even in the darkness, he could see the initials—TME.

Chapter 17

"**A**melia," Fleur said, wrapping her arms about her tiny friend. Three days had passed since she'd made a fool of herself in Gardner's woods, and she had a deep-seated need to put it behind her. "You look radiant."

Amelia's wedding gown was made of fashionable white linen, her headdress was crafted of finest lace. "My heartfelt congratulations to you."

"Thank you, Fleurette. Thank you ever so much. I am so happy," she breathed.

Despite the festivities, Fleur's mood was dark. What was wrong with her? It was bad enough that she'd let some foolish cravat upset her, but to dash into the woods like a mindless ninny . . . And then to snuggle up to the barbarian as if he were the answers to her prayers . . . Had she learned nothing? Men were deadly. And the Highlander . . . He could break her in two, snuff out her life without even . . . She shut her mind from the trailing thought. "And I pray you shall always be just as happy," she said.

"But of course I shall be. Marriage is . . ." Amelia turned her gaze, finding her husband through the crowd of well-wishers. Tears filled her eyes, and she spread her fingers across the delicate lace that embellished her bodice. " 'Tis like an intoxicating magic. Like the first day of spring after a harsh winter."

"What a lovely sentiment," Lucille said, appearing from behind. "I couldn't agree more."

"Truly?" Amelia asked, and abandoned Fleurette to wrap Lucy in an enthusiastic embrace. "I am so very happy to hear you say so. I feared that after your union with Lord Anglehill, you did not feel that way about marriage."

"Marriage?" Lucy asked, drawing back and looking aghast. "I assumed we spoke of a nice bottle of Chablis."

"Shame on you," Amelia chided, but at that moment, her bridegroom appeared. He had buckteeth, the beginning of a paunch, and was already balding. Amelia loved him to distraction.

"Lady Glendowne, Lady Anglehill," he gave them a bow and beamed at his bride. "I am delighted you could attend this happiest day of my life."

"Our lives," Amelia corrected, and hooked her arm through his.

"Our lives," he agreed, then they were surrounded by well-wishers and pulled into the intoxicated abyss.

"So." Lucille turned to Fleurette with abrupt aplomb. "How is your Celtic neighbor?"

Fleurette took a glass from a passing tray. "I wouldn't know," she said, and took a sip. Her nerves had been a tangle for days. The crushing wedding mob was doing little to unravel the condition.

"What do you mean?" Lucille asked, and relieved the server of another glass. "Surely you've seen him. He would be difficult to miss."

Fleurette skimmed the crowd. She wanted nothing more than to be home, beneath the Black Celt's soothing shadow. But she closed her mind to that line of thought as well. "He is not what you think," she said.

"Truly? Because I think he's a man. And quite an intriguing man at that." Lucille raised her brows as she took her first sip. "Am I wrong?"

Memories rushed at Fleur like a dark tide: tobacco smoke, hoofbeats in the dark, terror. "Excuse me," she said, feeling frantic and moving rapidly away. "I think I see Lord—"

"Fleur," Lucille said, and grasped her arm. "What's wrong?"

Worries tumbled in her head. Terror knocked at her heart.

"What is it?" Lucy asked. For once, the countess's face was devoid of the bored mask she often wore at such occasions. Honest emotion shown in her eyes. "Forgive me. Did I do something to upset you?"

"No," Fleur said, nerves jumping wildly. "Not at all. I simply have to go."

"What happened?" Lucille tightened her grip, following along. "Was it the Scot?" Her face paled, her eyes widened. "Did he hurt you in some way?"

Fleur shook her head. "No. No, I just . . ." She was dreadfully close to tears. Adrift in a sea of uncertainty. She turned to the countess with a start. "I don't know what to do, Lucy."

"What's wrong?" Lucille shifted closer and glanced about. "You're not with child."

"With child!" Fleur gasped, then lowered her voice and almost laughed out loud. "No. What would make you think . . . Why would you—"

"Why?" Lucy asked, her tone stunned before she lowered her own voice. "Do you think I'm blind?"

"I've never actually considered the—"

"I've seen how you look at the Highlander."

"The . . ." She huffed a laugh, caught off guard and stunned. "Sir Killian?"

"Is there another?"

"I—" Fleur shook her head, feeling crazy. "You're mad," she said, and pulled out of Lucy's grip, but the countess was not so easy to lose.

"What is it then? Please, Fleurette." She caught her arm again, her grip firm. "I know I act the fool sometimes—as if I do not care, but . . . You're my only true friend in the world. Please, forgive me if I've wounded you. I swear 'twas not apurpose. Let me help you."

Fleur shook her head. "I can't . . . I don't think anyone can help me."

"What troubles you? Is it finances? Do you need funds, because I can—"

"Lady Lucille."

Fleurette shifted her gaze toward the floor, trying to hide her emotions as Stanford stopped beside them.

"How lovely you look tonight. I was wondering—"

"Something's wrong with Flurry," Lucy interrupted.

"What?" Stanford asked, his tone immediately worried. "What's amiss?"

"Nothing. All is well," Fleur said, then cleared her throat and forced a smile. "I'm fatigued is all. It has been a long day."

"That's because you work far too strenuously," Stanford said. "You must let your hirelings take more of the responsibility."

"I'm certain you're right," Fleurette agreed. "And I shall take your advice to heart. But for now, I fear I must return to Briarburn."

"Leave the festivities already? Surely not," Stanford said. "You still owe me a dance from Lady Anglehill's party."

"I'm sorry, Stanford. Truly." Her head throbbed with impatience, and her stomach roiled. "Might I repay you later?"

His brow was wrinkled with worry. "Of course if you—"

"No," Lucy said, pushing them together. "No. Dance with her, Stanford. Find out what ails her."

"Really, Lucille," Fleur said, and tried to laugh, but Stanford was already reaching for her hand as he stepped up close.

His voice was soft and kind in her ear.

"Please, my lady, I cannot bear to see you sad. Dance with me."

"Oh very well," she said, as if mockingly peeved, and allowed herself to be drawn onto the ballroom floor.

His steps were graceful and carefully refined. He remained silent for a while, moving them easily around the other couples.

"Please tell me I've not upset you," he said finally.

"No, Stanford." She found his eyes with hers. "Of course not. You've been nothing but kind since first we met."

He sighed. " 'Tis a relief," he admitted. "After you shunned me at Lucille's soirée I feared—"

"I am so sorry for that," she said, reaching up and touching his cheek. "You are ever so dear to me. I did not mean to hurt you. I just . . . I have not been myself lately."

"Truly?" he asked, and smiled. "Then who have you been? Someone just as lovely I'll warrant."

"Thank you," she said, and gave him a misty smile. "My apologies. I should not act so foolishly at Amelia's wedding."

" 'Tis not foolish at all," he said. "You are troubled. I can see it in your eyes."

She shook her head.

"Lucille can see it, and you know she is never wrong. Please, Fleurette, let me help. What is amiss?"

She wanted to deny it, but friends were a dear and rare commodity, not to be taken lightly or lied to out of hand. "It's just that . . . I've been thinking lately."

"I shouldn't wonder, what with all the hours you spend at Eddings Carriage of late."

She gave him a wan smile. "About Thomas's death."

"Oh." He squeezed her hand. "I am sorry, Fleurette. I should not make light. It simply pains me so to see you sad. Thomas's passing was a terrible tragedy."

"Yes," she agreed, "Yes, it was, but there's something you don't know. Something . . ." Her voice broke. "Awful."

"Fleur. My dearest." He pulled her closer, letting her hide her face against his shoulder. "What is it? Tell me. Are you in some sort of trouble?"

"I don't know," she breathed. "I may well be."

He drew back for a moment, glanced at her expression, then ceased his dancing and stepped toward the door. They were outside in a moment. The air felt cool and rejuvenating against Fleur's warm cheeks.

He drew her into the shadows of a sculpted

shrub. "Now tell me," he insisted. "What is all this about?"

"I just . . . I tried to be a good wife. You know that, don't you?"

Perhaps he was confused by her abrupt question, but he answered evenly. "Of course," he said. "And you succeeded. There was never a bride so pretty nor so loyal."

"I cared for him. Truly I did, even though . . ." She paused, her heart racing as she lifted her gaze frantically to Stanford's. "I cared for him."

"Of course you did. 'Twas obvious in everything you did."

"So you don't think . . . You don't think people believe his death was somehow my fault?"

"What! No." He squeezed her hand. "One would have to be mad to believe such nonsense. Why would you even think such a thing?"

"There have been . . ." she began, then shook her head. "Nothing. 'Tis nothing."

" 'Tis very obviously something, Fleurette. Someone has frightened you. Who is it?" His face had lost all jocularity. Indeed, gone was the innocuous Stanford she had known for so long. And in his place was a tough young man who cared deeply for her happiness.

"I don't—"

He tightened his grip and leaned closer so

that all she could see was his eyes. "Is someone bothering you?"

She drew a deep breath, steadying herself. "There is a man named Mr. Kendrick."

"Kendrick?" he echoed.

"I met him some nights past."

He waited for her to go on.

"He . . . He accosted me—"

"Accosted you! My God, Fleurette! And you didn't tell me. Didn't even—"

"No. No. Accosted is the wrong word. He . . . spoke to me, after Madame Gravier's party. I was walking to my carriage. He introduced himself. Said he was Thomas's cousin."

Stanford scowled. "What nonsense is this? Thomas had no remaining cousins. I was his closest kin, and that by marriage."

"That's what I believed. But he said . . . He . . ."

"Did he threaten you, Fleurette?"

She managed to nod, though she could not meet his eyes, but he put his fingers beneath her chin and lifted it until she was forced to look at him.

"I shall take care of this for you."

"How? I—"

He pressed a finger to her lips and smiled gently. "I know you think me something of a fop. And perhaps I am. After all, I do believe there are few things more important than the cut of a good coat. Unless it is the perfect cravat. But I am not entirely without influence, Fleurette," he continued. She found no reply. He drew a careful breath. "And surely you realize what you mean to me."

"You have been like a brother to me. I couldn't have survived those first months without—"

"I would like to be more."

Her world settled crazily around her. "What?"

He laughed, but it seemed to be at his own expense. "Very well then, perhaps you don't realize what you mean to me. But that hardly negates my—"

"Stanford." She reached for his hands. "If I've given you any reason to believe I wished to marry again—"

"Hush," he said, and placed a gentle finger to her lips. Their gazes met and held. "I love you. I have for a long while. But that need change nothing. I will learn all I can of this Mr. Kendrick, and I shall put a stop to his harassments regardless of your feelings . . ." He smiled again. "Or lack of the same, for me."

"Stanford," she began, but he leaned forward

and kissed her lips. The caress was as soft as a sigh, and he drew back in a moment.

She stood dumbfounded, and he laughed a little.

"Come now," he said. "I shall escort you home."

She shook her head, trying to think.

"There will be no pressure," he said. "Indeed, we shall never speak of this again, if that's your wish. I only want you to remember, if you get weary of being both man and woman, if you tire of battling the odds alone, I would consider it an honor to care for you."

He linked his arm through hers and walked her toward her phaeton. Horace opened the door and drew down the step, then backed away respectfully.

"Thank you," she murmured, not quite able to meet the baron's kindly eyes. "But I . . . I'm feeling much better already and I need . . . I think I need some time to myself. To consider your words."

He looked immediately worried. "I don't believe you should be alone, Fleurette. Not tonight."

"But I won't be. Not really." She forced a smile and found that she did feel somewhat better. "Horace will be here."

He glanced worriedly at the driver, who gazed carefully into nothingness.

"Are you certain?" he asked.

"Absolutely," she said. Reaching out, she touched his cheek again. "And 'tis because of you. You have my thanks, dearest Stanford."

He grasped her wrist and turned her hand so that he could kiss her palm. Not a flicker of feeling sparked through her.

"You are most welcome," he said, and handed her into the carriage.

In a moment, it was moving. She gave Stanford a wave and watched him slip from sight as her phaeton trundled away.

But a scratch of noise distracted her. She turned to the left and gasped just as Killian of Hiltsglen settled onto the seat opposite her.

Chapter 18

❦❦

"**D**unna scream," Killian warned.

But the lady's mouth was already open in shock and dismay. Thus he snatched her onto his lap and pressed his palm against her succulent lips.

She jerked toward him. Her eyes were as wide as forever in her pale face. The beveled lantern swayed from the carriage's corner, casting shadows and light across her startled expression. He remained silent, allowing the fear to leave her eyes and the anger to settle in. He didn't have long to wait.

"Are ye calm now?" he asked.

Her eyes snapped like green flames in the candlelight, and despite the roiling emotions that thundered through him, the storm in her bottle green eyes almost made him smile. Even so, he removed his hand with some misgivings.

"What the devil are you doing here?" Her voice was raspy, her cheeks diffused with rosy color.

"I've but come to ask ye a few questions, lass."

Her brows lowered angrily, making him wonder if, once again, she failed to realize the disparity of their size and strength. "Then you should have scheduled an appointment at my office, Sir Killian, or—"

"This be a matter that begs some privacy," he rumbled.

"I've but to scream, and Stanford—"

"Stanford," he repeated, and though he saw nothing comical in the situation, he snorted a laugh. It sounded harsh and low against the sharp click of her grays' steady trot, but he hardly cared. "What might ye think your bonny Stanford would do for ye, lass?"

Her lips twitched with suppressed rage. "I think he would come to my rescue if ever I needed—"

"Huh!" He could not help the derisive laughter anymore than he could contain the stir of desire against her taut bottom. Mayhap he had thought too highly of his own self-restraint when he had settled her upon his lap, for he now found it difficult to think. "Ye would be far more likely to save a milk-fed weakling like the baron than the other way about."

"That shows what little you know. He has come to my rescue on more than one occasion."

"Has he now?" Killian rumbled. "And what dire troubles assailed ye at the time, lass? Had yer hound gone astray? Or mayhap yer *foeniculum vulgare* was na blooming to yer satisfaction."

"*Foeniculum* . . ." She shook her head with manic frustration. "I've no idea what you're—"

" 'Tis the Latin name for fennel. If ye were na forced to labor like a penniless crafter, mayhap ye would ken something of the plants what grow in yer own—"

"Plants!" She skimmed his chest and arms with a derisive glare. "How the devil does a battle-scarred knight of the realm know so much about plants?"

He tried not to redden. Tried not to shift uncomfortably against the sweet curve of her bottom. "I've spent some days in the garden near—" he began, then deepened his scowl and turned the peats.

"The point be this, lass, your puny baron is na man enough to—"

"Lord Lessenton is gentle and kind. That does not make him weak."

"Nay. Methinks 'tis his lack of strength that makes him so."

"Power does not make a man a man," she hissed, turning more fully toward him.

Her hip pressed firm and intimate against his arousal.

Lust smote him like a broadsword, hard and low, stopping his breath, stealing any trace of civility. "In truth, lass," he rasped, "I believe it be the stones what makes a man a man. Does yer bonny Stanford have any, do ye suppose?"

She was momentarily silent, then. "He is more the man than you shall ever be."

He could not help the emotions that burned through him like a pitch fire. Neither could he stop his words. "Because he has lovely golden locks and dances divinely?" he asked.

"Because he has no need to overpower those weaker than himself."

"Mayhap that is because he canna find another to fit that description."

She growled as she jerked from his lap and turned about to face him from the opposite seat. He winced, maybe at the jab against his nether parts as she departed, or maybe simply because she was gone, lifted mercilessly from his lonely lap.

"Tell me, Sir Killian," she snarled, "have you come here simply to boast of your fabulous strength?"

He shook his head, but she was already storming on. "Because I must tell you, I've had my fill of men who control others with their fists."

He was about to speak, to defend his intentions, when the weight of her words struck him like a blow. But he kept himself absolutely still, calming his sharp-honed instincts as he studied her in the shifting darkness. As it was, he knew the moment she regretted her statement. Knew the instant she wished she could draw back her words.

Sir Killian of Hiltsglen was not a man of wild emotions. Indeed, he had found that feelings do not belong in a warrior's world. A knight must be cold, he must be calculating in order to survive. It was entirely possible she was lying, after all. Entirely possible she'd said the words in just that manner to make him believe they had slipped out unintentionally. Oh aye, he knew far better than to believe a maid's innocent suggestions. And yet anger rumbled through him like thundering chargers. He remained exactly as he was, holding himself steady, watching her.

"What might ye be saying, lass?" he asked.

She drew a slow even breath and raised her chin slightly, as though prepared for battle. "I am saying you are far too high-handed," she said. "You've no right to decide whom I should dance with or who—"

"Did he strike you?" His voice rumbled forth like distant thunder, though he tried to lighten the tone.

"What?" She drew dramatically back, but her hands were gripping the seat as if to hold herself steady. Her knuckles looked white and taut against the patterned velvet. "Whatever are you talking about?"

He controlled the unacceptable rage, quieted the simmering wrath, and kept his tone steady. "Yer husband." He said the words slowly, lest the possibilities spill him over the razor-sharp edge of control. "Did he hurt ye in some way?"

"No. Of course not," she said, her cheeks ablaze with sudden color. "What would make you ask such a ridiculous thing?"

He didn't answer immediately. Instead, he watched her in ruminative silence.

She laughed, but the sound was breathy and her hands suddenly fluttery. "Tell me true, Sir

Hiltsglen, do I seem the sort of woman to tolerate abuse?"

"Nay," he said, holding her gaze "Ye dunna. Indeed, ye seem admirably strong. I but wonder what put the steel in yer spine at the outset."

She shrugged. The movement was stiff. "I am what I am, Scotsman. If that threatens you in some way, 'tis—"

"I am not threatened by ye lass," he snarled, leaning suddenly forward. "I am set ablaze by yer—" He yanked his words to a halt and forced himself to settle back against the cushioned seat behind him.

"Where is he buried?" he asked, his tone steady again.

She tilted her head as if amused, but her face was still pale, and her breath halted. "What?"

"Yer husband," he said, keeping his voice quiet, restrained, lest all hell break forth and burn them to cinders. "I but wondered where ye saw him laid to rest."

She had gone deathly still. Even her gaze didn't flicker away. "He drowned, as I told you." She drew a deep breath finally and glanced down at her hands, as if the memory were too much to bear. "His body was never found, as you well know."

"Never?"

"I told you as much!" she snapped, then clasped her hands in her lap and soothed her tone. "This is not a memory I care to dwell on, Sir Hiltsglen. Indeed, I think it cruel of you to dredge up old pain."

"As cruel as he was?"

Her gaze flashed to his, her eyes enormous in the wavering shadows, but she forced herself to relax, to breathe normally. "I've no idea what you're talking about."

He did not call her liar, though he knew she was. "Why do ye na sleep in the chamber ye shared with him?"

"What?" Her voice was little more than a hiss in the shattered darkness.

"The master's chamber," he explained. " 'Tis a fine room. Why do ye choose to occupy the one what lies at the far end of the great, long hall?"

"It's none of your concern where I sleep."

"And why alone?" he asked.

Her lips opened and moved. He could hear her draw a shuddering breath. "I think you should leave."

"Surely 'tis na because of a dearth of swains," he said, and though he knew better, he could not help but allow his gaze to skim her bonny form. Her hair trilled down in gentle spirals to her milky shoulders. And her breasts! Below his plaid, his erection throbbed with lonely insistence. He shook his head, silently denying his own heated desires. "Even London's foolish will-gills would na be daft enough to turn aside a woman such as yerself."

"I . . ." She paused, breathing hard and shaking her head with a huffed laugh. "I can't seem to tell for certain, but . . . Might you be paying me a compliment, Hiltsglen?"

He lowered his brows, disturbed by the unseemly fact that he may have been doing just that. "I am na a man for bonny words, lass. If I say a thing, ye can be assured, 'tis na meant as flattery, but as a fact unpolished and true."

"Well . . ." She chuckled again, but the sound was breathy. " 'Tis good to know." She seemed a bit more herself now, controlled, sure. "Tell me, sir knight, what is your purpose for being here?"

"I would know the truth."

She pursed her lips and kept her back perfectly straight. "Concerning what exactly?"

"Do ye sleep alone because the memories of yer husband be so fair to yer mind or because they be so hideous?"

"My husband," she said, her voice perfectly level, her irresistible lips slightly pursed, "was a gentleman."

"I've known those called gentle men," he said, remembering back. "Indeed, it seems they are oft the cause of great sorrow."

Her lips parted, and she blinked as if temporarily lost, but she found her way in an instant and brushed a wrinkle from her skirts, as if wishing she could be rid of him as easily. "I believe, Sir Hiltsglen, that you may very well be quite mad."

He nodded slowly. " 'Tis possible," he said. "Indeed, I've thought the same meself in the few days just past, but this I'll tell ye, lass, I've na struck a maid. Na in all me considerable years."

"Why would you assume—"

"There is fear behind yer eyes when ye speak of him."

She laughed. "I hate to disagree, but you cannot see behind my eyes, Sir—"

He slapped his palm against the seat, and she jumped, startled from her haughty expression.

"Why na call a bastard a bastard?" he snarled.

"Because he was supposed to cherish me!" she spat, then covered her mouth with a gloved hand and stared at him. Her eyes had gone wide with shock, and her fingers trembled the slightest degree against her rose red lips. For a moment she remained absolutely still, but finally she lowered her hand and leaned back against the cushion behind her.

He said nothing, but watched her in silence, and when she next spoke her voice had gone soft.

"And if he did not . . ." Her eyes looked lost and haunted. "What did that say of me?"

Sorrow as old as time burned through him, and though he knew he must not, he wanted nothing more than to take her into his arms. "That ye had married a fool."

She watched him, then filled her nostrils and gave him the smallest hint of a smile. "You are a difficult man to decipher," she said.

"I am what ye see," he argued. "Na more and na less."

She shook her head, but her eyes were soft now. "Why have you come here?"

He wished to God he knew. "Tell me of yer husband, lass," he said.

"Did Kendrick hire you?"

"Kendrick?" he asked and narrowed his eyes. "The . . . *gentle man* what attacked ye on the night of our first meeting?"

She nodded, then scowled at the memory as if trying to work out the possibilities.

"Would I na have sided with him at the outset if that were the case?" he asked.

She shrugged. "Maybe you are more clever than you look."

"I know it seems likely," he said, picturing his own inelegant features. "But I fear 'tis na true."

A smile flickered across her candlelit face. She was as bonny as the sunrise, far too beautiful for a battle-scarred warrior such as himself. Far beyond his reach.

"I am what ye see," he said quietly.

"And what do I see?" Her voice was like music, her scent like a warm garden, and sitting thus, with her golden hair framing her bonny face, she looked all but irresistible.

He tightened his fists and kept himself carefully on his side of the carriage. "Ye see a warrior what will learn the truth, lass, whether ye wish it or nay."

"The truth?" She exhaled heavily, letting her eyes drop closed for a moment and looking suddenly weary. "The truth is often a slippery thing, Scotsman. Slippery and dangerous."

"Nevertheless I shall find it."

She laughed. "Might you think there are some deep dark secrets hidden here?" she asked.

"Mayhap."

She watched him in silence, her expression somber. "What will it take?"

He narrowed his eyes at her, wondering at her meaning.

"To convince you to leave," she explained, her chin high again. "And never return. What is it you want?"

He had known another like her in the past. Just as haughty, just as dangerous, and because of that, if for no other reason, he should detest her, and yet it was the furthest thing from the truth. Indeed, he ached with a longing so ferocious it all but consumed him. And yet he knew, even now, in the dark throes of lust, that it would not be enough to lie with her. Nay, he wished to protect her, to hold her, to touch her very soul, but he was not fool enough to admit such horrid weaknesses. For weakness killed.

"I think ye know what I want, lass," he said, and felt her draw him like a beacon in the darkness, but she was shaking her head, her eyes uncertain.

He watched her in silence for a moment, trying to understand. "Might ye think I want coin, lass?"

"What else?"

He could not help but chuckle, for even now, when he knew she was deadly, he could think of nothing but how she would feel in his arms, in his bed, in the very heart of his life. "Could it be that men have changed so much through the ages?" he mused.

"What?"

"Can you believe I would prefer coin to your . . ." He drew a careful breath and loosened his fists, letting them lie flat against his thighs. The muscles there were hard with tension. He tried and failed to relax. "Ye are all but irresistible," he said evenly, "as ye very well know."

She canted her head as if examining him. "I fear you are quite wrong," she said. "Indeed, men seem to have little trouble resisting me. My bank account, on the other hand . . ."

"Ye are beauty itself."

Perhaps she had meant to go on, for her lips were still parted, but her words had ceased.

"Ye are like ice set ablaze."

"I just . . ." She laughed, but her face was pink. "I don't know what that—"

"Ye are like a goddess of yore. Spirit and wit and beauty so intense I can barely breathe for the sight of ye."

Her eyes were round and bright in the shifting candlelight.

"And I want naught more than to hold ye in me arms, even though I know ye could well be the death of me."

"Yer death?" she breathed.

"He did na drown," he rumbled.

"What?"

"Yer husband, the baron of Briarburn. He did na drown, lass," he said, and reaching out, touched her face.

"Why do you say that?" she hissed.

"Because 'tis true. I would but know how it is that he died."

"I've no idea what you're talking about," she rasped. "We were on the river. I . . . I was feeling unwell and left him there alone."

"Lass, I ken he was na what ye say—"

"You know nothing," she said, and scooted back, away from him. "He drowned. While I was away. He—"

"Lass." He reached for her again, but she was already at the door. "Stay back," she warned, "or I'll scream for Horace."

He shook his head. "I've na wish to harm yer wee driver."

"Then go away," she pleaded, her eyes suddenly haunted. "Go and don't come back."

"I canna do that," he said, and tried to grasp her arm, but she wrenched the door open just as the carriage rumbled to a halt. And then she was gone.

Chapter 19

~~~⌒⌒⌒~~~

"Millie," Fleurette stood in Lessenton Halls's lovely morning room. "How are you faring?"

"Very well, my lady," said the maidservant, and spread her fingers over her expansive belly. "But as fat as a puppy."

"Not fat at all," Fleur argued. "You look radiant. When is the wee bairn due?"

"Bairn?"

Fleur held her breath, but refused to show her mortification. The idea that she was beginning to speak like the barbarian only confirmed the fact that she was doing the right thing. "Baby," she corrected, and forced a laugh. "When is the baby due to arrive?"

"Four months' time. Have a biscuit, my lady. Eloise just now took them from the oven."

"Thank you but no," Fleur said, and steadied her hands against her skirt. "If I—"

"Lady Glendowne," Stanford said, hurrying into the room.

Fleur turned toward him with a groomed smile. Her lungs felt tight and her head ridiculously light, as if she couldn't get enough air.

"How long have you been waiting? I hope 'tis not long. Millie, you must inform me the minute my lady arrives."

"Yes, my lord," said the maid and, setting the tray on a small table nearby, bustled from the room.

"Fleurette," Stanford said, and reached for her hands once they were alone. "What brings you by at this hour of the day? Is something amiss? I've been ever so concerned."

She laughed. The noise sounded high-pitched and flighty. Not at all like herself, but she wasn't herself lately. She was someone else entirely, someone frightened and needy. There was no other explanation for her irrepressible attraction to a man wholly unsuited to her. He was a barbarian, for pity's sake, an overbearing, opinionated warrior who had horned his way into her life. But that didn't mean she could afford to become accustomed to his ever-protective presence. Having him near was akin to keeping a large bear on a short string. 'Twas likely none would trouble you whilst you were out for your constitutional, but you would forever rue the day when you caused his ire. For he could devour you without warning.

No, she dare not trust Hiltsglen, but she was damnably weak, and she knew beyond a shadow of a doubt that she would do just that. If he kissed her again, if he stood as her protector one more time, as brave and solid as a stone, she would crumble like a house of sand. And that she could not afford to do. Thus her journey to mild Stanford's home.

"Everything is fine," she assured him. "Whatever were you concerned about?"

"Well . . ." His expression proved his worry. His hands felt gentle and soft against hers. Not at all like the callused fingers of the barbarian, who took her breath while setting her teeth on edge. "Ever since Amelia's wedding, I've been dreadfully afraid that I disturbed you. That I was too forceful, too—"

"Disturbed me? No. In fact . . ." She paused. Her stomach turned, but she made herself go on. "In fact, I've given your words a good deal of thought."

His expression froze. His hands trembled. "My words?"

She took a deep breath. "Your . . . kindly proposal," she said.

"Fleurette . . ." he breathed, his eyes wide. "Dare I hope that you've . . ." He shook his head. "Might you be willing to accept my humble suit?"

She smiled and squeezed his hands, though her stomach was still knotted up fast and hard. "Are you certain that is your wish, dearest Stanford?"

"Am I certain . . ." He laughed and glanced about as if searching for someone with which to share the moment. "Of course I'm certain. My lady . . ." He dropped spontaneously to one knee. Tears filled his eyes as he looked up at her. "Will you do me the honor of becoming my bride?"

Shame and worry melded messily with hope and fear. "Yes," she said. "I will."

The shadows were as dark as eternity beside the ancient statue of the Celt. Killian remained unmoved, waiting.

The scents of foxglove and oxslip teased his

nostrils, and though those fragrances had soothed his tired senses for many long years, anger and frustration still brewed like potent grog in his soul.

But she would come. He was certain of that, and he had learned to be patient. Hours slipped by. From somewhere in the woods a kit yipped. Another answered. An owl swooped down in the still night air, unconcerned by Killian's presence. A mouse squeaked as it died, then there were footsteps.

Killian knew Fleurette came, though he was unsure how. It seemed as though he could smell the sweet lavender scent of her skin, could hear the quiet rush of her breath.

And then he saw her.

She wandered slowly through the garden, wearing naught by a night rail. It seemed to gleam in the mercurial light of the besieged moon. Mists rose silently from the dell, wreathing her in silver. He watched her come until finally she was there, lifting her gaze to the Celt's eyes, settling her hand on his thigh.

Killian felt the burn of her touch in his own soul. Gritting his teeth against the weakness of her nearness, he stepped silently forward.

"So 'tis true then," he said.

She startled like a frightened doe, almost fled, then settled, watching him.

"Tell me, Sir Hiltsglen . . ." Her tone was taut, but she remained as she was, the sweet curves of her silvery form almost visible through the fragile fabric of her gown. "Do you ever announce your coming?"

"Tell me if 'tis true," he rumbled, and stepped forward, though he knew he should not.

She hustled back, her face pale in the darkness. "I don't know what you're talking about."

"Aye, ye do," he said, and crowded toward her so that her back was against the statue. "I would but know the truth. Are ye planning to marry yer weak-kneed sop?"

She bristled instantly. "Lord Lessenton is not a sop," she snarled. "He is a gentleman of the first water. Indeed—"

"Why would ye take another coward into yer bed?"

"He is not—"

"Aye, a coward he is, as was yer husband afore him, and na strong enough to manage the likes of ye."

"Manage! Is that what you think marriage is?" she growled. "Management?"

"He is not the man for ye."

"Then who is?" she asked, and laughed out loud. "God knows a woman cannot handle her own affairs. So whom shall I marry, Scotsman? You tell me. Who do you think might be able to manage me?"

He drew a breath through his nostrils and clenched his fists against his thighs lest he reach out and snatch her against his chest. "He is na yer match," he said simply.

"Well . . ." She laughed again. "I just happen to disagree."

He gritted his teeth. " 'Twould be like mating yer mare with me gelding."

"Do I forget, or did you not extol me with the gelding's many fine attributes."

"Aye, well, here's the truth then, the gelding is a hapless nag with na more spirit than balls."

"And maybe that's what I want."

He stared at her for a moment, but finally he shook his head. "Nay, lass. Ye want a mate whose strength matches yer own."

"Do I?"

"Aye," he said. " 'Tis just that ye dunna want his strength set against ye."

"Do you think strength is determined simply by the muscle in your arm?" she asked. "For 'tis not true. A man can be as strong as Hercules and still be weak. There is such a thing as character, you see. Such a thing as—"

He laughed. "So ye think the cut of a man's coat determines that character?" he growled.

"More so than how far he can toss a . . ." She searched for the proper word, gesturing wildly. "Whatever it is you foolish Scotsmen toss about."

"Ye've na idea how to judge a man's character."

"Oh?" She was all but panting into his face. "And pray tell, barbarian, how does one go about such a thing then?"

" 'Tis what's in his heart," he said, and curled his hand into a fist. " 'Tis the strength of his will."

"Lord Lessenton has a good heart."

"Does he, lass?" he asked, and took a single stride forward so that he had to bend his neck to look down at her.

"Yes," she breathed. "He loves me."

Killian snorted and let his gaze skim down her delicate form. In the moonlight, her gown was all but translucent. "Any fool with eyes and half a mind would love ye, lass. But will he set ye ablaze?"

He watched her eyes flare with emotion, watched her lips move. "Yes."

"Me thinks ye lie," he said and stepped forward again.

She retreated, skittering sideways along the

Celt's towering form. "You're wrong."

"Verra well then. Ye find him irresistible. But will he protect ye, lass? Will he stand beside ye when ye need a hand? Before ye when ye need a shield?"

A dozen images stormed through her mind—his firelit expression as he lifted her from the blazing stall and onto his charger. The rumble of his voice when he sent Kendrick fleeing. The tenderness in his hand when he touched her.

"Behind ye," he said, "when ye need naught but adoration."

She blinked, breathing hard, struggling for the strength that had abandoned her at the first sight of him. "Yes," she said, but the single word was no more than a whisper.

"Then where is he now? Polishing his boots? Berating his tailor?"

"How would I know?"

"If ye were mine, I would na waste time on footwear and clothiers," he vowed. "And ye surely would na be here with another, looking up at him as if . . ." He gritted his teeth against her nearness.

"As if what?"

"As if ye long to be touched."

She huffed a laugh. "Is that what you think,

barbarian? That you have some sort of allure that I can't resist? Some sort of—"

But at that moment his control burst. He snatched her against his chest and kissed her. She pressed her hands against him, pushing hard, and though it took all his force of will to release her, he did so.

She stumbled back, her eyes bright in the darkness. Her breath came hard and fast. Her lips were parted, but suddenly she leapt toward him, and in an instant, she was crushed against him once again. Her fingers curled like talons in his tunic.

"Damn you!" she swore, and kissed him. Her fingers were fast and warm against his belly. His belt loosened, but he caught her hands in his. She moaned something, but he kissed her again, slowly this time, deeply.

He loosed her hands. They fell away, and he bent to lift her into his arms. She felt like heaven against his chest, like golden magic. Striding down the darkened path, he found a bed of moss where the fragile scents of teasel and poppy caressed the night air. Bending reverently, he laid her there. She reached up, but even as she did so she shook her head as if defying her own wishes. "I'm sorry," she said. "I must n—" she began, but he kissed her again. She trembled against him, and he slipped his fingers down her ivory throat and onto her arm.

"Killian." She breathed his name. "I've lost my mind. I'm sorry. I'm not a wanton. Truly. I don't usually—"

Reaching down, he pulled his tunic over his head. He heard her soft hiss in the darkness as her gaze settled on him, then she reached out, tentatively touching his aching chest. Feelings licked him like living flames. He cocked his head back, reveling in her velvet touch.

Her fingers skimmed a scar. He moaned at the burning feelings, but her hand was still moving, bumping over his nipple.

He jerked beneath her touch, breathing hard, wanting desperately. She slipped her hand downward, rippling over the battle-hardened expanse of his belly. But he caught her fingers before he lost control and burst forth like a loosed trebuchet.

Her gaze met his in the darkness. "You are beautiful," she breathed.

He breathed a laugh of sorts. "Lass, I fear—"

"Nothing," she murmured. "I think you are as fearless as the ancient Celt himself."

But he shook his head.

"Then tell me, Scotsman," she said, and eased his belt loose. "What is it that frightens you?"

He could barely breathe. Could certainly not think. "I'm scairt ye'll change yer course," he admitted, skimming his knuckles along her arm, "and leave me here alone. Aching and desperate to feel ye around me," he said, and let his plaid fall away.

Her eyes lowered and widened.

His cock blushed and danced against his belly. Reaching tentatively forward, she skimmed her fingers over its head.

"Please—" He caught her hand again and shivered like a weakling lad.

"What's wrong?"

"Naught." He shook his head. "Naught is wrong." He tried to relax, to think, but there was little hope for either. "All is right. 'Tis simply that . . ." He tried to draw an even breath. "It has been a long while for me."

"As it has for me," she said, and reached for him again, but he shook his head and drew her arms up over her head.

"I fear ye may not know the meaning of the words, lass," he said, and, leaning down, kissed her lips. She moaned beneath the caress. He moved lower, kissing her jaw, her throat, the elegant sweep of her shoulder, then drew her gown lower, exposing more satiny flesh. She shivered, and he eased reverently against her, warming her with his burning heat. Their lips met again. He reached for the hem of her gown and she bent her knees, then lifted her hips to assist him.

In a moment she was naked. The moonlight gilded her like a golden halo, shining on her glorious skin, gleaming on her tumbled hair.

Reaching out reverently, he smoothed his palm over her breast. She tilted her head back. Moonlight licked her throat. He slipped his fingers over her nipple and watched her shiver in response. His body quaked in unison. He parted his fingers, letting her nipple peak between them, and there was nothing he could do but kiss it.

She bucked against him. He lapped his tongue across her and heard her hiss of need, then drew her gently into his mouth.

Her gasp of pleasure trilled through him like fine wine. She arched against him, and now there was nothing he could do but lay himself against her, to reach around her luscious body and grasp her buttocks in his hand.

Cocking against her, he eased inside.

They hissed in unison. But age-old memories burned him like a living flame.

He froze, remembering the endless darkness of betrayal. But in that moment she pressed against him with a low moan of desire. He quivered on the edge of control.

"Killian." His name was a raspy entreaty. Her succulent lips parted, and 'twas that entreaty that pushed him past the edge of caution. He jerked into her. She gasped and froze.

Too hard. Too . . .

He gritted his teeth against the aching desire and pulled out, but her eyes were wide as if she were horrified.

"No. Please," she rasped.

He rolled to his side and though he told himself to withdraw, to save himself, he pulled her atop him.

She straddled him, her thighs strong and slim, her bottom wet and warm. And it was easy, so damned easy to slip inside.

She jerked her head back, hissing as she did so, and he froze. 'Twas she who moved first. She who rocked against him. He gritted his teeth against his aching impatience and tried to go slowly, but she was building the tempo, riding him astride, pressing around him.

She gripped his biceps and he clasped her thighs. Her head was thrown back, and her hair, a wild tangle of golden curls, flowed like spun gold across her outthrust breasts, just revealing the pebbled nubs of her rosy nipples.

He growled as he drove in harder, and she snarled back, arching into him, driving ferociously, reaching ravenously.

They exploded together, reaching the pinnacle with a groan and a hiss.

She fell against his heaving chest. Her hair felt like satin against his bare skin. Her fingers curled loosely against his biceps. His muscles twitched, battle-weary, sated.

Reaching weakly to the side, he pulled her night rail over her body, protecting her from the mists. She slipped to the side, one gloriously long leg thrown over his, one arm soft and limp against his chest.

And it was there, in the shadow of the Black Celt, that she fell into dreamless sleep.

Chapter 20

Fleurette awoke with a long, heavy sigh. For the first time in some nights, no nightmares had assailed her. Indeed, she felt rested and strangely content. She smiled and stretched, then froze.

Jerking upright, she tried to separate fact from fantasy, but sharp memories were already crowding in. Memories of bulging muscles, of whispered words, and . . .

"Dear God." Her heart hammered like a gong in her chest. "Dear God," she hissed again, but one glance around assured her she was in her own chamber, in her own bed. Her night rail felt warm and soft against her legs. The laces were tied neatly at her throat. Indeed, nothing was out of place. All was well. It was just a dream. Just . . .

But reality would not be denied. There was no forgetting the raging passion, the soaring emotions, the muscles, hard and straining against her.

She closed her eyes to the thought. Damn it all. She'd cuckolded her betrothed. She'd broken her vow to Stanford even before it was spoken, she thought, and buried her face in her hands.

She had no idea how she had arrived in her own bedroom. In fact, she shuddered to think. Had Killian brought her there? Had he carried her up the stairs? Had he still been naked?

The idea stirred something hot and liquid deep inside her. Good God, he was built like a god, like an ancient statue, as hard as stone, as alluring as the very Celt that graced her garden. Like a—

Leaping out of bed, she paced wildly.

She'd lost her mind. That was it.

After all, she was engaged to be married. Engaged! She covered her mouth with a trembling hand and stared at nothing.

There was only one thing to do, only one possibility; she would go to Stanford. She would tell him everything. After all, it wasn't as if he had been completely pure since his wife's death. Perhaps he would understand. Perhaps he would forgive. And if he did, then she would know he was the man she had always thought him to be, the man whom she should marry.

She drew her hand slowly away from her face and drew a deep, even breath.

Yes, that was what she must do, and there was no time like the present.

"My lady." Stanford entered his parlor. He wore no jacket, but his stock was perfectly tied, his hands tender when he lifted hers and kissed her cheek. "My dear, I had hoped to see you, thus I stopped by your place of business, but you were not there."

Fleurette felt pale and weak. "I hope I'm not disturbing you."

"Don't be absurd. Of course not. I can meet with my tailor anytime."

Killian's words about footwear and tailors came storming back to her. She pushed them irritably aside. "Commissioning a new coat?" she asked.

He shook his head. "I wish it were so simple. 'Tis a garment I had sewn weeks ago. At some expense, I might add. But the cut was not quite right."

She almost winced.

"But I doubt you've come all this way to talk about my wardrobe, fascinating as it is." He gave her a smile, then sobered handsomely. "Is something amiss, Fleurette?"

"No. I . . . No," she repeated, then cleared her throat.

An unknown housemaid entered the room, bearing a platter of biscuits and a silver tea set. And though she was gone in a minute, Fleur fidgeted and glanced toward the hall.

"Would you mind if we walked for a bit in the garden?" she asked. Uncertainty gnawed at her like a hungry hound, but the guilt was just as ravenous, and she would not let it consume her. Not when the truth could make her free.

Stanford glanced outside. The clouds were gray and heavy with rain, but he acquiesced easily. "Of course not, my love. Let me fetch a jacket."

He was back in a moment, the garment firmly buttoned in place.

His gardens smelled of lavender and violets.

They walked side by side for a spell, both quiet. Stanford clasped his hands behind his back. He looked thoughtful and sober in profile, but he turned to her finally.

"Have you come about our engagement?" he asked.

She felt sick to her stomach, weak and foolish. "No. I mean, well, yes, in a manner of speaking."

He was silent a moment, then, "If you've changed your mind, you needn't worry, Fleurette. You can tell me."

"No. It's not that . . . 'Tis simply . . ." She stopped to face him, then wrung her hands and forced herself to meet his eyes. "You're such a good man, Stanford. In fact, I fear you may be far too good for me."

He smiled. "I've not known you to drink to excess before, my dear."

"I mean it, Stanford. I don't deserve you."

His smile turned wistful. "My dearest Fleurette," he said, and gently took her hand in his. "Could it be that you do not yet comprehend the depths of my feelings for you?"

"I know—"

"I don't think you do," he said. "For there is nothing you could say that would make me change my mind about our impending union."

She swallowed and closed her eyes against the gnawing guilt. "I believe you are wrong," she whispered.

"How long have we known each other?"

She shrugged. "Since well before my marriage. Near eight years I suspect."

"And in all that time do you truly believe I have not become accustomed to your every nuance?"

"Stanford, I—"

"I know of your indiscretion," he said.

She reared back. "What?"

His expression was somber, his eyes sincere. "As I told you, I had hoped to see you. Thus I traveled to Briarburn last night."

"No," she whispered.

He closed his eyes for a moment. "It was late and dark. Still, I could not wait to be with you once again. But before I reached the house . . ."

He paused.

"Stanford." She felt sick to her stomach, weak and ashamed. "I'm so sorry. I didn't mean to—"

"I know that. I know," he said, and touched her cheek. His fingertips were soft and gentle. "And that's why I forgive you. I know he's not the sort of man you would choose to wed." He laughed. "My God, you're a lady of the first water and he's . . ." He let the sentence drop as he slipped his fingers into her hair. "It's not as if my own record is without blemish."

"You know," she breathed, unbelieving. "You were there. And you forgive me?"

"What are my options, Fleurette?" His expression was haunted, but his eyes kind.

"I don't—"

"Would you be happier if I flew into a rage?"

"No!" Memories reared up, ugly and painful. "Of course not. But . . ." What would the Scotsman have done? Certainly not stood there and watched while his betrothed lay with another. But perhaps Stanford's actions were those of true love. Perhaps that was mature . . . and perhaps that wasn't what she truly wanted. Despite everything, maybe she longed for passion, for feeling, for heat. "Don't you care?" she asked.

"Care!" He gritted his teeth and squeezed his eyes shut as if attempting to close out the burning memory. "You think I could see you with—" He paused, drew a breath, and found her gaze with his. " 'Tis my caring that makes me forgive," he said, and suddenly she saw that his eyes were filled with tears. "For 'tis that or lose you forever."

"Oh, Stanford." She touched his face. "I am so very sorry."

"Just say . . ." He skimmed his hand down her arm to take her fingers in his. "Just swear you will not do so again."

She tried to say just that, to promise fidelity, to swear to everlasting faithfulness. But memories of the previous night lingered like scented mists in her mind—the swell of hardened muscles beneath her hand, the roar of emotions, the inexplicable feeling of belonging.

"Kiss me," she said suddenly.

He blinked, uncertain. "What?"

"Kiss me," she said, and held her breath as she watched him.

His eyes showed his doubt, but finally he leaned in. His lips met hers. The kiss was filled with tenderness and caring, with promise of forever and eternal security.

She felt nothing.

He drew away.

"I'm sorry," she whispered.

"Fleurette—"

"I just . . ." Her mind was whirling, but one thing was certain; she could not marry this man while she longed for another, no matter the consequences. "I cannot marry you, Stanford. I'm so sorry."

"Please," he entreated, squeezing her hands and holding her gaze in his limpid stare. "Don't do anything you'll later regret."

"Forgive me," she said, and, turning, ran from the garden.

She was astride *Fille* in a matter of moments, galloping madly toward Briarburn. The mare's hooves beat a quick tattoo against the hard-packed road. But neither speed nor distance would drive Stanford's forlorn expression from Fleur's memory.

She slowed the mare to a walk and swiped at her face, smearing tears across her cheek.

What was wrong with her? All these months, all these *years*, she had told herself she had no time for overbearing men. She respected gentle men, kind men, those who could nurture and cherish. Those who weren't afraid of a woman with strength and drive. But now the truth was out. She cared for neither goodness nor tenderness. Indeed, she was attracted to the opposite— to a man who was barbaric and callused, who wanted nothing more than to overpower her.

But was that the truth of the matter? If Killian had wished to harm her, to take her against her will, he could have done so without effort. Instead, he seemed forever to be beside her when she most needed him, to guard her body just as the Black Celt guarded her home. Memories of the night before filled her mind. Feelings of belonging swamped her, as if she had ever been in his arms, as if she were destined for his touch, his . . .

Hoofbeats shattered her heated thoughts. She turned in the saddle. A horse raced around the bend behind her, ears flattened back with its speed. In a moment she recognized its rider.

"Stanford." She breathed his name even as he drew his gelding to a halt some yards away.

"Fleurette." His voice was breathy, his face flushed.

"Stanford? Whatever are you doing here?"

"I could not let you go," he said. His expression was mournful now and his eyes haunted. "Not without trying one last time to change your mind. Not without—"

"Please," she interrupted, unable to bear to hear his words. "Stan, I'm so sorry. Truly I am, but I cannot marry you. Don't you see? It would be wrong. Selfish. You deserve more."

"Perhaps," he said, and smiled wanly. "But I want you."

She shook her head. "When you've had time to think it through, you'll see that I'm right. You could never forgive me. Not really."

"And yet I love you," he whispered. "Marry me, Fleurette."

For a moment she almost weakened, almost crumbled. But surely she had learned better by now. The wrong marriage was far worse than no marriage at all.

"I can't. You must understand. For the rest of our lives, I would wonder if you're thinking about what I've done. If you resent me. If—"

"I could never resent you."

She scowled, baffled and lost. "How can that be? After what you've seen. After—"

"After what I've seen?" He sighed and, closing his eyes, shook his head with a wistful smile. "Believe me, love, I've seen far worse."

"I can't believe you . . ." she began, then paused. "What?" she asked.

"I am saying that I know you killed Thomas, Fleurette. Indeed, I saw you do it."

Chapter 21

$\sim\!\!\circ\!\!\circ\!\!\sim$

"What?" Fleurette's world was spinning. All was madness. She shook her head, trying to clear it, trying to think. "What are you saying? My husband drowned. We had a . . . a disagreement, yes. But I didn't . . . I wouldn't . . ." Her chest felt tight around her heart. "I left him in the boat and walked back to Briarburn alone. I thought he would follow me. But he didn't. He never came home." She felt panicky and stiff, as if Thomas were watching her even now, accusing her. As if he knew everything she did. Everything she had done. "He never returned to Briarburn."

"So you told one and all that he had been drinking," Stanford said.

She nodded woodenly. "He was intoxicated."

"Everyone knew he couldn't hold his liquor."

"Yes."

"It was easy for them to believe that he must have become inebriated and toppled into the river."

" 'Tis the only explanation."

"But 'twas not true was it, my dear?"

"Yes. He—"

"I was there, Fleurette," Stanford said. His tone was sad and soft, his expression pitying.

"What?" The single word was barely audible to her own ears.

"I was there. In the woods, just out of sight."

She shook her head, but he continued on.

" 'Twas a lovely afternoon." His eyes looked far away, as if he walked a dream. "Not like to-day." He shivered. "How I detest the rain. So gloomy. A fellow can neither keep his spirits up nor his footwear unstained. But I digress." He turned back toward her, almost as if startled to find her there and gave her a wistful smile. "You and your beloved were picnicking on the River Nettle. You had packed a luncheon with your own sweet hands."

"How do you know that?" she breathed.

"You had packed a lunch," he repeated "But you had forgotten the wine. Or maybe . . ." He scowled a little as if thinking. "Maybe 'twas an act of self-preservation. Thomas was a fine man. God knows I loved him like a brother. But he could be . . ." He shook his head, as though the truth pained him even now. "Unpleasant when intoxicated. He had already been drinking when you drew anchor. And that is to say nothing of the bottle he brought along."

Memories crowded in, dark and haunting, smothering Fleurette like a blanket of smoke. "I begged him not to drink," she whispered.

"I know you did, love. I know," Stanford crooned, leaning toward her from his chestnut. "And he should have listened. Should have realized you only wanted what was best for him."

She tried to nod, but her neck felt stiff and her head was spinning. "You were . . . watching us? Spying on us?"

"Perhaps you could call it that. Perhaps I was wrong to be there at all. But the truth is this . . ." He paused momentarily and let his eyes fall closed. "Even then I longed for you. Indeed, I had for years. My Fleurette, my lovely flower, so beautiful, so elegant. I tried to deny it. You were, after all, my Clarice's sister by law and the wife of my very dear friend." He shook his head.

"Poor Clarice." His eyes shone in the lowering sun. "She could hardly hold a candle to your luminous beauty. Still it was a terrible pity when she died. Except that it gave me more time to be near you. To watch you. You and Thomas."

Fleurette felt the hair lift eerily along her arms.

"Such a lovely couple. Everyone said so. He cut quite a dashing figure, did he not?" His smile was wistful. "And you . . . always so demure . . . so refined. Until that afternoon."

Terror leaned in with the memories, crushing her, turning her cold. She cringed away as if they were a visible force. "You saw him strike me," she whispered.

He held her gaze, then closed his eyes again as if the memories pained him. "I did, Fleurette. I did, and I wanted to help you. Truly. But . . . He was your husband. You were bound to him, both legally and morally. What could I do?" He winced, then gave her a wan smile. "But in the end it matters not, for finally you fought back."

She wanted to deny his words, but it was too late. The pain was too real, her need to confess overpowering. "I was so afraid," she whispered. "I thought . . ." She winced, seeing it all again, his anger-reddened face, his clenched fists. "I was certain he was going to kill me."

"So you struck him with the oar."

"I didn't intend to hurt him." Her words came out in gasps. "Only to . . . to stop him, to bring him to his senses."

"No one can blame you for attempting to protect yourself, Fleurette. Indeed, if anyone is at fault, it is I."

"You?"

"I knew," he murmured. "I knew he beat you."

"No." She shook her head though she had no idea why. The truth was out, and yet the pain of her humiliation was almost too much to bear.

"I saw the bruises, Fleurette."

She was still shaking her head. "I often fell. I am so clumsy sometimes. 'Twas—"

"Please, my love," he entreated. "There is no need to protect him. Not anymore."

She stared into space, remembering back against her will. Her hands shook on the reins, but she did not care. "Why did he hate me so?"

"Hate you! No," Stanford argued. "He could not have hated you, my love. No one could. He simply . . . He was troubled. And the drinking . . ." He shook his head. "I should have done something. I should have come to your aid."

She heard him speak, but his words failed to register, for she was back on the river, and she was small again. Small and young and defenseless. The air was warm, the sky a blue so brilliant it all but hurt the eyes, and yet she was cold with fear. Death stalked her. She could feel its breath. And she did not wish to die. Thomas was rising clumsily to his feet, his handsome face distorted with rage. The boat wobbled erratically beneath her as he approached. She clutched the gunwale, trying to steady the vessel, to scoot backward, to survive.

"I tried to reason with him," she whispered. "I tried to calm him." He'd not heard her. Not then, not ever. His rage was all-consuming. She tripped over the oar and scrambled backward. "I grabbed it," she rasped. She could feel the rough wood against her palms once again. "It was heavy, and I was terrified. I swung with all my might. There was a noise." She jerked at the echoing sound. "And then blood." It dripped down his face in tiny rivulets, diverted around his nose, darkening his lips. "He looked so . . . surprised. He staggered back." She held out a hand as if she could still catch him, could start anew, make things right. But things had never been right, though she'd been too naïve to realize that until it was too late. "I thought he would stop. I thought . . ." She swallowed, but the terror remained, twisting her gut, shaking her hands. "But he came toward me again." She was breathing hard. Her muscles ached with tension. "He was so strong. Much stronger than he looked. Much stronger than I."

"So you struck him again."

She nodded, remembering. She had screamed, had begged him to think, to be merciful, but he'd kept coming, staggering toward her, drunk, wounded, incensed. She had swung without thinking, without intending to. Indeed, even now it seemed as if it had been someone else. Someone strong. Not her, not the frightened girl with the too-big eyes and the scrawny figure.

"He fell into the boat." Her voice was very small. She saw it all, as if it were happening again. He'd crumpled slowly, fighting the debilitating weakness. Down against the keel, his fingers splayed harmlessly against the boat's ribs. "I thought he'd get up. I thought I only had a moment to escape before he recovered." She winced. "I didn't think he'd drown. He always seemed . . . invincible."

She glanced frantically down the road, remembering her scrambling flight over the gunwale and into the water. It was shockingly cold, despite the heat of the day, but she hadn't cared. It splashed around her, the droplets shining like crystals in the still air. She'd gasped at the shock of it, then slipped on a rock. Water drenched her face, soaking her, pulling her under. For one horrible moment she'd thought he'd caught her. Terror ripped at her heart. But she jerked to her feet. Mud tugged at her slippers. She was sobbing when she reached solid ground. She jerked about, certain he was behind her. But she was alone. Scrambling up the rocky riverbank, her face wet with tears and mud, she scurried into the woods.

"I hid," she whispered, as though she were doing the same now. As if someone was searching for her even as she relayed her sins. "I hid and waited, trying to think, trying to . . ." She scowled. "But he didn't follow me. Darkness came on. I was certain he was watching me the whole while. Laughing. The proud Lady of Briarburn, covered in mud, shaking in my hole." She smiled. The expression hurt her face, as if it were breaking. "He always said I was too prideful. But pride was all I had left. And even that abandoned me . . . alone and shivering as I hid." She nodded brokenly. "I thought he'd come at any moment, but the seconds dragged on. Then minutes, and hours. I was freezing." She shook with the memory. "So I . . . I sneaked back through the woods toward the river." Her body felt stiff, as if she were doing it all again, knowing he was there, knowing he would find her. "I had to see him, to know what he was planning. Maybe if I apologized . . . If I begged for forgiveness . . ." She scowled and shook her head. "But the boat was empty." It was bobbing just a few feet from shore, like a cork on the sea. It had taken all her nerve to approach it, to peek over the side. But when she looked in, she found him gone. She remembered the panic like the taste of rancid wine. She'd jerked about, certain he was behind her, certain she would die. "The boat was all that remained. The boat and one shoe. But he was gone." She glanced up, blinking, half-surprised to find herself safe on the road. No blood stained her hands. No mud marred her frock.

"I didn't kill him." She shook her head, wincing. "Not . . . not really. He must have fallen into the river somehow and been swept away." She glanced up, terror sharpening her senses suddenly. "Right?"

Stanford remained absolutely silent.

"I'm right, am I not?" she rasped. Fear was making it difficult to breathe, impossible to think. "He's dead. Isn't he?"

"I'm certain he is," said the baron, but her stomach had clenched up tight in sudden agony.

"Dear God," she breathed. Terror swept her anew, like the cold waves she'd waded through to peer into the empty boat. "You've seen him haven't you?" Her throat hurt from the effort to force out the words. "He's come back for me."

"No." Stanford shook his head "No. You needn't worry, my love. He's dead. Still . . ."

"What?" Her hands were like claws against the reins. "Still what?"

"There are those who might think you responsible for his death."

"Kendrick," she breathed, remembering.

He glanced down as if troubled, then looked up again. "I've checked into that a bit."

"Into Kendrick?"

"Yes."

She held her breath. "And?"

"I don't want to frighten you, Fleurette. Or to hurt you. Truly. You must believe me."

"What is it?" she asked, and felt a bit of latent courage seep slowly into her frozen system.

"I believe the Scotsman may be somehow involved."

She felt the blood drain from her face. "Killian?"

He nodded. "I'm sorry. Truly. But I fear . . . I believe Mr. Kendrick hired him to learn the truth about Thomas's death."

She shook her head, but he was already continuing.

"Don't you wonder where the Scot came from? Why he's here out of the blue?"

"He said he wished to settle down. To find a bonny place to spend his days. He—"

"To settle down on the property adjacent to Briarburn, just when Kendrick shows up to threaten you? You're an intelligent woman, Fleur. Don't you find that strange? Coincidental? No one has ever wished to buy the quarry before. And suddenly he wants it desperately. Indeed, he paid an exorbitant price."

Fresh pain diffused her. So she'd been betrayed. Again. But she was being absurd. The Scotsman was nothing to her. Still, she could not forget the deep soothing burr of his voice, how he seemed to hold the troubles of the world at bay. "He took a liking to the land."

"Maybe you're right, my love," Stanford said. "You're probably right." He glanced away as if wounded.

"But where did he get the money?" Fleur whispered.

Stanford winced, but didn't look at her. "Kendrick is wealthy."

She felt her stomach twist.

"What if he spills the truth, Fleurette?" He murmured the question as though it hurt him to say the words aloud. "I couldn't bear it if something happened to you. What if he knows the truth and tells others? Thomas was well loved. Indeed, he—"

"So Killian . . . He was paid?" She whispered, for speaking out loud would be too painful, too real. "He was paid to learn my secrets?"

"Yes," Stanford said, and gave one brief nod. "I'm sorry. I believe he plans to accuse you of your husband's murder."

"I didn't mean to kill him," she breathed. "I only wanted to be loved, to . . ." Her voice broke.

"I know," Stanford murmured. He reached out, covering her hand with his own. "I know, my dearest, but others might not see it the same. They might not believe you were only protecting yourself."

"But you do?" She whispered the words like a tortured child, needing to know he believed her, trusted her.

"Because I love you. Because I couldn't take my eyes off you. Even then . . . when you were another man's wife." He squeezed her hand, his eyes intense. "Perhaps I should apologize for that. But I cannot. I can only attempt to make things right now. To keep you safe from Kendrick and any other who might wish you harm."

"How?"

"Marry me, Fleurette." His hand trembled

slightly with the strength of his emotion. "Let me help you. Let me take care of you."

"But . . ." She scowled, her mind spinning. "Once Kendrick spills the truth—"

"We'll marry this very night. I don't care about the scandal. My title still holds some power in the House of Lords," he said. "I shall issue a statement saying I saw Thomas alive and well after you left him on the river. I shall say that he was drunk. 'Tis the truth, after all. Everyone knew of his weakness. No matter what Kendrick has discovered, I shall swear you had nothing to do with Thomas's death."

"Stanford . . ." She breathed his name like a prayer. "You would do that for me?"

"For you?" His gaze held hers. "My love, my bride . . ."

She winced as the weight of his words squeezed her heart, and slowly pulled her hand from beneath his.

"I'm sorry." She closed her eyes and breathed the words. "But I can't marry you, Stanford. Not after what I've done."

"It was self-defense, Fleurette. I cannot, *will* not hold that against you."

"Perhaps not," she murmured, and caught his gaze with her own. "But what of last night? I fear you cannot help but hold me accountable for that."

"The Scotsman," he said.

She nodded slowly.

He winced as if fighting the pain of the memory. "I do not mean to say that this is easy for me." His eyes looked immeasurably sad. "I do feel betrayed. Indeed, I feel as if my very heart has been torn asunder, but I can forgive. If I must. If it means having you beside me."

"You could forgive," she said. "Even that."

"Marry me," he said, "and I swear I shall make you happy."

Safety. Marriage to a decent man. She opened her mouth to agree, but in that moment something rustled in the underbrush beside the road.

They turned in breathless unison.

A black steed stepped out of the woods, and on his back, straight as a lance, rode the dark knight.

Chapter 22

⟨◦◦⟩

"**K**illian." Fleurette whispered his name, for even after all she'd learned, she could not help but want him, his strength, his touch. He met her gaze with steady deliberation,

"What the devil are you doing here?" the baron snarled.

The Scot's eyes glimmered dangerously in the dim light as he turned them toward the other. "And why should I na be here, laddie?"

"I told—" Stanford began, then paused and straightened in his saddle. "You've dishonored my lady, sir."

The Highlander turned his gaze on Fleurette

again, his eyes dark and unflinching, as if he had nothing to hide, nothing to regret. Or perhaps it was that he would bear whatever consequences came his way. "Methinks the lass be her own lady," he said, "and deserving of the truth."

"I've told her the truth," Stanford rasped. "It's you who have lied. You who have ruined her."

" 'Tis a strange thing," Killian said, his words slow, as if he was just realizing the truth of them. "For I think she be the ideal of womanhood and na ruined a' tall."

She was lost in his eyes, in the old-world cadence of his voice, but she had been fooled by a man before, and that mistake had almost destroyed her.

Killian turned slowly away, as if he could read the doubts in the depths of her soul. "Did ye tell her 'twas ye what hired Kendrick?"

"That's not true," Stanford hissed.

Fleurette sat breathless, frozen in place. "What? No. He—"

"I spoke to the cur just this morn," Killian said.

"Of course he spoke to him," Stanford rasped, his tone strained. "He is in the man's employ."

"Nay, I am na," Killian said, "but he was kind enough to stop by me cottage nonetheless. We had a wee bit of a talk, and after a time he admitted that a Lord Lessenton had sent him to me." Some dark emotion sparked in his eyes, but his hands remained absolutely steady on the stallion's reins. " 'Twas kindly of ye to think of me, laddie, but mayhap it would have been kinder still had ye sent him by during the daylight hours." Curling his right hand into a fist, he flexed his arm as if it ached. "And without the wee weapon."

It wasn't until that moment that Fleurette noticed the blood on his sleeve.

"You're hurt," she breathed.

He didn't turn from the baron. Instead, he remained exactly as he was, his eyes deadly steady. " 'Tis naught but a scratch lass. Still, 'tis a clever little contraption, these pistols. Or would be in the proper hands. Unfortunately, yer hireling was a weakling, laddie. And na up to the task ye set afore him."

"I don't know what you're talking about," Stanford hissed. "I didn't send anyone."

"Kendrick disagreed. Indeed, he said ye had hired him some weeks afore to frighten the lass here."

"That's preposterous."

"I'll na claim to know much of gentlemanly behavior," Killian said. "But it seems a poor way to convince a maid to marry ye."

Stanford twisted about in his saddle, pinning Fleurette with his gaze. "Don't listen to him. He's insane."

"Mayhap," Killian said, and urged his mount nearer. The stallion tucked his head and pranced forward, battle-ready, intense. "But I am na the murderous coward ye have proven to be."

"What?" Fleur rasped, but in that instant Stanford yanked a pistol from beneath his coat.

Fleur reared back in shock, but Killian sat perfectly still, his gaze never leaving his adversary's.

"How clever you are," the baron hissed. "For an unwashed barbarian."

Killian said nothing. Instead, he sat unmoving, holding his charger at bay with one steady hand. "Ask him how yer husband truly died, lass."

"I don't understand," Fleur breathed. "What do you mean? What are you talking—"

"You little fool," the baron rasped, but didn't bother to turn toward her. "Yes, I killed him. And you should thank me for my efforts."

"You . . ." She laughed foolishly, her breath gone, her mind swimming. "No. He . . . he drowned."

"He couldn't drown, you twit. You knocked him unconscious. He fell to the bottom of the boat. The river was still. It wouldn't have capsized. Even you must have realized that much."

"But I thought . . . I assumed . . ." She shook her head. "You killed him? Why?"

"Why?" He laughed. "Why the devil not? He certainly deserved it. Even you will admit that. The fabulous Lord of Glendowne. So handsome, so charming. And his wife . . ." He flipped his free hand at her and chuckled. "All elegance and good breeding. So happy they were together. The perfect couple. Or so people thought. But they didn't watch him beat the life out of you time and again, did they?"

"You . . . watched?"

"Of course I watched. I was transfixed. 'Twas quite entertaining."

She shook her head, floundering in a sea of roiling uncertainty. "But how—"

"How? Easily. When he was not concentrating on taking you, he was busy with his fists while you were just as busy fending him off. Or trying to." He laughed. "Though not very effectively, I'll admit. Not until that lovely day on the river." He shook his head as if thinking back with fondness. " 'Twas a sight to behold. The timid little baroness rising up against the odds. It did my heart good. Indeed, when I saw him fall, I thought for a time that you were the answer to my prayers."

She shook her head, trying to understand, to take it all in, but facts and memories and questions spun like whirling dervishes in her mind. "What prayers? What—"

"He planned to be rid of ye and yer husband the whole while," Killian said. "And to take you and Briarburn as his own."

"No," she said, and Stanford laughed.

"I know, 'tis difficult to believe. A gentleman of the realm having aspirations. But, as you know, my family's funds have been dwindling. Thus I thought it perfect when I saw you strike him. Indeed, I thought you had done my task for me. Even after you scrambled toward home whimpering like a whipped pup, I was certain I owed you my thanks, but then I heard him moan." He scowled as if miffed. "What else could I do but finish the job?"

"You killed him?"

"Still not understanding my words?" He sneered. "Yes, I killed him. And quite handily I might add. For all his bravado, he died with surprising ease."

"You killed him and let me think his blood was on my hands."

"It worked out quite perfectly. You so needed a friend. Poor little baroness, wracked with a guilt she could not admit."

"You killed him and left him in the river. Left him to—"

"Don't be a fool, Fleurette," he said. "He would have surely washed ashore, and though most people are deplorably daft, I feared they might very well realize he'd died of rather unnatural causes, since the left side of his head had been bashed in with a rock.

"Now true . . ." He waved an elegant hand. "They would have certainly blamed you. After all, you were with him that day, and if they knew of the abuse you had endured at his hands . . ." He shrugged. "But I could hardly let you take the blame. Not after I had spent so long earning your trust, getting rid of Clarice, assuring my eventual place by your side. So I got rid of the body and I waited." He smiled.

"You made an adorable little widow. I must admit that I was not pleased to see my future property pawned off like pickled herring in the public market, but then you bought a carriage company and began showing a tidy profit. I was impressed. Truly. And you needed a friend." He smiled. "Good old Stanford." Anger flashed in his eyes. "Seven years I've waited, Fleurette. Seven years."

Terror reached for her, spurred by the madness in his eyes, but she pushed it back, trying to think, to stall, to survive. "So it wasn't Thomas," she breathed. "In my bedchamber. In my garden."

Stanford laughed, but the sound was raspy.

"Nay, lass," Killian rumbled, his voice low and steady against the baron's maniacal chuckle. "Yer husband was long dead and buried in the woods beside the quarry. I found his grave some days past."

Fleurette turned woodenly toward Stanford. "'Twas the simplest way to dispose of the corpse. I visited him quite often. Tied his favorite cravat around a nearby tree, in fact." His face twisted. "I couldn't bear to lose my dearest friend. But I looked after his widow, and I was patient. Seven years passed. You could remarry, and I had you in the palm of my hand. Then you came." He turned his sneer toward Killian. "And ruined all my lovely plans. You shall regret that."

Fear made Fleur's throat feel tight and raw, but she forced herself to speak, to search for the man she had thought he was. "Don't do this, Stanford. I'm your friend. I'll help you. We'll tell the truth, go to magistrate. I'll tell him of my abuse. That you were protecting me. That—"

His laughter stopped her words. "Little Fleurette. So clever. And kind." His smile twisted. "I appreciate the offer. Truly. But forgive me. I do not care to be hanged for ending a worthless life. No. I believe I shall take my chances. I shall mourn the fact that you were murdered by this barbarian, of course. But I shall be brave. And there will be other women." His smile brightened until it almost looked real. Almost looked sane. "Other heiresses."

"So you will kill me," she whispered, but it was Killian who answered.

"Nay, lass." His voice was low in the darkening stillness. His eyes were as steady as the earth beneath his mincing stallion and the muscles in his arms hewn like ancient stone. "He is na," he rumbled.

Stanford watched him, then threw back his head and laughed out loud. "Such chivalry. Such drama. 'Tis just like the days of yore. The gallant knight come to save the lady fair." He sobered, and his expression grew ugly. "But I fear you're perfectly wrong, old chap. I shall kill her. But first, I fear, I must kill you," he said, and raised the pistol.

Something snarled from the woods. Stanford twisted to the left, and in that second Killian spurred his stallion forward. The destrier struck the baron's gelding head-on.

Fleur screamed, but the men were already falling, tumbling to the ground in each other's arms, the pistol gripped in Stanford's hand between them.

They twisted wildly, then rose, facing each other. The gun exploded, Killian jerked. He took one faltering step forward, then he fell. Slowly, like a toppled statue, Killian dropped to his knees.

Fleurette whimpered. He lifted his gaze to her, tried to recover, then felt silently onto his back.

"No!" Fleur shrieked, and suddenly she was ripped free from her trance. Leaping to the ground, she raced toward the Scotsman.

Stanford wiped his mouth with his hand and stumbled toward the fallen knight.

"Damn you!" he snarled, and loading the pistol, aimed again.

Rage and fear roared through Fleur like a flame. Unthinking, she leapt between them, straddling Killian's legs, sheltering his body with her own.

"No! No!" she sobbed. Her hand was shaking as she held it with placating desperation toward Stanford. "Please. Let him be."

Blood trickled down the baron's forehead. His grin looked ghoulish. "I fear I can't do that, my love."

"Let him live," she sobbed. "I'll not tell anyone about Thomas. I swear it."

He laughed.

"I'll marry you," she rasped.

He canted his head at her.

"I will. I'll marry you and continue to make my company prosper. It'll be worth even more in time." Behind her, Killian rasped for breath. "Let him live," she whispered, her voice breaking, "and it will all be yours."

Stanford stared at her, then shook his head slowly. "I would like to accept your offer, but I don't believe the barbarian here is the sort to stand idly by while I do so. I've seen how he looks at you. Indeed, I've seen him do much more than that," he snarled and raised the pistol.

Fleur braced herself against the inevitable impact, but suddenly the world jerked. She tried to remain on her feet, tried to hold her position between the two, but Killian had swept her legs out from under her. She struck the earth with a gasp.

The gun exploded. She screamed, but when she'd twisted about, Stanford was already stumbling backward, his fingers splayed around the black hilt of a blade that protruded from his gut. The pistol drooped, then fell to the ground. His knees struck the earth a moment later, and he toppled onto his face.

Pivoting toward Killian, Fleur scrambled to him on hands and knees.

"Don't die!" She was crying and pleading at the same time. "Please, don't . . . You shouldn't have come." Blood was oozing into his tunic. She glanced frantically down the road, desperate for help, but they were alone. Yanking up her gown, she balled it in her fist and shoved it shakily against his chest.

He moaned a staccato grunt and forced his eyes open. A muscle jerked in his cheek.

Her free hand fluttered to his face. Her fingers were sticky with blood.

"Why did you come?" she whimpered.

"And what should I have done, lass?" His mouth twisted into the parody of a smile. "Leave ye to face the bastard alone?"

"Yes." A tear tripped down her cheek and onto his chest. "Chivalry is dead. Don't you know that?"

He chuckled. "Well, 'tis surely dying," he corrected, and let his eyes fall closed.

She tightened her grip desperately on the rag against his wound. "Killian!"

He dragged his eyes open again. "Aye, lass?"

"Please." She was crying in earnest now. Her hands shook on his chest, parchment white against the crimson flood of his blood. "I would ask a favor."

He closed his eyes.

"Scotsman!" she rasped.

His eyelids fluttered and opened.

She gripped the rag in desperate fingers, as if she held his very life in the palm of her hand. "You're a knight, a man of honor, sworn to guard and protect."

He scowled. "I'm a wee bit . . ." He drew a few ragged breaths, "Weary . . . just now."

"Well . . ." She chuckled, feeling crazed, feeling lost. "That's unfortunate, because I need your help."

His fist tightened as it lay against the ground, but there was no weapon there, no hope. His eyes stuttered closed.

"Sir Killian!" she cried.

"What is it?" he asked, and managed to look at her once again.

"I need you," she demanded, her voice strident, her hands atremble. " 'Tis your duty as a knight to come to my aid."

His lips quirked slightly. His fingers curled against the earth as if he longed to touch her one last time, but he failed to lift his arm. "Methinks ye will be fine on yer own, lass."

"No." She clutched his shirt in bloody fingers. "No, I won't. I need you to live. I beg you . . . please . . . Killian. It's . . . it's a long way to Briarburn. And . . . it's growing dark."

He found her eyes with his, though his gaze was unsteady. "Are ye saying yer afeared of the night, lass?"

"Yes," she whispered, and nodded jerkily. Another pair of tears splattered onto his shirt. "I'm afraid, Killian."

He sighed. His eyes fell closed. She leaned against him in abject panic.

"Very well then," he said, "I shall accompany ye as far as yer gardens."

Chapter 23

❦❦

"To my..." Fleurette's heart fluttered wildly against her chest. "To my gardens?"

"Aye, lass. The Black Celt's resting place," he rasped, and groaned as pain wracked him. The cords in his broad throat contracted like living roots as he arched his head back into the dirt, then relaxed slowly. "And were I ye..." His words were barely audible, his breath came hard and fast. "I would na dringle."

"But how will I get you there?"

A nerve ticked sharply in his cheek. "Yer a clever lass," he said. "And braw." He tried to smile, but the expression was lopsided. "May-hap ye could carry me."

She laughed. The sound echoed on the edge of hysteria. But he was all right. He was fine. Making jokes. Her hands quaked like autumn leaves. She glanced toward the stallion, who waited nearby. "I'll get you on Treun. Can you stand?" she asked, but he didn't respond. "Can you—" she began again and turned abruptly toward him. But he had gone completely limp. "Killian." His eyes were closed, his hands lax.

"Please." She grasped his shirt and leaned closer. "Please, Killian. Just this one thing. I'll not ask another of you," she vowed, but he failed to respond.

She glanced frantically at the horses. *Fille* tossed her head, flicking her ears nervously toward the woods even as a wolf stepped out of the trees.

Fleur gasped, but remained where she was. "Go away!" she ordered. "Go."

The animal stopped, lifting his muzzle as he tested the scents.

"Leave!" she shouted, and digging up a handful of clay, heaved it at the beast.

It leapt sideways, then remained where it was, watching.

"Killian!" she gritted, but he didn't stir.

"Scotsman," she rasped, then, in desperation, slapped her open palm against his wound.

He awoke with a raspy roar and jerked upright.

Fleur scrambled backward. He stumbled to his feet, following her, his eyes glazed with pain, his hands grasping.

"Killian . . ." She scooted away on her hands and feet. "Please. You must get on your horse."

He reached drunkenly for her. She shot to her feet and dodged toward Treun, but he caught her easily, dragging her to his bloody chest. She hung in his fist and let her tears fall on his hand.

"Please," she begged.

He scowled, then sagged as coherency shifted slowly into his feverish brain.

"Don't. Don't quit," she ordered.

Their eyes met and held, then, nodding weakly, he stumbled toward his stallion. Grasping the pommel, he dragged himself shakily upward.

Fleurette heaved her weight against him until he was draped over the seat. Cursing and praying, she pushed harder. His hands moved slowly, grasping the mane in stiff fingers as he dragged his leg over the cantle. It seemed an eternity before he was astride, and once there he weaved like a drunken sot.

"Hold on. Hang on!" she ordered, and racing to *Fille*, loosed her reins from her bit. Running back, she strapped Killian to his saddle and put her foot in Treun's stirrup. The saddle tilted toward her. Killian slumped to the left. Shaking and praying, she managed to prod him upright as she swung up behind him.

Once there, she braced an arm on each side of him and pushed Treun into a walk.

Killian's head bobbed at the motion, and when he spoke his words were naught but a whisper.

"What?" she rasped, struggling to hold him upright. "What did you say?"

"Hurry," was all he said.

Fleurette closed her eyes and prayed as she set her heels to the stallion's barrel.

The horse leapt forward. Killian jerked in Fleur's arms, but somehow she held him aloft.

Painful miles thundered beneath them. Fleur's arms ached with the effort. But finally Briarburn appeared. Treun rounded the corner of his own accord. His hooves rang like death knells against the cobblestones.

She was yelling for help even before they slid to a halt. Mr. Smith burst out of the house.

"My lady—"

"Take him!" she rasped. Her arms quivered with the effort. Her chest ached with fear.

"My lady, where?" he asked, already reaching for the ties that held Killian in place. "Where shall I take him?"

And in that moment her gaze was drawn toward the Black Celt. He stood brave and solid, watching her from the serenity of his adoring roses.

"To the garden," she whispered.

"The garden, my lady?"

Other servants rushed up from behind to give assistance.

Killian slid limply into their arms. They staggered dizzily under his weight.

"My lady . . ." Mr. Smith looked into Killian's pallid face, then glanced up, his eyes worried. "I fear he is already—"

"No!" she snarled, and dropped to the ground to face him. "You'll not say those words. Do you hear me?"

He nodded jerkily.

"Tessa, fetch blankets. Horace, drive to Mayfair and bring back the doctor. Do not return without him. You others . . ." She dared for the first time to glance into her warrior's unconscious face. "Lay him in the shadow of the Celt."

"My lady . . ." Dr. Simpson dipped his head in respect. "I have done all I can for him."

Fleurette sat in Briarburn's parlor with London's premier physician. Tessa had served them tea. Etiquette, after all, must be observed, even if the world was shattering into a thousand irreparable shards.

Fleurette clasped her hands and remained perfectly still and upright. "And what is the prognosis, Doctor?"

His eyes looked weary and sad. He shifted them momentarily away. "I was able to retrieve the bullet."

She knew that much, had heard it before, which meant he was avoiding the question. She twisted her hands together, but would not be weak. "You expect him to die."

He shook his head. "My lady, I fear he is already—"

"He's not dead," she said, and straightened her back to look him full in the face. "You said yourself that you thought you felt a pulse."

"Yes, but that was some hours ago, just after dawn when first I arrived."

"Horace heard him moan."

Simpson looked pained and shifted uncomfortably, holding his cup and saucer like a china shield before him. "Sometimes the body will make sounds even after—"

"Thank you." She jerked to her feet and

paced the few steps to his chair. "Thank you, Doctor."

He looked troubled as he set his cup aside, but he rose to his feet and glanced out the window toward the shadow-shrouded garden. "You must, at the least, bring him inside."

Her gaze followed his. She could see Killian from there, his face pale, his body still beneath the shadow of the ancient Celt. "Of course," she said. "I shall see to it immediately."

He faced her as if to speak, then took his hat from Tessa, who stood in the doorway, and left without another word.

"My lady." The maid's voice was very small. "Shall I tell the men to bring the knight inside?"

The statue stood solemn and silent, towering above the quiet glory of the garden, keeping vigilant watch over the fallen warrior.

Tessa cleared her throat. "The master's chamber would make a fine place to view—"

"No!" Fleur snapped, then closed her eyes and turned toward the maid. "Do not say the words." Her heart felt slow and heavy in her chest, but she drew a deep breath and faced the maid with something akin to normalcy, as if she could survive this. As if she could hope to live if he did not. "He is not dead."

For a moment Tessa looked as though she

would object, but then she bowed her head. "Of course not, my lady." There were tears in her eyes. Fleurette ignored them. She would not cry. Would not wail against injustice. "But surely we should bring him safely out of the damp."

He hadn't moved a muscle, not even at the doctor's harsh ministrations.

"Before he catches a chill," Tessa continued.

Fleurette turned back toward her. "We shall not dishonor him with the master's chamber."

Uncertainty flickered across the maid's face. So they thought her mad, Fleurette thought, and almost laughed out loud. "He shall remain in the garden."

The girl winced as if struck, but finally she nodded and left.

As for Fleurette, there was little she could do but return to the Celt.

The day slipped away like the curtains of hell. Night settled in, and with it came the clouds, dark and thick and somber. Lightning crackled in the distance, but Fleur remained in the garden.

Killian yet lay on his back, his expression blank, his eyes closed.

Fleurette turned. Standing silently between the statue and the wounded Celt, she clasped her hands in uncertain supplication.

"I don't know who you are," she said, looking into the ancient stone face.

No one answered. Thunder rumbled quietly, like the growl of a distant beast.

"And I do not pretend to understand why you came."

The night was utterly silent for a moment, the darkness heavy and damp.

"I did not think I needed help." She took a stuttering step closer to the statue. "Indeed, I did not think I needed anyone." The Celt gazed silently down at her, impervious to the world, unmoved by her troubles. But when she put her hand on his thigh, the stone felt as warm as life beneath her fingers.

"I was happy alone."

He watched her in grim silence and she glanced at her hand, lying flat against the powerful thigh.

"Content at least," she corrected. "I was content. You cannot deny that."

It almost seemed as though she could hear the restless rustle of the destrier's hooves in the foliage at its feet.

"But there was much I didn't know."

The Celt waited patiently. Misty droplets sprinkled from the darkened sky.

"Love," she said and cleared her throat. She

was, after all, no weak-kneed wench, crying like a broken fool because her hero had fallen. "Perhaps I did not know love." He did not argue. "Gentleness," she whispered. "True gentleness . . ." She laughed a little, for she had thought she was wise. Thought she was clever. So independent. So strong. " 'Tis a rare gift. I see that now, despite what the . . ." She winced and swiped at her cheek with the back of her hand. "Despite what the peerage may think, a gentleman is not born, he is made. His value is not determined by the cut of his coat or his ability to waltz."

The hewn muscles almost seemed to shift beneath her hand.

"I love him," she whispered. "Please." She raised her gaze in tortured supplication and moved closer, pressing desperately up against the rocky leg. "Let him go," she begged. Her tears mingled with the raindrops that fell soft and steady from the leaden sky.

There was a groan behind her. She turned with wooden breathlessness, and even in the darkness she could see Killian shift beneath his blankets.

She dropped to her knees. Their gazes met with a velvet clash. She reached for his hand, and her hair, wet and wild, slapped against his skin.

"Killian." She breathed his name like a prayer and pulled his hand to her breast. "You're back."

He scowled. "Ye said ye were scairt of the dark," he rumbled.

She hiccupped a laugh and squeezed his hand against her chest lest her heart leap from her body. "Yes. Yes, I am."

"Then hie thee inside, lass. 'Tis raining bloody hell out here."

Chapter 24

"As I heard it told, the lass here carried ye to Briarburn after ye were wounded by the wee pistol. Is that the way of it?" O'Banyon asked.

Killian turned his attention irritably from Fleurette to watch the Irishman in silence. He sat in a chair next to the sickbed, his foolishly elegant fingers long and tapered against the tiny cup he held aloft. What the hell kind of man had hands that pretty?

"Tell me," Killian rumbled. "Have ye yet been shot with one of the wee weapons?"

O'Banyon's lips quirked slightly, etching a

dimple into his cheek. "Nay, I canna say that I've had the pleasure."

Killian watched him from beneath lowered brows. " 'Tis something every man should experience."

O'Banyon's laughter was deep and quiet. "If ye were na stretched out flat on yer back with naught but the wee lass here to keep ye from death's door, I would think ye were threatening me, old man."

Killian snorted and shifted to stand, but Fleur was there in an instant, placing a surprisingly strong hand on his arm.

"You must remain still," she said, "or you'll tear open the wounds."

Killian opened his mouth to assure her all was well, but despite her firm tone, her eyes were filled with such soft caring that he found himself hopelessly falling under her spell once again.

"Please." She smiled tremulously. His muscles quivered beneath her touch, aching to drag her onto the bed beside him. There could be no earthly reason to be lying abed like a withered gaffer if she wasn't there with him. Their gazes melded, promising pleasure and hope and a thousand unspoken vows. She smoothed her hand up his biceps to touch his cheek. He covered her delicate hand with his own, and even that simple touch was nearly his undoing, for there was nothing he wanted more than to take her in his arms and spend eternity in the shelter of her love. But she shook her head as if reading his thoughts. "The doctor said you must rest if you are to return to your full strength."

The Irishman chuckled quietly. Fleurette smiled mistily and drew away. Killian scowled and shifted his gaze back to his tormenter.

"'Tis said," O'Banyon added, laughter in his voice, "that the king's own physician declared ye to be dead already."

"Mayhap even ye can see he was mistaken," Killian rumbled and shifted uncomfortably beneath the blankets. He could not be near the maid without desire burning him like a brand.

"Well aye, ye do still seem to be breathing," O'Banyon said and shrugged. "But if ye were felled by such a small missile, most any wee problem may well be yer undoing. An ache in yer tooth. Fatigue. 'Tis na too cold in here for ye is it, Scotsman? Methinks I feel a draft."

Killian deepened his scowl.

O'Banyon's smile brightened. "And ye look a wee bit flushed," he added.

Fleurette rushed forward to lay a hand on his forehead. "Are you chilled? Do you need another blanket? Shall I—"

"Lass." Killian caught her fingers in his own, and even the feel of those delicate digits made him squirm with unanswered desire. "All is well. Do not listen to the Irishman's foolish prattle."

She held his gaze until Killian shifted his toward O'Banyon's.

"Ye will na worry the lass again," he rumbled. "Are these words ye understand?"

The Irishman grinned, then set his cup aside and rose to his feet with the litheness of a hunting hound. "Me apologies, me lady," he said, bowing gracefully. "I did not mean to alarm ye. The truth is this, the bastard Celt here—"

Killian cleared his throat and darkened his scowl.

O'Banyon shifted his gaze toward the bed as if surprised, then bowed again and took Fleurette's hand between his own. "Me apologies again. 'Tis simply what his friends called him in days of yore." He cleared his throat and began anew. "As I was aboot to say, yer brave, beloved knight . . ." He shifted his gaze toward Killian as if his presence in the elegant bed were naught but cause for constant hilarity. "He is all but impossible to kill. Indeed, I have tried it meself on more than one occasion and—"

"What?" Fleur snapped, and yanked her hand from his. "You tried to kill him?"

"He jests," Killian said, sprinting a glare at the Irishman before turning his gaze back to Fleurette. "O'Banyon here could na kill a midge with a long pike."

"He tried to kill you?" she breathed. Her eyes gleamed with protective zeal, and there was something about her bloodthirsty expression that caused him, more than ever, to long to drag her into the bed beside him and promise love and protection and everlasting happiness.

But O'Banyon was still damnably present. Killian gave a mental sigh. "Lass, me apologies, but I would have a few words alone with the damned . . ." He stopped himself and nodded toward the other. "With me friend here."

Her eyes were worried as she stared at him, but finally she pursed her wild strawberry lips and nodded. "Of course." She turned her back to him and brushed past O'Banyon with a murmur. The Irishman's brows lifted with a snap, then she was gone, closing the door quietly behind her.

An instant of silence lay between them before Killian found the other's gaze with his own. "And what did she say to ye?"

The blue eyes danced with dangerous joy. "I

suppose ye would na believe me if I said she had begged to meet me in the stable loft in one hour's time."

Killian kept his body carefully relaxed and tilted his head. "Nay," he said, "but I might see ye gelded."

O'Banyon laughed lightheartedly and slouched back into his chair. "She said that if I harmed ye, she would throttle me with her own hands." He glanced toward the door, his smile faded, his eyes showing an odd meld of admiration and jealousy. " 'Tis a strange thing, though, her ire might well be worth the trouble just to feel the touch of—"

Killian cleared his throat and silently debated murder.

O'Banyon's grin lifted merrily. "A bonny lass ye've found yerself there, Scotsman. Mayhap a bit bloodthirsty for me own taste, but who are we to resent that, aye?"

Killian's chest swelled so that he had to steel himself against the burgeoning emotions, but he carefully tamped down the unfamiliar feelings. For now, he would concentrate on the business of keeping her safe. But later . . . He scowled and locked the thoughts firmly away. "What of Kendrick?" he asked, hoping to hide the weakness she spawned in him, the desperate need to look into her eyes, to feel her hand in his.

"I have seen to him," O'Banyon said offhandedly. "Ye've naught to worry on, old man."

"Seen to him?" Killian growled. "What the devil does that mean? 'Tis na the Dark Ages, Banyon. Did I na warn ye. Ye canna simply murder a man these days, na matter how surely he deserves—"

"I spoke to him," the Irishman corrected, and laughed. "God's truth, man, she's made ye as soft as a Yuletide pudding."

Killian relaxed marginally, no easy feat, since O'Banyon had indeed been known to attempt to kill him from time to time. "What did ye say to him?"

The Irishman shrugged. "Na so verra much. Simply that 'twould be unwise to show his face in England again if he hopes to keep his head above his shoulders."

"Ye did him na harm?" It was not easy for Killian to keep the disappointment from his voice. But Fleurette deserved a civilized man, a forgiving man, and he was determined to be just that. "Na even a broken bone or two?"

"Nay," Banyon said, then grinned. "But I hear there was a wolf what followed close on his heels until he reached the docks."

Killian could not quite manage to contain his grin. Surely, even a civilized man would enjoy the idea of Kendrick's reaction to being hounded by a wolf the size of a Russian bear. "He boarded a ship then?"

"Aye, paying double the usual fare to sail at first tide."

Killian nodded and drew a calming breath. His Fleur would be safe so long as he breathed. "And what of ye?" he asked. "What be yer plans?"

A flash of hopelessness shone in the Irishman's eyes for a moment, but he bundled it quickly away and shrugged. "It seems I have little choice. I shall remain near the Celt."

Memories slinked in—endless darkness, eternal hopelessness. But there was light, was there not? He remembered the feel of Fleur's hand on his thigh, remembered being drawn into sunlit hope.

"Your curse may yet be broken," Killian said.

The other shrugged as if it was of no concern. "Unlike yerself, I dunna have me liege lord's death to avenge. Indeed, I seem to have been dragged into this world as a sort of afterthought."

Killian glanced out the window. From his vantage point, he could see the statue. Old memories stirred dark and tumultuous in his soul, but at that moment Fleurette stepped into view. Her gown was daffodil yellow, her hair as bright as sunlight. And at the sight of her, something as old as time stirred in his soul.

So this was love. Who would have dared hope it would come to him at this late date? He watched her as he spoke. "Ye know then that her husband was the Master's kinsman."

"Aye," said O'Banyon. "His only remaining blood. 'Twas his death what finally stirred ye from yer slumber."

She bent to pet the spaniel that had avoided the Irishman like the plague, but now bounced about her feet.

" 'Twas what I thought at the start," Killian admitted, his words half to himself as he watched her.

" 'Twas the curse what was cast," Banyon reasoned. "Ye were to live in darkness, captured by the stone until ye found a way to make amends for betraying the Master. Surely avenging his final heir's murder would do just that, na matter how long it took."

"Evil," Killian said, his mind spurred back to old wounds, old nightmares. "The Master was evil, and thus he cast an evil curse. But now I wonder . . ." The spaniel bounded after a hare, and Fleurette bent to gather a bouquet of roses. Lifting them to her nose, she shaded her eyes with the edge of her hand and smiled up at his window. "Might not love be the stronger force?"

"What's that?" O'Banyon asked.

Killian did his best to quell the rush of feelings in his chest, but there was no hope for it. Happiness rocked his very soul, overwhelmed him, undid him. He turned toward the Irishman with brusque nonchalance, as if his heart was not swelling within the tight confines of his chest. "Her touch is surely as strong a magic as any the Master could concoct."

"Ye think 'twas she what woke ye from the blackness?"

"I felt her presence when all was darkness," Killian said. "I felt her force like the sun upon me face."

"God's breath!" O'Banyon said, and sadly shook his head. "I did na think I would live to see the day when the Celt spouted poetry like a milk-fed farm boy."

Killian scowled, but his gaze was once again drawn to the lass in the garden. "We shall see how cavalier ye be when ye are touched by joy itself."

O'Banyon snorted, but when he spoke he could not completely quell the edge of wistfulness in his tone. "I dunna think that path be for me, old man."

The sadness was there again, hidden but visible beneath the Irishman's golden veneer.

"Ye dunna know that for certain," Killian said, turning regretfully from the window. "Indeed, there is much we cannot foresee."

"Mayhap," said the other, and shifted his gaze away. In the garden below, Fleurette was laughing with her maid, and when Killian turned to the Irishman, he saw that the other's eyes glistened. "Well . . ." He rose abruptly to his feet and turned toward the door. "I shall leave ye to her coddling then."

"O'Banyon," Killian said.

The Irishman turned back.

"Mayhap there is more good in the world than ever we knew."

A smile flickered across the Irishman's face, but it was weary and old, as ancient as the earth itself. "Mayhap," he said, and disappeared through the doorway.

Fleurette appeared a moment later. Killian could sense her presence long before he could hear her approach, and turned breathlessly from the window. She was framed in the doorway, her expression soft, her tender body lit from behind.

"All is well?" she asked.

She looked as bonny as springtime, and when she smiled at him, his heart felt young and hopeful in his chest, unimpaired by wounds and ancient worries. Aye, he had fallen back into the darkness, had been contained by the stone, and there he had lain until the Celt had felt the warm brush of her tears. "'Tis now," he said, and felt hope bloom like Highland roses in his heart.

Her eyes gleamed. Glancing down the hall, she stepped silently inside and closed the door behind her.

Killian's arousal reared like a restive stallion as she paced toward him.

"Are you tired?"

He lowered his brows and eyed her askance. It was true that he knew little of this time and place, but he must assume there were some moral boundaries, and he had no wish to compromise her. Indeed, he had not meant to do so the first time, but circumstances and her own vibrant beauty had contrived against him. Still, he would not let it happen again. "Nay," he ventured cautiously.

She cleared her throat. "Weak?"

He raised a brow. "As I've told ye before, lass, I'll na have others gossip about ye."

She sat down beside him on the bed. Her hip brushed his thigh, and the foolish barrier of the blanket made no difference, for his skin burned as if they were flesh to flesh.

"Killian," she said, and placed a gentle hand against his bare chest. "I do not think you need worry what the *ton* will gossip about."

He stared at her.

"You dress in tartan skirts," she explained, "and—"

"I dunna mean to start a bullirag, lass, but me ancestral plaid be hardly a skirt."

Her lips twitched. "You speak as though you've just arrived from a forgotten century and—"

"There is naught amiss with me speech."

Her smile peeked at him as she lifted her hand to settle one tender finger upon his lips.

"And you basically rose from the dead. I think, perhaps, we have already given the gossipmongers some grist for the mill," she said, and, skimming her fingers over his chin, ran a fiery trail down his throat to his chest.

He swallowed and held on to his resolve. He was a knight, for God's sake, tested in battle, trained in fire. Surely he could fend off one small maid.

"Besides," she murmured, "if I do na disremember . . ." She smiled at her own antiquated speech. "I have already been compromised."

He cleared his throat and tried not to squirm. "I was na thinking properly then."

She slid her hand across his chest. He hissed air between his teeth and held himself rigid.

"Perhaps you're not thinking properly now," she said, her eyes all innocence. "After all, we are to be married."

"Aye, well . . ." He gritted his teeth against the sweet spark of feelings. "We shall wait upon the nuptials."

Her smile was like the light of the sun. "Shall we?" she asked and bumped her fingers across his nipple and over his rippling abs.

He caught her wrist in a trembling grip. "Lass . . ." he croaked.

"Yes, my love?" she whispered, and leaned close so that her lips were inches from his. "What can I do for you?"

"'Tis bad enough that ye have taken me into yer house without chaperone. I'll not have people know ye were closeted alone in me chambers with me."

"I won't tell them," she murmured, and kissed the corner of his mouth, "if you—"

"Lass . . ." Good God, was he panting? "I am a knight of the realm. When I make a decision, the decision stands. 'Tis best ye ken this at the outset if we are to be wed."

She drew back slightly, eyes dancing. "Oh aye," she murmured, picking up his brogue with perfect aplomb. "And I would na dare to gainsay ye." She tugged her arm from his grip and he let her go, lest she feel the tremble in his fingers. "Unless I have an excellent reason. And this . . ." she began, and suddenly her hand had disappeared below the blankets. It felt soft and firm as it curled about his throbbing member. He gritted a groan, and before he could stop her she was stretched out against him, her eyes suddenly somber. "This be an excellent reason."

"Please, lass . . ." Damn it all, and now he was pleading. "I've na wish to see ye shunned by others."

"And I've no wish to wait to share my love with you."

Their gazes caught and smoldered. He shook his head, trying to breathe. "I dunna deserve ye, lass."

She smiled, and the sun, as bright as a promise, shone with sparkling glory on the garden below their window, warming the dark Celt that stood watch below.

"On the contrary," she breathed, and kissed him. "I think I may be exactly what you deserve."